Turned towards them, seen more and more
clearly as the flare sank towards the ground, was
a face. In the bluish light the teeth seemed to be
bared. The face was broad and hairy with a
flattened nose, and heavy brow-ridges. The
reddish hair which fringed it grew thickly round
the large ears and head. As the light from the
slowly sinking flare became more intense Harry
saw that the desperate eyes were fixed on his.
For a moment an extraordinary sense of urgent
communication filled his mind ... It was
something like a gorilla, something like a man ...
covered in hair. It was hard to estimate height
while the creature was still crouched in the
shadows, but it was probably around six feet.
The body was barrel shaped, squat and obviously
powerful ...

Also by John Gribbin in the Abacus imprint published by Sphere Books:

FUTURE WORLDS

Brother Esau

**DOUGLAS ORGILL AND JOHN
GRIBBIN**

SPHERE BOOKS LIMITED
30–32 Gray's Inn Road, London WC1X 8JL

First published in Great Britain by
The Bodley Head Ltd 1982
Copyright © Douglas Orgill and John Gribbin 1982
Published by Sphere Books Ltd 1983

All characters in this book are imaginary, except
those whose names are already celebrated in the
chronicles, past and present, of science.

Printed and bound in Great Britain by
Cox & Wyman Ltd, Reading

And Isaac intreated the Lord for his wife . . .
and Rebekah his wife conceived.

And the children struggled together within
her; and she said, If it be so, why am I thus?
And she went to inquire of the Lord.

And the Lord said unto her, Two nations are
in thy womb, and two manner of people shall
be separated from thy bowels; and the one
people shall be stronger than the other people;
and the elder shall serve the younger.

And when her days to be delivered were
fulfilled, behold, there were twins in her womb.

And the first came out red, all over like an
hairy garment; and they called his name Esau.

And after that came his brother out, and his
hand took hold on Esau's heel; and his name
was called Jacob . . .

And the boys grew: and Esau was a cunning
hunter, a man of the field; and Jacob was a plain
man, dwelling in tents.

Genesis 25

PROLOGUE

The snow leopard had twenty seconds to live. Satiated, half-asleep, he stretched beside a spur of rock which buttressed the first few feet of a sheer drop into the Himalayan valley. His belly was comfortably full of the feral goat he had killed a hundred feet lower, twenty minutes ago. Far, far below, the silver thread of a river cut across the green-brown patchwork of the valley floor. Although the ledge where the leopard sunned his eighty pounds of flesh and bone and muscle was fully 12,000 feet higher, the midday air was warm. Two bright orange butterflies skipped over the thin grass, endlessly spiralling for position in an intricate game of territory or sex or something more unknowably complicated than either of these. Lazily, the leopard blinked his yellow eyes as they passed within paw-length, but he was too relaxed to cuff at them in play as he sometimes did. He was safe, supreme, in the heart of his own territory . . . the undisputed ruler of three desolate square miles of the Great Himalaya.

White clouds, driven by air currents funnelled from the mountain walls, moved steadily down the valley, hundreds of feet *below* the ledge where the leopard lay. Yet above them the air was still. The autumn sunlight gilded the fronds of a cluster of ferns sprouting from the base of the spur. It etched sharp shadows from the wrecked trunk of a long-dead pine which lay a few feet along the ledge. The whole world seemed set in the stillness of a trance. There came the very faintest phantom of a sound. Instantly, in that first thousandth of a second, the snow leopard's ears pricked. In the same splinter of time, the rock beside which he sprawled seemed to blur and alter shape.

The leopard was seized through the thick mottled fur of his neck, and below the muscles of a hind-leg. Even as he struggled, snarling, to turn his jaws behind, his back was arched uncontrollably, helplessly. With a sharp snap, his spine broke. He twitched on the turf, his eyes clouding. The butterflies drifted back, still intent on their private manoeuvres. The white clouds navigated on down the valley towards China and

Ladakh. For a moment or two, a higher cloud passed across the sun, and the ledge was chill. As though pulled down by invisible strings, the orange butterflies sank to earth, the flying veins in their wings contracting as they cooled. Nothing now moved on the ledge. The leopard was dead.

1

Kneeling uncomfortably on the flinty ground, Prakash Chowdhuri thrust the fingers of his right hand through the scum-like crust which remained in the lee of the rocks from last winter's snowfall. There was definitely something there. He could feel it, embedded in the volcanic tuff under the overhang of the rock. A gust of wind, with a first scattering of rain, blew up the valley, fluttering the plastic tags on the grid of one-meter squares which made up Bed Four. He glanced over his shoulder. On the other side of the dig Mohammad, the foreman of the Kashmiri workmen, was watching him covertly. Chowdhuri sat back, squatting on his heels.

'Bring me the sieve,' he said sharply. 'And then go down to the tents and fetch my camera.'

As soon as Mohammad had placed the sieve beside him and disappeared down the old stream bed towards the camp, Chowdhuri turned back to the overhang where he had been working. He took from his belt the pointed, flat-bladed chisel that a back-yard foundry in Srinagar had made for him from a fifteen-centimetre nail. Delicately, he began to probe the point into the shale, working it steadily back and forward until the tuff began to break up. Then he put his hand back under the overhang and drew out handfuls of powdered, crumbled tuff—the residue of a volcanic eruption long, long ago, when the Himalayas were still young. One by one the handfuls went into the sieve. At last he sank back on his heels and gently shook the sieve. Something lay greyish-white against the red ash.

He picked it out of the sieve, holding it between finger and thumb. There was no doubt what it was . . . a tooth. With mounting excitement he turned it over, holding it now in the cupped palm of his other hand. It wasn't one of the frequently-encountered fossil fangs from the ancestral form of hyena which had roamed here ten thousand centuries ago, but a large primate molar, from a monkey or an ape. Unbelievingly, he counted the bump-like cusps around its edge. Yes, there were five. Its owner, then, had been an ape. He was no specialised anatomist, but he knew enough anatomy for his job. Men and other apes, like chimpanzees, had five cusps. Monkeys had four.

The rain-gusts were settling into a steady drizzle, scudding up the valley and soaking the shale around him. Heedless of this, he lay full-length on the ground and thrust his wrist further into the overhang. His fingers met with a hard smooth surface, and then, exploring lower, with a curved row of jagged indentations. A jaw . . . he was sure of it . . . it was a jaw. His trousers and anorak were now sodden, but he pressed himself up against the overhang, unclipping a small pencil-torch from his belt. With his head wedged under the overhang he positioned the torch against his ear and switched it on. Little more than a foot away the empty eye-sockets of a skull stared into his.

The blood rushed to his head, and he felt physically sick, almost faint. He wriggled into a better position, his heart pounding, and looked once more at the skull in the thin light of the torch. It seemed to be wedged awkwardly between two layers of hardened tuff. The upper half, with the eye-sockets and the great brow-ridge, was mostly in shadow, and however he manoeuvred the torch in the few inches of space available, he could see no more of it. The jaw, both mandible and frontal teeth, was broken away, embedded in the lower level of tuff, at the edge of which his fingers had found the single molar.

Chowdhuri forced himself to be calm. Even on this shadowy inspection it looked as though the frontal dentition, at least, was almost complete. He peered again at the upper half. The torch battery was beginning to fade, and the shadows around the empty eyes were deeper than ever. There was something alien about that brow-ridge . . . no matter, no matter, that would have to wait for Liliane. It was going to be a difficult skull to move. But Liliane would deal with that.

As he rose stiffly to his feet he saw that Mohammad was back from the tents. Silently, the Kashmiri held out Chowdhuri's camera. The light was poor, but Chowdhuri took four pictures of the general site from various angles, and then tried to position the camera, with its flash attachment, under the overhang of the rock. There was no way he could get his eye to the viewfinder, but he took four more flash pictures with the lens pointing to where the two halves of the skull were wedged. The pictures were unlikely to be of much value, but at least he would be able to tell Liliane he had obeyed her rules. He looked round. Mohammad was standing beside him.

'Is there something there, *sahib*?'

There was no point in completely evading the question, though Chowdhuri was not eager to have the find talked about yet among the workmen. If that happened, he reflected, it would be all over Srinagar, the next time one of the Kashmiris went into the little Kashmir summer capital for supplies.

'Yes, there is something, Mohammad. What it is—' he hesitated for a moment—'I am not sure. We will leave it until the *memsahib* returns.'

'Shall I make a shelter for it, *sahib*? As we did for the hyena bones? It is a time of rain.'

Chowdhuri considered for a moment.

'No,' he said at last. 'It—whatever it is—is well sheltered by the rock.'

Better, he thought, not to indicate too closely either what or precisely where it is. He had no especial reason to distrust Mohammad or the other four workmen, but after all, they were Kashmiris. Any Indian from further south knew that Kashmiris were a treacherous, dishonest, swindling race.

When he reached the huddle of tents on the grassy expanse of the mountain *merg*, two hundred feet below Bed Four, Harry Kernow was waiting for him. His eyes rested on the camera which swung from Chowdhuri's shoulder.

'Have you found something, Prakash?'

Chowdhuri nodded, hesitating for a moment. 'Yes, I think it may be important. You're picking up Liliane tomorrow?'

'Yes, I'm leaving early in the morning. Mohammad can take the ponies down and wait for Liliane and me to get back in the Land-Rover from Srinagar. Unless the plane is late we'll be back before dark. Or we might stay on the houseboat. Anyway, Mohammad has a friend who runs that old dak-bungalow in the valley. He can wait there. But what have you found?'

'I'd rather not say yet, Harry. I think we should wait for Liliane. She'll be back tomorrow, or the next day.'

11

The Englishman grinned. 'Have it your way.'

'It's not my way, Harry, it's Liliane's way. She made the rules. You know that.'

'You always obey the rules, don't you, Prakash?' said another voice, behind them.

Chowdhuri swung round. It was the American, Tom Meachem, looking at him, half-smiling.

'What's to stop me or Harry going up there and looking as much as we want?' said Meachem.

Harry laughed, patting Chowdhuri on the shoulder. 'Count me out, Tom. You and Prakash and Judy and Liliane are the palaeontologists. It's you who're rooting around here for human beginnings, not me. I'm just here to run the camp. I don't join the in-fighting.'

Chowdhuri looked at Meachem and swallowed. 'I don't think you should go up there, Tom. Liliane wouldn't like that.'

Never certain whether Meachem was joking or serious, Chowdhuri was always nervous of these exchanges with the American, though they usually fizzled out and came to nothing.

'I'm asking you not to go,' Chowdhuri said again. 'I am second-in-charge here. I hope you will agree not to go up there yet.'

Meachem looked at him for a moment, shrugged, and went back into his tent. Harry turned to Chowdhuri.

'He won't do it, you know. He just likes to assert his independence from time to time. But he won't cross Liliane.'

'How is Judy?' asked Chowdhuri, to change the subject.

Kernow jerked his head towards the second of the six tents. 'Asleep at the moment,' he said. 'But I think she's going to be all right in a day or so. I've given her a couple of tablets, and she can have two more this evening. They should do the trick. We all get a touch of tummy when we first come out here. That's where you're lucky, Prakash.'

'Oh, I've had it, too, last year,' said Chowdhuri. 'These damn Kashmiris—they never wash the fruit . . .'

Almost four hundred miles south of the tents on the mountain meadow, Liliane Erckmann lay awake in her hotel room in Chandigarh, listening to the quiet hiss of the punkah blades revolving on the ceiling above her. She was annoyed—with herself as much as with others, though the realisation did not soothe her. Why, for three days, had she wasted her time here in the Indian Punjab, when she ached to be back at the dig in Kashmir? Surely Harry could have had enough perception to see that she ought to have stayed at Shalamerg at this stage of the operations, now that they were beginning on Bed Four. It's mostly my own fault, though, she reminded herself. When they put me in charge, I made up my mind that I'd behave like a man, take no privileges, lead from the front. I ought to have known that's precisely how a man would *not* have behaved —that he'd have taken all the privileges he wanted, having led from the front just long enough to prove himself to the other men. It was ridiculous. Here she was, with a doctorate in anthropology from Berkeley and another in palaeontology from the Sorbonne, by far the best qualified investigator in the party—and the best brain, too, she told herself firmly— wasting time and nervous energy on a hot sticky return trip to the University of the Punjab to dump a load of not-very-exciting specimens at the Institute, simply because it was her turn for that particular job. Somebody else could easily have done it, but nobody else had offered. Harry Kernow was supposed to be in charge of administration. He could have managed it so that she stayed at Shalamerg, even if it meant altering the rota.

Yet perhaps it had a bonus side after all. The University here was important—its prestige in India was the deciding factor which had persuaded the Government in Delhi to give permission for the dig. Kashmir was a very fraught area, politically speaking, as Chowdhuri sometimes reminded them. Chowdhuri was observer as well as colleague, acting as the University's representative in the party. So maybe it was no bad thing that the Indians at the Institute should see that she, the leader, didn't mind coming down to Chandigarh every so often. If she'd sent Chowdhuri again, out of turn, they—and he— might have thought he was being used as a messenger boy.

I don't like Chandigarh, she thought sleepily. Too modern, too rectilinear, a battery city for battery human beings. No, that's unfair. Indians aren't battery humans. They've been what they are for a long, long time . . . longer than the American half of me, or the French half, for that matter, can properly comprehend. Not battery humans at all. Just humans in an intolerable situation, like the rest of us. A situation that's been developing steadily for five thousand years. And even that's a totally inadequate concept. Of all the people in the world, I should be one of the few who know better. Not five thousand years. Not fifty thousand years. Something, give or take a few millennia, closer to a million years.

As she turned on her side to sleep her mind flicked for a last drowsy moment to the rocky slope in Kashmir, marked with its red and blue plastic tags, that was now known as Bed Four. Perhaps Bed Four was one of the places where it had all begun.

'How much longer do you imagine Erckmann will be able to carry on out there?' asked the Directeur of the Musée de l'Homme Primitif, looking absently out of his high office window, watching the tops of the lime trees shake in the sunshine. Somewhere to the east roared Paris, but here in the great museum's administrative annexe it was peaceful. The man opposite shrugged, wagging his grey head with wry amusement.

'Who knows? She's got American money, of course—as well as our own grant. And it's a small party. Not too expensive . . .'

The Directeur reached out and stirred his tea. This cup in the afternoon was an English habit—almost the only Anglo-Saxon habit he liked.

'Oh, Émile, it's always expensive in Kashmir,' he said. 'I remember ten years ago. We were working on that new area for *Ramapithecus*, you recall?'

The other nodded.

'It was expensive then,' said the Directeur. 'We were fifteen per cent over budget. The costs must be horrific now.'

'And *we* got results on *Ramapithecus*,' said Émile.

The Directeur laughed. 'Well, we confirmed other people's findings, at any rate, Émile. That jaw—the best yet. Eleven million years ago, and it ate like a man—well, something like a man. More like a man than an ape, at any rate.'

'You should see some of my students eat,' said Émile

14

morosely. 'And so . . . what are you going to do about Erck-mann?'

'Give her another month, and then put the whole thing to the Committee,' said the Directeur. 'I think they'll conclude she's had a fair chance. They'll have to refer everything to Berkeley, of course, but even in America the optimism must be running a little low. And American money . . . it isn't endless, these days. I think we'll be seeing *la Liliane* back in Paris within a few weeks.'

'I'm sorry for her,' said the other. 'No, I mean it. I know she has a royal arrogance, but she's clever, M'sieu Directeur. She's more than clever. She's brilliant.'

The Directeur smiled. 'Too much like the Maid of Orléans for my taste. But I know what you mean. In any case, she'll get work soon enough. She could go out to the Fayum Depression with the Germans, Stross and Rindt.'

'She doesn't like Germans.'

'There's a new project in Tanzania, with that young English-man everybody talks about . . . Kemble.'

'She's not too enthusiastic about the English, either,' said Émile.

Impatiently, the Directeur stirred his tea. 'Then if she wants to work in France and not in America, she'll have to settle down here at the Musée, though God knows she's not the easiest of colleagues. But she can't go on spending a lot of money looking for human origins in the Great Himalaya, following up what is basically a purely personal theory. She's got this absolute obsession that the Himalayas were the cradle of mankind. But we could use the same money to send out a party to Tanzania. And get better results in a month than Erckmann has managed in half a year at Shalamerg.'

'No doubt,' said Émile. 'But I'm glad it's you, not I, who'll have to tell her.'

2

Harry Kernow waited out on the edge of the dusty concrete apron in front of the airport administration building at Srinagar. Reaching a howling crescendo, an ochre-coloured MIG 21 wearing the green insignia of the Indian Air Force hurtled off the far runway and climbed steeply, trailing a streamer of expended fuel across the hard bright blue of the Kashmir sky. It was followed by another . . . and another . . . and another. They're putting on a bit of a show for the old man today, thought Kernow, looking beyond the apron to where a group of medalled Indian air force and army officers stood beside a brown, bald man in an elegant grey corduroy suit. Three camouflaged army cars waited nearby and, as Kernow watched, the party arranged itself inside them and drove slowly off the airfield, preceded by a couple of smart despatch riders on motorcycles.

From long habit Kernow looked at them critically as they rode by, sitting upright in the saddle in attitudes of rigid attention. We British left India one thing that was really good, he thought, with a faintly absurd sense of pride. The Army. It was good when my father was in it, and it's good now. He wondered what the man in the corduroy suit, an Indian Deputy Defence Minister, thought about that. Long, long ago, in the days of the King-Emperor, the Minister had been a *subadar*, a captain, in the Mahrattas. That was a regiment that could take its place beside any in the world.

Kernow jerked his mind back to the present. Now that the Minister's party had left the tarmac, the passengers were being allowed off the jet from Chandigarh. A grubby yellow bus pulled out from the aircraft steps. Kernow walked back to the gates where it would unload. For a moment or two he could not see her. Then, suddenly, there she was, striding through the Indian crowd, looking questioningly towards where he stood at the barrier. He felt his usual twitch of reluctant admiration.

'Good morning, Harry.'

She was always so unnecessarily formal. He looked at her more closely. Maybe she wasn't in a very good temper.

'Hello, Liliane. Good trip?'

She shrugged, smiling. 'It wasn't a bad flight. And they were pretty good to me at the Institute—though I think they were disappointed with the specimen. Probably hoping for something more interesting than ancestral mongoose bones.'

He nodded. 'Well, it's good to see you, Liliane. Listen . . . if you want, you could stay overnight on the houseboat, just down the road. We could go on tomorrow. It was raining up above Shalamerg when I left—the weather forecast isn't good. We could get away early tomorrow—have a quiet evening tonight and get our heads down. Do you good.'

Liliane hesitated for a moment, and then shook her head. 'No . . . I want to be out early at Shalamerg tomorrow morning. Has . . . has Chowdhuri got any further?'

'Well, he's pretty keen to see you. You know what he's like . . . he doesn't think it necessary to tell me very much. Something's getting him excited, though. But I don't see that a night on the houseboat would—'

'No, Harry,' she said decisively. 'I can't spare the time. Besides, it would not be proper.'

'Not proper?'

'Of course not. You and me—alone on the boat, except for Abdul. And even he sleeps on the bank . . .'

He looked at her without expression. 'Do you really mean you think I'm going to try—'

'Of course not,' she said again, impatiently this time. 'But people talk—you know how they talk. I . . . we . . . can't afford that to happen. You, of all people, should know that.'

God, he thought, why do Anglo-Saxons imagine French women are sexy? Did she seriously think . . . but no, she'd given the real reason. She was absorbed with her image as leader of this particular little party up at Shalamerg. That was why he hadn't risked changing the rota when it was her turn to go to Chandigarh. For anybody else—well, he'd have fixed it without a second thought. But not for Liliane. She'd have pushed back that heavy dark hair off her forehead and looked at him and said, 'When it's my turn, Harry, I do it.' She'd said it before, and he wasn't a man who enjoyed being snubbed. He was always the outsider, anyway, in this little squad of scientists. He couldn't really accompany them mentally on their trips digging back to Adam and Eve, up there on Beds Two, Three and Four. He simply didn't talk their academic language. He was the fix-it man, the hired hand, the one who was there because he knew the people and the country . . . and because twenty years in the Army was supposed to have taught him how to organise life in the wild.

'Are the others all right?'

She seemed to be speaking more to break an awkward silence than because she wanted to know.

'Tom Meachem's fine. He gets a bit stroppy from time to time, but he'll learn. The new girl, Judy—she's got a touch of tummy, and I've given her some pills. She'll be better in a day or two.'

His leg was hurting a little, in the way he'd become used to, as they walked out through the crowded reception hall of the little airport. But he was careful not to limp. He hated Liliane to see him limp.

The unmistakable scent of Srinagar, a compound of spice, heat, dust, flowers, fruit and sweat, pricked once more at their noses. Nearly half a million people lived in this grubby river-threaded city, in houseboats, corrugated iron shacks, tiny rooms above shops, and tall red villas of carved sandstone, each with a fountain and a herd of goats in the shaded gardens. Harry, leading, pushed his way through the crowd . . . women in bright saris, children in dazzling white tunics, young men in cheap, European-style suits, old men wearing the astrakhan hat that was almost a trademark of Kashmir. These old men—most of them barely more than sixty—moved with a kind of eager dignity, straight-backed. Over their shoulders hung the wide-sleeved dun-coloured woollen *pheron*. Under the ample folds of these cloaks, in winter, they held little pots of hot charcoal to warm them against the cold.

Outside was Harry's old Land-Rover, and beside it stood a *saddhu*, a beggar-priest, vivid in his saffron-yellow robe. Almost absently, yet politely, Harry gave him a couple of small coins. Harry always manages that so well, Liliane thought grudgingly. When I do it, I feel either slightly ashamed, or slightly superior. The *saddhu*, watching her with unexpectedly bright eyes in a dirty face, brought his hands together in front of his throat, and inclined his head to Harry.

'May your life prosper, *burra-sahib*,' he said.

Once she'd asked Tom Meachem what was the difference between *burra-sahib* and just *sahib*. Paradoxically, although Tom was American and a relative newcomer to India, he'd majored in Eastern languages and spoke both Hindustani and the Kashmiri dialect better than Harry, who in every other respect knew far more about the Himalayas than the rest of the party put together. *Burra-sahib*, Tom had told her, meant 'great lord'. And it wasn't a title that Kashmiris conferred on everyone who gave them a half-rupee. Plain *sahib* or its feminine equivalent *memsahib* was good enough for the rest of them.

She glanced out of the corner of her eye as Harry sat beside her at the wheel of the Land-Rover. How old was he . . . thirty-eight? He was good-looking in that clipped, English military way—not that it's the way I particularly like a man to be, she told herself. All that quiet authority raises my hackles. Still, they'd been lucky to get him. Harry was known throughout the Himalayas—before the accident which had taken him out of the British Army, and had also left him with that slight limp, he had climbed twice on Everest—reconnoitring, a French mountaineering friend had told her with respectful awe, the Great Central Gully on the south-west face. And an American who himself had climbed on Annapurna had said to her, on hearing that Harry would manage the Shalamerg party: 'Kernow, eh? You couldn't do better. He's a good guy—a first-class rockface man, safe and careful. The kind of man the Brits say they'd go into the jungle with . . .' That, it seemed, was high praise.

Harry drove into the city, down the side of the sprawling channels of the Jhelum River, along a road lined with fruit stalls, and shaded at intervals by giant chenar trees. The Land-Rover crossed a bridge and nosed carefully through the traffic of patient buffaloes, wandering bullocks, battered taxis. Down in the waterchannels the living-boats were moored in rows, thin columns of cooking smoke rising from their galleys. The *shikara* taxi-boats, high-prowed, were busy as they arrived at the glittering stretch of the Nagim Lake. Somewhere over on the far bank lay the spacious houseboat that the digging party used as a headquarters for rest and recreation when they came down, at intervals, from the austerity of life at Shalamerg. There would be a bath and a shower, and Abdul the house-boy would make tea in a silver pot. Cool sheets waited on a comfortable bed. Resolutely, she thrust the thought from her mind. There was a lot to do at Shalamerg.

She turned to Harry.

'Chowdhuri gave you no message for me, then?'

'No, but I've got a fair idea what he's been doing.'

'Yes?'

'He's well down into that tuff. You know, the section that sticks out of the rock overhang on the north end of Bed Four?'

She nodded. In her mind's eye she could see the welded mass of tuff . . . volcanic ash which millions of years ago had fused hard from the heat of its own eruption. The tuff had preserved fossils, in some cases, in a protected natural store-place over hundreds of thousands of years.

'At that far end, he's digging under the tuff,' Harry said. 'I gave him a hand when Judy was sick. There was a bit of the usual material. An unmistakable hyena . . . what do you call it, *Hyaena hyaena*?'

She nodded again. 'Yes, the ancestral form.'

'Well, there was that, and a few scattered mongoose bones —at least, Chowdhuri said it was mongoose. I'm damned if I'd know. But yesterday he found something else.'

'What was it?'

Harry shrugged. 'I don't know. He shut up about it—told Mohammad and the rest of us to stay away until you came. You know what Chowdhuri's like. He keeps a poker face. He simply said you'd be interested, and nobody must work there until you'd seen the site. So Tom and he are at the other end today, clearing some pretty basic tuff. There was one interesting thing, though. Last night, when he thought nobody was noticing, he went up to Bed Four and stood there, brooding. God knows what's going on in that Indian mind.'

'It's a very good mind—an excellent mind,' she said, half-annoyed.

'All right, all right,' he replied peaceably. 'I'm not arguing. I'm just a simple soldier—*was* a simple soldier.'

'There's nothing simple about you, Harry,' said Liliane.

He smiled without speaking more, concentrating on picking his way through the last outskirts of Srinagar. They were heading away from the city, out into the Vale of Kashmir. For miles the road wound through a checkerboard of rice paddies and bright yellow fields of ripening rice. Every so often a grove of willows sheltered a little farm, until at last the landscape began to change as the Land-Rover climbed into the foothills of the Great Himalaya. Liliane, still tired from the previous day, half-dozed, half-watched, conscious of Harry's steady hands on the wheel, and more relaxed than she had been for days.

It had begun to rain in swift little flurries. The mountains ahead seemed lost in dark mist. Far away the thunder muttered. At about 8,000 feet they rounded a bend on the mountain road to find themselves in the muddy main street of a small village, decrepit in the wet. Men in loose brown woollen gowns sheltered under roadside awnings, talking and chaffering beside open boxes of apples piled on the ground, or over the cheap shirts and blankets offered on rickety booths.

There was a long travellers' bungalow in the centre of the village, perched on an escarpment looking over the Vale far below. Harry climbed stiffly from the Land-Rover to buy a couple of bottles of Campa-Cola. The usual knot of children, hands outheld, was gathering round the car. To avoid them, Liliane followed him into the bungalow. It was as seedy as the rest of the village—a long verandah of shabby armchairs, a bar piled with dusty crates of soft drinks and boxes of sweet cakes, with a couple of grubby toilets at the far end.

In some indefinable way, the tawdriness of the bungalow put her out of tune again with Harry, and although he made one or two attempts at conversation when they got back to the car, she pretended to be asleep. And then Harry was shaking her gently by the shoulder, and they were there, below Shala-merg. She *had* been asleep . . . it must have been for more than an hour. The rain had stopped, but up here at more than 10,000 feet the late autumn afternoon was chill.

She shivered as the blanket Harry must have tucked round her fell away. She got out of the Land-Rover and looked around. Mohammad and his boy Jinni were standing a few yards away with the four ponies. Mohammad himself came forward, clasped her hand between both of his, and said a few

21

conventional words of greeting. It had been hard for Mohammad to accept her as leader of the party, but he seemed to be coming to terms with it. Her own pony, Bulbul, was waiting —a sturdy little Himalayan animal that knew every rock on the path ahead. You didn't try to ride or guide Bulbul—you simply sat on her back and let her take you her own way.

In a straggling single file they jogged away from the Land-Rover up into the steep valley which rose above them . . . Jinni proudly leading, then herself, then Harry, then Mohammad last of all. Within a few minutes they crossed a shallow stream bed, littered with the great boulders of an old glacier, and trotted on over the short grass and mossy stones, climbing steadily higher. Ahead of them, the tall mountains gleamed with a covering of unbroken snow, though the snowline itself was fully two thousand feet above them. Soon, she reflected, it would have reached down to the stream beside which they rode. The brown, ribbed flanks of last year's snow, protected here and there by overhanging rocks, were all around them. There was no sign of animal life apart from a white-tailed goshawk which swung overhead on its ceaseless hunt for snow-pigeons, though Harry had told her that there were wild goats and bears and even, very occasionally, a leopard in these hills.

Bulbul picked her way along the stony paths which skirted the mountainside, unhesitating even when, every so often, the way was no more than three or four feet wide, with a long rolling drop on the other side. Behind her Harry's pony slipped and scrabbled for a moment, and then recovered itself. It was probably Harry's fault, she thought—sometimes he thought he knew better than the pony and tried to guide it. He was nearly always wrong.

It was already dark and beginning to rain again when, two hours later, they reached the mountain meadow of Shalamerg. Stiffly, she slid from the pony, and Jinni came forward to lead it away. The tents were white against the dark of the mountain. The door of the little log hut where they stored the specimens opened abruptly, and Chowdhuri peered out, his olive face breaking into a grave smile as he saw her. But before either of them could speak the flap of the nearest tent parted and the small slim figure of Judy Agar came through it quickly, her short dark hair tousled and her face alive with pleasure. She ran to Liliane and hugged her.

'How lovely to see you—I imagined you might have stopped over on the houseboat. Have you heard the news?'

'What do you mean?'

'Prakash Chowdhuri has found something. He's being very mysterious about it.'

'Yes, Harry told me. But how are you? Harry said . . .'

'Oh, that. I took four of his wonder-pills, and it all seems to be over.'

'Good.'

Liliane looked up as Chowdhuri joined them. He was certainly excited, his eyes glinting behind his spectacles.

'I am glad to see you, Liliane. I thought perhaps you might not come until tomorrow.'

'Not if you have news, Prakash. I couldn't wait.'

Chowdhuri smiled nervously and began to speak very quickly.

'I've got a skull. Up on Bed Four . . . you know where the overhang . . .'

She nodded.

'It looks like the best skull imaginable, Liliane. Almost complete, I should say. But it's quite a long way under the overhang and I couldn't see it very clearly. The cranium and the jaw seem to be there, though they're in two pieces. The teeth, too—I've got one of them.'

'You don't mean you knocked one out?' Her voice was sharp.

His reply was reproachful. 'Of course not. It was the tooth that led me to the skull—I was probing behind the overhang when I found it. It was at least a foot away. Probably detached from the jaw long ago. I have it in the hut. Come and see.'

The tooth lay on a sheet of yellow blotting paper pinned to the top of an old trestle table. Carefully, Liliane picked it up. Her heart began to beat faster.

'Pongid,' she said almost absently. 'Ape-like. It looks like a first molar.'

'The cusps?' Chowdhuri's voice was triumphant.

'Yes. I had no idea of anything like this, though. Harry was

23

talking about *Hyaena hyaena*. He didn't say anything about apes.'

'I didn't show it to Harry, or to anyone else.'

'Why not?'

'It's your own rule,' he protested, indignation sounding faintly in his voice. 'You've always said that when anything is discovered there must be a sequence, beginning with you personally seeing the place it was found, and then the find itself. And no chatter about it until then. That's your rule.'

'Prakash has been a good boy.' It was Tom Meachem's voice. He had joined the group unnoticed. In spite of his tall, thin, angular body, which sometimes made him look clumsy, he had a disconcerting capacity for silent movement. Now he was smiling in a way calculated to make Chowdhuri feel uncomfortable.

Liliane felt a prickle of annoyance. At twenty-seven, Tom was already a first-class palaeontologist—one of the best of the new generation, his professor at Columbia had told her when she was choosing the party. He'd worked at Jebel Kafzeh in Israel and in central Java—and he wouldn't have lasted long at either dig if he couldn't get along with non-Americans. But somewhere in Tom was a schoolboy sense of humour that could be irritating enough even to Americans, and that Chowdhuri found completely incomprehensible. Luckily, the open friendliness of Judy Agar, the other American, helped to balance Tom's occasional abrasiveness. Judy was there mostly because her father had founded the Agar Scholarships, and still poured money into university campuses from Boston to Berkeley. She was very young—only twenty-three—and she wasn't the world's greatest palaeontologist, but she was a tireless worker and her cheerful little face usually bubbled with fun. Even though Tom didn't really approve of little rich girls who got places on their father's money, he was on good terms with Judy. But now he must not be allowed to make Prakash feel the odd man out. Liliane put her hand on the Indian's arm.

'You were absolutely right, of course.' Well, he *was* right. Her strict procedure with any find sounded an arrogant rule, and she knew that Meachem sometimes felt it was exactly that. But it was the only way she could keep a clear mind about anything found.

Chowdhuri was watching her eagerly. 'You will come and see the place now?' he asked.

She shook her head. 'Better to wait for morning. I won't get much idea in the dark.'

His face fell, but she was firm. If she went up to Bed Four in the twilight she would be able to see very little by the light of a torch. And then she'd have to spend the rest of the evening talking about it with the others—and that was something she did not want to do. She wanted to think. As soon as was possible without rudeness after the evening meal—the usual curried lamb, cooked by Mohammad's assistant Zareer—she went to her tent, taking the tooth with her. From the box beneath her bed she took the big green volume of Tobias's report on the man-like ape, or possibly ape-like man, nearly two million years old, whose bones were found by the Leakey family and their co-workers at Olduvai Gorge in East Africa in 1959. Almost feverishly, she turned to the tables which measured the size of the creature's individual teeth. There it was . . . first molar . . . mesiodistal diameter 15.2 millimetres. She looked down the table for comparison. A modern American white man had a figure of 10.7. In spite of herself her fingers trembled as she measured the tooth Chowdhuri had found. It was 12.9 millimetres—almost exactly half-way between the Leakey's *Australopithecus* pre-man and modern man himself. It wasn't remotely conclusive, she told herself firmly. Not nearly enough was known about the dentition of ancient apes. But was it what she had gone there to find? Was it?

3

Lying beside the overhang on Bed Four, Liliane turned her face up to Chowdhuri, blinking her eyes against the bright autumn sunlight which had followed the rain.

'Do you have a spatula with you, Prakash?'

Chowdhuri tut-tutted, spreading his hands in a gesture of self-annoyance. Silently Tom Meachem took a spatula—it looked like a flattened tablespoon—from his belt and handed it down. She scraped at the tuff for a couple of minutes. There was a sort of powdery material there—thank heaven, it was so far under the rock that the rain hadn't washed it away. Was it bone residue? She'd never seen anything quite like it before. She took a small plastic pillbox from her pocket and spooned a little of the residue inside it. Then she put her face back to the rock. There was something else there, something bulky behind the upper half of the wedged skull, but even with Harry's more powerful torch she couldn't see what it was. And there was another small, loose object . . . gently she slid the spatula beneath it and brought it out. It was another tooth, an incisor this time. Silently, she held it up to the others, and Tom Meachem picked it up carefully.

'My God,' he said slowly. 'This is a whole new ball-game.'

He turned to Chowdhuri, grinning.

'Well, you've got your name in the history books, Prakash. It looks like you've found a hominid. That's a mighty small incisor, to belong to an ape. That tooth could cut up meat. Maybe it's small enough to have eaten cooked meat.'

Liliane scrambled to her feet. She smiled at Chowdhuri, but she spoke to Meachem.

'Have a good look down there, Tom. It's going to be difficult to get those two halves of skull out without bringing down the rock and crushing them.'

Meachem took five minutes to make his examination, before he nodded briskly.

'I can do it. I'll need Mohammad and two of the others. We'll have to build a scaffolding to hold up the rockface. We could burrow underneath, of course, but I guess you don't want that?'

'No, don't go underneath. There may be something else there. That skull is so complete there could well be other bones.'

'OK. Then we'll start building.'

Liliane spent the next six hours at the camp, trying to shut Bed Four from her racing mind. Tom was a superb excavator —the best she had ever known—and Mohammad a good foreman. Neither of them liked an audience when they were working, especially on a site as difficult as this. She noticed that, with seeming casualness, Judy Agar climbed up there from time to time, and even Harry occasionally disappeared without explanation. And it was Judy who eventually came running across the *merg*, half-gasping, half-laughing.

'They're ready. And Tom says he thinks there's something else there . . . something behind.'

The others were already grouped round the overhang when she reached it. Tom handed her the biggest spatula available in their equipment. His smile obliterated the slight irritation she had felt with him since the small episode with Chowdhuri.

'I guess you should do the honours, Liliane,' he said. 'It's your dig.'

'It's an Indian dig,' she said, and proffered the tool to Chowdhuri. He shook his head. She knelt down beside the overhang. All the debris at its front had been cleared, and a jointed metal scaffolding, perhaps two feet high, was supporting the rockface. The skull was now clearly visible, and although most of it was still deep in shadow all the tuff in which it had been embedded was now loose. With infinite care she pushed the spatula beneath the loose shale under the skull and drew it out on the broad blade. There was a soft 'aaah' from Judy behind her, but Liliane was staring, transfixed, into the overhang beyond. Tom squatted beside her, busy with a feathered dusting stick. He looked up at Liliane and she nodded. With infinite care, he drew out what appeared to be the cranium of a second skull.

'I thought there was something else there,' he said slowly. 'But not this . . .'

*

27

The two skulls—the larger one still partly embedded in the matrix of tuff which had encased it for many thousands of years—lay on the blotting paper in the wooden hut. While the others crowded round her, she stared at the skulls, her stomach heaving. Carefully, she picked up the upper half of the first one, trying to make her voice as dispassionate as possible. All her life she would remember the shock of first seeing these bones.

'This is almost the whole of the brain-vault,' she said quietly. 'Look at the size of it. It will be measured properly later, of course, but it must be around the size of the brain of a modern man—it looks to be about 1400 c.c. It's fantastic . . .'

'I thought . . . I thought . . .' stuttered Chowdhuri excitedly. 'I thought—but I could not be sure.'

He did a little hopping dance in front of the table. At any other moment it would have seemed absurd, but now it served to lessen the tension. Harry stretched out his hand. Liliane hesitated, and then passed him the cranium, relaxing when she saw how carefully he handled it. His face was puzzled.

'You mean,' he said at last, 'that it was a very intelligent sort of ape?'

Liliane laughed. 'Ape? It's no ape, Harry. The brain-case is enormous—nearly that of an average modern man, and certainly twice that of a modern gorilla. This was a creature not so very unlike us. There are modern humans with a brain-case smaller than this.'

She picked up the other, smaller piece of cranium. It was very slightly less massive than the first piece, and suddenly she had the totally irrational conviction that it had belonged to a woman. And I mean a woman, she told herself fiercely. Not a female.

'Look at this one,' she said. 'There's not quite so much of it, but it looks to me as though the brain-vault would have been virtually identical with the other. These . . . creatures . . . must have died together.'

'And how old are they?'

It was Judy Agar's voice, and it sounded strange, strained. Liliane glanced at her curiously. Judy made no move to look more closely at either cranium, or to hold one in her hand.

'If the hyena bones Prakash found in the area and at the

same level are contemporary—and they almost certainly are —I would guess around a million years old,' said Liliane.

Judy sounded almost angry.

'But that's impossible. A million years ago is far too early for a brain like that.'

Her voice was tense. Alone of those round the table she now seemed to experience no sort of pleasurable excitement.

'They'll have to be dated, of course,' said Liliane. 'We'll get potassium-argon, fission-track, the lot. There's going to be a lot of argument about these two skulls. Unless, of course, we can find more bones.'

'What about the teeth?' said Harry.

Liliane picked up the lower jaw of the first skull, examining it carefully.

'Whatever he, she or it was,' she said at last, 'these teeth ate a mixed diet. Look at the canine—it's a long tool for tearing flesh. And the incisors—short and sharp. It could cut. This was a creature that ate vegetables and meat. And it didn't use its teeth for self-defence. Not that it would have needed to, with a brain of that size.'

Alone on her camp-bed in the darkness of her tent two hours later, Liliane lay awake, her thoughts spinning round and round the problem of the skull fragments from Bed Four.

Well, she'd known there was something in these mountains. That was why she was there. But not this . . . not this. Never in her wildest . . . what was that noise? For a few moments she listened hard. But there was nothing save the distant whisper of the stream in the old glacier bed, and an occasional tug of the wind at the tent canvas. She settled back to her thoughts. There was something else, almost unbelievable, about the skulls. They could virtually have belonged to modern man, yet they might well be a million years old.

What had brought super-brained modern man up the evolutionary scale from the 1000 c.c.-brained varieties of *Homo erectus*, the upright-standing proto-man—also around a million years old—which had been uncovered in Africa? There was only one generally accepted answer . . . speech. The ability to teach, to ask questions, to learn. The power to store and expand a culture with each successive generation. Yet the forebrain portions, as far as she could see, of both the craniums from Bed Four were quite small—far too small to have contained the Broca's Region which controlled the motor area of speech. Neither of the creatures from Bed Four—man, woman or ape—could speak, could communicate concepts. Possibly they couldn't even form concepts. Each had a big brain, but it was going nowhere. Was it a new species? It would have to be named, of course. *Homo kashmiriensis erckmann*, perhaps. God I'd love my name on it, she thought. But maybe it ought to be *Homo kashmiriensis chowdhuri*. Prakash had found those bones, and perhaps a compliment to India might pay off. If what had seemed impossible only a week ago now turned out to be true, they were going to need a lot of Indian goodwill.

The two skulls should go back for dating as soon as someone could take them. England, perhaps . . . Cambridge. That would be best. They had a good dating laboratory, and there would be less publicity, because the skulls weren't really their concern.

Of course, she was guessing about the dating at present, and she could be wrong. But somehow, it didn't seem . . . There was that noise again. On an impulse she slid out of her sleeping bag and knelt at the tent-flap, shivering. A cold wind blew down the glacier, and the stars were bright above. The sound came again. Its source was the next tent, and its nature was now unmistakable. Puzzled and concerned, Liliane crept back to her sleeping bag. The next tent was Judy Agar's. Inside it, in steady convulsive sobs, Judy was weeping.

'There's something very, very odd about those two bits of skull, Oliver. Either that, or somebody's playing a damn stupid game.'

The young scientist at the Cambridge radio-carbon laboratory looked across the wooden trestle to where his partner was adjusting the twelve-chambered mechanism of the laboratory's particle accelerator, which stood like a Gatling gun at the far end of the room. Through the open window came the sound of sparrows quarrelling in the clematis on the wall: the radio-carbon laboratory had been built four years ago over the old tennis court of a large Victorian villa on the outskirts of the city. The other man shrugged.

30

'We haven't even done the tests yet, John,' he said. 'Don't let's jump to conclusions.'

'I'm not jumping to conclusions,' said John patiently. 'But you have the report of the potassium-argon test they did at the Cavendish?'

The older man nodded. 'I know what you mean. It *is* curious.' He looked again at the report. One skull gave a clear potassium-argon age of 1.1 million years. The other did not register at all.

'Well, you know what potassium-argon's like,' he said, his voice doubtful. 'That second sample may have got contaminated. Maybe the minerals with it weren't contemporary. There could be a score of things.'

'No, there's something very strange. Both those skulls should register on the same test. Erckmann apparently says they were found within four feet of each other, at exactly the same stratigraphic level. So potassium-argon dating should give identical results—for God's sake, all the test is doing is measuring the rate at which potassium 40 is converted into argon 40. It simply must be the same for both of them.'

Oliver straightened up from his machine. 'I keep telling you,' he said, irritation in his voice, 'that something probably went wrong. Either at the Cavendish lab, or perhaps even in Kashmir. If Erckmann sends a few more bones, the potassium-argon people can try again.'

'Then why are they asking us to try radio-carbon? They know perfectly well that even with this machine radio-carbon dating's no good for anything more than 100,000 years old.'

'Somebody may be a bit suspicious about Erckmann,' said Oliver. 'You know what I mean . . . that she's trying a Kashmir version of the Piltdown Man. Something faked up with a couple of old teeth and maybe a very young cranium.'

'Surely she'd never do that? I know she's got a reputation for being totally obsessive about her theories . . . but not an actual fake?'

'It's been done before,' said Oliver, 'and by people whose names were once household words. Suppose you were Erckmann, and you were really sure you were right, and that the Himalayas are the cradle of mankind. And you go out there, spending a lot of other people's money, and you don't find very much at all. And then the people with the money start getting restive . . . well, you might be tempted. You could always justify it to yourself, that you were merely anticipating the truth.'

'Not me,' said the young man. 'A fake is a fake—no good to anybody. Anyway, it still doesn't make sense, because one of those craniums has been potassium-argon dated at more than a million years old. Nobody's arguing about the accuracy of *that* test. And a million-year-old skull, even all by itself, is a hell of a find.'

He watched as Oliver loaded the pinhead graphite samples obtained from the disputed, undated Kashmir skull into the chambers of the accelerator. It was a procedure he had seen many times before, but he felt again the familiar twitch of excitement at the knowledge that they were about to lift a window on the past. Already every particle of matter that was not part of the test-fragment of the original living skull had been cleared away. The contaminants—mostly humic acids produced by the rotting of vegetation—had been chemically eliminated so that the 'clean' carbon atoms could be removed.

While he had lived, the owner of the skull had absorbed tiny amounts of radioactive carbon-14 from every animal or plant he or she had eaten—a process that had ceased the moment he died. The proportion of carbon-14 to all the other carbon that was in his bones on that unknown day could be calculated now by accurate scientific precedent. And after death, it would have decayed at a steady, regular rate: for every 1000 original atoms of carbon-14, 500 would be left after 5,730 years, 250 after a further 5,730 years, 125 after 5,730 more years, and so on down the scale. The progress of decay could be measured accurately for about 100,000 years back, but not beyond. If the owner of the skull was less than a thousand centuries old, the accelerator would find out. The amount of carbon-14 now in his bones, compared with what had been there when he died, would determine, within about fifty years each way, when he had lived.

Oliver made a last-second adjustment. He nodded to a technician on the far side of the room, who closed a switch. There was a low purr from the input mechanism as the carbon atoms began their run, bombarded first by caesium ions, and then hurled away down the long vacuum tube of the accelerator which ran along the base-line of the long-ago tennis court. Somewhere deep in there they would strike a three million volt-charged plate, to be shot down more tubes, separated, and finally measured at the end of their journey. The differences in weight between the flying atoms would reveal which were carbon-14 and which were not. The machine would have reached back up to 100,000 years to find the era in which the owner of the skull had met his death. And the whole process would take about an hour.

It was, in fact, nearly two hours before the two scientists returned to the laboratory. By then, the micro-computer on line with the accelerator had already ejected the narrow pink sheets of its print-out. Oliver, the senior man, picked them up, and read through them slowly, pursing his lips in a soundless whistle. The other watched him impatiently.

At last Oliver passed the print-out across and said wryly, 'Well, John, you were right. There's something very odd. It doesn't make sense. That skull is dated 180 years Before Present—around 1800. It's no more prehistoric than Napoleon.'

The young scientist read slowly through the print-out. 'There's something else,' he said slowly.

'Oh?'

'We know one of these two skulls is around a million years Before Present—the potassium-argon test on it can't be far wrong. And given the usual fifty-year error margin for our own radio-carbon testing of this second skull, its owner could, in fact, have died around 1750.

'Well?'

'Or, alternatively, the error may have run the other way. That could give a date of 1850.'

'In other words,' Oliver said, 'we have two identical prehistoric skulls. One's a million years old, and the other could have been alive within living memory.'

'God help Erckmann,' said John.

Extract from a letter from Dr Liliane Erckmann, field director at the Franco-American excavation at Shalamerg in the Pir Panjal mountain range of Kashmir (Indian Zone) to Dr Richard Kimbell, Professor of Primate Anatomy, University of California, Berkeley, CA., U.S.A.

. . . and so, darling Kim, not for the first time or the last. I'm in a mess. Sometimes I lie awake at night and wish we'd never found that second skull. Because without it—well, I'd got all I came for. An astonishing species of *Homo*, far in advance of anything of similar dating found in East Africa—and supporting my original theory that decisive steps in human development were taken in the Himalayas. You've heard my reasoning often enough, Kim, since the days—too many years ago! —when you taught me the tiny but rather vital differences between Plato and a chimpanzee.

But that second skull changes everything, doesn't it? I expect you've heard by now that already there are idiots who accuse me of planting it at Shalamerg, like that stupid English Piltdown fraud. And there's a German science magazine that says the first skull (the undoubted one million years Before Present cranium) was also planted there by me—I apparently having obtained it (just imagine!) from East Africa. They think I smuggled it to Shalamerg to back up my theories. Thank God the popular Press hasn't really picked it up in a big way yet—the Indian Government isn't giving out any permits for Press visits to Shalamerg at the moment.

Still, there are some like you who'll give the matter really serious thought. Because the second skull is the one we have to account for, somehow. All by itself it could overturn most of the thinking about human evolution since Darwin. That skull, logically speaking, *cannot be there*. And yet there's no mistake on the date. We've had samples through half the radio-carbon labs in the western hemisphere, and the same result comes up, mocking, every time . . . 1800, give or take fifty years.

Incidentally, both the craniums had a capacity slightly in excess of 1430 c.c.—the 'modern' one very fractionally the larger of the two. Both have distinct sagittal and occipital crests. Tom Meachem (he's being unexpectedly co-operative, by the way) made full-size clay models of our rough projection of the appearance of the original heads. He says the older skull's crest was so pronounced that it would look rather like an Apache haircut moulded in bone. I have a curious feeling that this older skull is male, and the younger one female. If you look at my sketch of the older skull (I also enclose a photograph of Tom's clay models) you'll see that the temporal lines curve away behind the crest. I think this could indicate . . .

4

With a sigh, Richard Kimbell folded the letter and slid it into the small drawer at the top of his desk. Before he did so he touched it to his nose, fancying for a moment that he could still sense, faintly, Liliane's own scent. I see her maybe once a year, he thought, and it's strictly business nowadays. But she can reach out across half a world and make me stir. I'm sixty now, and still it happens.

He picked up the big glossy black and white photograph of Meachem's clay models which Liliane had sent with her letter. Meachem had made no attempt to simulate the eyes. Blankly, blindly, the clay faces stared into his. On both heads the ridge of the sagittal crest ran sharply back, beginning a little behind the heavy overhang of the brows. And that was very puzzling indeed.

The usual evolutionary explanation for such a crest was that it acted as reinforcing support, on top of the skull, for massive, hard-working jaws—jaws like those of a modern gorilla, which needed to consume a great deal of uncooked vegetation to sustain life. The crest had disappeared in modern man because his superior brain-power had enabled him to evolve less demanding and time-consuming ways of eating and a more efficient diet. So why had creatures with brain-capacity equal to modern man not themselves evolved ways of living

35

which would have phased out these crests? One of these skulls, moreover, was dated as belonging to recent times. If that date was correct, the original crest had lasted for a further million years. What then, had Liliane's ape-men—or men-apes—eaten to justify their evolutionary retention of this ancient crest? And why were both skulls so remarkably similar, in spite of the immense time-gap between them?

He put the photograph away, touching Liliane's letter once more as he did so. He couldn't face going home just yet. The house up the hill seemed empty since his divorce, though that was what he'd imagined he wanted, when Jane—it was still hard to think of her as his ex-wife—was still there six months ago. Supposing he had married Liliane, instead of Jane? Could they have made a success of it? Well, better than Jane and I managed, he thought. I never wanted any woman like I wanted Liliane, and we could talk to each other, too. I think that's what she liked . . . the talking. I don't think she really wanted me, though she let me have her. It was a rather incestuous professor-student relationship—like that Hemingway character who always called his mistress 'daughter'.

He got heavily to his feet and went out of the book-lined room, locking the door behind him. In spite of his daily jogging, he was still more than ten per cent overweight, and he knew he'd never be anything else. Probably without the jogging he'd be twenty per cent over. Anyway, he'd stopped smoking.

Down in the parking lot he got into his blue Volvo and drove slowly, carefully away from the Berkeley campus, past the broad grassy slopes where the students sprawled among the scattered eucalyptus trees. It was about time for the usual afternoon traffic back-up on the main approach to Bay Bridge, so he took his own roundabout route into San Francisco, picking up Highway 580, and cutting through North Oakland until he got to the toll-booth on the Bridge. It was a safe route, he thought, and he was a safe man. He was paid $45,000 a year for being a safe man. He was no research high-flyer, but he could teach. And people listened to him—because he was safe. Nevertheless, he was going to have to back her. He couldn't stand by and watch Liliane pulled to pieces by a pack of those people. But what about the science of what she said she'd found? It all seemed such contradictory non-sense. To hell with the damned science. He was going to back her.

The Prime Minister stood at the broad window of the official working room of her home in York Road, deep in official Delhi. Outside the garden sweltered in the hard Indian sun, but the *asoka* tree in the lawn, beyond the well-kept borders, shook slightly in an unexpected breath of wind, so that the fading coral-red flowers on its branches trembled against the long, dark-green leaves. A house-crow flew out of the tree, arched its grey neck as it landed, and then hopped purposefully along the lawn towards the small kitchen garden which lay beyond. Carefully, the Prime Minister smoothed a fold of her apple-green sari, while the man opposite watched without speaking. No wonder they call her the Mantis, he thought wryly—she looked just like one of those disconcerting stick-like insects, with her long thin arms and column of a neck. Her predecessor, Indira . . . her nickname had been the Iron Butterfly. Indira could be tough, too, but the Mantis was an altogether different proposition. Like the creature she was named for, she could eat an enemy—or even a friend—alive. As the thought passed through his mind she turned back from the window and spoke to him.

'Well, Amrit Singh, what do you recommend?'

She studied him carefully while he smoothed his dark beard before he spoke. She was longing for a cigarette, but Amrit Singh was a Sikh, and would take it as an insult if she smoked in front of him.

'If I may summarise first, Prime Minister?' he asked.

She nodded.

'That which this . . . this party claims to have discovered in Kashmir is altogether ridiculous. It is making fools of us. We have provided facilities, permissions, transport, quite a lot of the party's administrative apparatus. We are indubitably associated with them, and we cannot afford that this should continue. We shall be a laughing stock.'

'Afford?' said the Prime Minister. She seemed to pluck the word from the air.

'I am not speaking of money,' said the Sikh. 'That has come

from France and America, of course. But we ourselves have a scientific representative in the party.'

'Dr Chowdhuri?'

'Precisely, Prime Minister. From Chandigarh.'

'I do not know him.'

'He is a Kashmiri Brahmin,' said Amrit Singh, careful to keep his voice and face expressionless. The Prime Minister's family were also originally Kashmiri Brahmins, who three centuries ago had fled from Moslem overlordship in the Vale of Kashmir. Like most Brahmins, they had done well since.

'Ah,' said the Prime Minister. 'And the leader, this Dr Erckmann. Half French, half American, I believe?'

The Sikh nodded.

'She seems to have put her hand into a nest of snakes,' said the Prime Minister.

The Sikh leaned forward. His voice was angry. 'We must throw her out of India. She is a fraud and she is doing us no good at all, not a bit of good.'

'You are sure she is a fraud? I do not myself know enough about the origins of the human race to make such a judgement.'

Her voice had the very slightest tinge of irony. Amrit Singh had become her Minister for Science because, like many Sikhs, he had a clear grasp of technological principles. Discuss with him the choice between two types of nuclear reactor and his views would be valuable. But palaeontology was hardly his subject.

The Sikh had not missed that faint twitch to the Prime Minister's mouth, and he looked at her defiantly. 'I listen to expert advice, Prime Minister. As you do.'

She made a slight, mock acknowledgement of the thrust, and then stood, placing her hands palm to palm in a gesture of polite dismissal.

'Thank you, Amrit Singh. I shall consider most carefully what you have told me.'

'And then?' he persisted.

'And then, Amrit Singh, I shall come to a decision.'

He inclined his blue-turbanned head in a compromise between a bow and a nod before he left the room. Left to herself, the Prime Minister riffled absently through the pages of the report on the finds at Shalamerg which Amrit Singh had placed on her desk. Amrit Singh was right, of course, the whole affair *did* seem ridiculous. But a woman with Erckmann's qualifications—why should such a woman attempt an absurd fraud? Any undergraduate could have worked out something more convincing than that. And no one was disputing that one of these skulls, at any rate, was a million years old. And it seemed to be a skull far in advance, in evolutionary terms, of anything already known from a million years ago. Was India, then, to be acknowledged as a crucial area in the development of *Homo sapiens*? That would be a feather in our cap, she thought . . . and imagine the foreign currency it could bring. Scientific funds, more tourism, perhaps.

And yet so many scientists had turned on Erckmann, turned to rend her. It was almost as though they did not *wish* to believe her. Why? Was it because she was a woman? Amrit Singh, for instance—there was something about the way he said 'she' and 'her' when he spoke about Erckmann. Damn the man, he was little more than a jumped-up taxi-driver, anyway. All Sikhs were taxi-drivers at heart.

She closed the Shalamerg report. Her mind was made up. In her heart, she knew she had decided even before Amrit Singh had left her. Erckmann could stay in India, and work on at Shalamerg . . . for the moment. She glanced at her watch as her secretary knocked at the door and came in.

'The first petitioners are here, Prime Minister,' he said. She sighed, and sipped at a glass of water. This was her open-house morning—the one day a week when any ordinary person could make an appointment to discuss a grievance. They think it is democracy, she thought, as a bent, white-bearded man was shown in. But it has nothing to do with democracy.

'How is Judy?' asked Liliane, looking up from where she sat on her camp-bed as Harry Kernow came into the tent.

He shook his head, his face puzzled. 'Still pretty listless,' he said. 'I don't really understand it—she's been like this for nearly a week now. It's not the usual trouble at all—nothing to do with her tummy. I think she'll have to go back to Chandigarh if she doesn't shake it off soon, whatever it is.'

'She won't improve much at Chandigarh,' said Liliane.

He looked angry for a moment. It was almost the first time she had seen Harry show genuine annoyance. 'Well, that's where she'll have to go, nevertheless. I'm not a doctor, just a first-aid man. I can treat a broken arm or a case of Delhi-belly, but I don't know anything about women or their troubles.'

'No, you don't,' said Liliane, and then smiled, touching his arm. 'I don't mean that, Harry. I agree—you can't be expected to know what's wrong with Judy. If there *is* anything seriously wrong, that is—she seems apathetic and out of sorts, but the symptoms don't seem to develop into anything, do they?'

'No. But it bothers me. I'd like her to see a real doctor.'

'Give her another couple of days. Then we'll decide.'

'Have it your way,' said Harry tonelessly, and went out of the tent. She watched as he disappeared up the track which led to Bed Four. As she turned back inside the tent one of the ponies grazing on the slopes of the *merg* beyond the camp suddenly gave a long, frightened neigh and galloped sharply away to the edge of the drop into the valley. As Liliane watched it put its head down and began to tear once more at the thin grass, giving an occasional little whinny as it became calmer. Nothing else was to be seen on the bare expanse of the *merg* save the other ponies, which had shown no reaction. Above them, in the hard bright blue of the autumn sky, the inevitable goshawk swung, ceaselessly hunting.

On a sudden impulse Liliane walked across to Judy Agar's tent. She and Judy were the only ones left in camp. The others were all up at Bed Four.

Judy was sitting on her camp-bed. She looked apprehensive, and stared at Liliane without speaking as the older woman parted the tent-flap and peered inside.

'Feeling better?'

Judy sank back on the bed, turning her face away.

'I'll be OK soon, but right now I feel like being left alone.'

Liliane closed the flap of the tent. Harry was right. There was something odd about Judy's behaviour. Ever since that strange night when Liliane had heard her weeping, Judy seemed in some curious way to have distanced herself from the rest of the party, almost as though she was exhausted. Frowning, Liliane turned back towards her own tent, but then changed her mind, and began the long climb up the stony path which led to Bed Four.

When she reached the site, Tom Meachem was talking to Harry. Tom had obviously been digging. He was sweating slightly, although the air up here was distinctly chill. It was still early afternoon, but little puffs of grey cotton-woolly cloud were already gathering around the peak of the mountain above them, sure messengers of the fast-approaching autumn night. Tom saw the look of enquiry on her face as she reached them, and shook his head.

'Nothing more so far. There's not a bone anywhere near. Just those two skulls, ancient and modern.'

He saw the momentary spasm of feeling on her face and added hastily, 'Don't get me wrong, Liliane. I'm not knocking them. I know what I found when I got here, and I'm damn sure it wasn't planted by you or anybody else. You know what I mean . . . you get kind of a feel for these things, after you've been on one or two digs.'

She nodded abruptly, but he persisted.

'But it *is* mighty curious, isn't it? Two near-perfect skulls, and nothing else. There should be something, surely?'

'Perhaps some movement in the mountain?' Chowdhuri had joined them quietly, still holding the pointed steel trowel with which he had been probing the sub-soil exposed beneath the rock overhang. 'The other bones could have shifted— perhaps they are ten, twenty yards away, down the slope.'

'No sign of any movement that I can see,' grunted Meachem. 'And it would have had to be a recent one. One of those skulls isn't more than two hundred years old.'

Harry Kernow watched them, interested. It was strange how the little scientific crisis into which they had all been plunged seemed to have united them, instead of splitting them still further, as he would have imagined. Meachem was even polite to Prakash Chowdhuri nowadays, and Chowdhuri himself—though he was harassed by constant queries from Delhi —appeared to have lost that chip on his Indian shoulder. The reason, reflected Kernow, was simple enough. They were united now by faith in Liliane. Not one of them believed she had planted any kind of fraud in the rocks above Bed Four —even though each of them, including himself, knew that she would have had plenty of opportunity in the past few weeks. Criticism and suspicion from outside had fused them into a tight, outward-facing little group . . . all of them except for Judy. She alone had withdrawn. It was as though she knew something the rest of them didn't.

A few minutes later, walking in silent single file, they reached the bottom of the path, where it led out on to the flatter ground of the *merg*. Harry felt a slight prickle of unease as his gaze took in the tents. There was something wrong . . . something missing. He looked hard to where the ponies were grazing peacefully in the far corner of the *merg*, and said quietly to Mohammad, who was walking just behind him, 'Where's Bulbul?'

Taken aback, the Kashmiri stopped, and then called sharply to one of the other porters. Zareer came out from the porters' tent, looking around, surprised. By now the others had realised what was wrong, and were crowding round him. Liliane's pony Bulbul was no longer on the *merg*. Oppressed by a sense of dread, Kernow walked to the edge of the long line of rocky scree which marked the two-hundred-foot drop into the valley. The twilight was gathering fast, but with a sick feeling at his stomach he could just discern the pale-cream hide of Bulbul far below him. She lay on her back, her legs in the air, and there was no movement.

'Is she down there, Harry? I don't really want to look.'

Liliane was at his side, her face apprehensive. He took her arm, and moved her back from the edge.

'Yes. There's nothing to be done for her. She was startled by something . . . an eagle, perhaps. Or maybe she just made a mistake. It was a quick death, anyway.'

She nodded, but he kept his hand protectively on her elbow as they walked back to where the others watched silently.

'The *memsahib* had better have my pony Ayesha now,' he said to Mohammad. The man looked frightened.

'And see that I get something better than Bulbul,' said Harry with deliberate brutality. 'I don't want another animal that jumps over a cliff because it sees a big bird, or gets stung by a wasp.'

Mohammad nodded silently, and disappeared into the Kashmiri communal tent.

Jumped over the cliff? thought Harry. He'd never known a Himalayan pony to do something as stupid as that. He remembered how Bulbul was lying—fully ten yards out from the bottom of the drop. Jumped? It was more as though she'd been catapulted down into that valley.

5

Puzzled and wary, Kernow stood back from the pony's huddled corpse. The morning sun was warmer in the shelter of the cliff than had seemed possible in the expanse of the *merg* far above him, and two or three late butterflies drifted past, one settling for a moment on Bulbul's glazed, dead eye.

The first thing Harry had done when he woke was to take one of the other ponies down to where Bulbul lay. He had chosen an animal called Zenoba which he had not ridden before. Cautiously, he had tethered it some distance away from its dead companion, so that it would not take fright. Again he put his hand through Bulbul's thick rough mane. There was no doubt about it. Her neck had been broken by a blow—not shattered, as might be expected from a two-hundred-foot fall, but neatly snapped. The broken ends were cleanly severed. Moreover, to judge from the condition of the rest of the body, she had landed not on her head but on her rump and rear legs, which were crumpled under her. Of course, the whiplash effect of such a landing might have snapped the powerful neck bones. But somehow it looked like a blow.

Suddenly he shivered, standing motionless. It was a totally still day, yet the leaves on a big sprouting juniper bush thirty yards away seemed to be trembling very, very slightly. And he could have sworn there had been the very slightest sound. His eyes searched the ground in the way he had been taught as a soldier. But nothing now moved, and a moment later the silence was broken by a call from above him.

'Harry . . . what are you doing?'

It was Liliane's voice. Shading his eyes with his hands, he looked up and could just see her head, outlined black against the sky where she peered over the parapet-like edge of the drop.

'Just checking old Bulbul. I'm coming back to camp now.'

She nodded and disappeared. He went slowly back to where Zenoba stood tethered, nibbling daintily at the short turf.

Whatever had disturbed him did not seem to have bothered the pony. Nevertheless, he was frowning as he urged Zenoba up the stony path to the *merg*, and as soon as he arrived at the tents he sent for Mohammad. The Kashmiri was washed and scented, fresh from prayer. Kernow motioned him to the spare canvas chair in his tent. Mohammad sat, and waited silently.

'I have been down into the valley to see Bulbul,' said Kernow at last.

The Kashmiri nodded. 'I also, at first light.'

Kernow leaned forward intently. 'What did you think?'

Mohammad shrugged. 'Back broken, *sahib*. Neck also. It is—' he gestured expressively with his hands— 'a long fall.'

'Why did you go down?'

Again there was a flicker of unease in Mohammad's dark, handsome face. 'I was . . . curious, *sahib*.'

'And now you are satisfied?'

Mohammad was silent, uneasy.

'You're not satisfied, any more than I am, Mohammad,' said Kernow briskly. 'And I think you know something . . . suspect something, at any rate. What in God's name was it, then, that threw that pony off the cliff?'

'A bear?' Mohammad's voice was doubtful even as he said it, but Kernow noted with interest that he said nothing to challenge the statement that the pony *had* been thrown over.

'It was a damned odd bear that tackled Bulbul with Zareer awake in his tent twenty yards away, and the *memsahib* Agar in her own tent, and did it so silently that neither of them heard a sound. Not a grunt, not a squeal.'

There was another pause, while Mohammad elaborately picked at a bit of dirt under his fingernail. Kernow had learned to wait, and said nothing. At last Mohammad spoke again, in a polite, conversational way.

'Before the time of Hari Singh, this meadow was not called Shalamerg.'

Hari Singh was the one-time Maharajah of Jammu and Kashmir, whose princely rule under the British Raj had ended with Indian independence nearly forty years ago.

'In the time of Hari Singh,' repeated Mohammad, 'the name was changed. The Maharajah loved the flowers. He called this meadow Shalamerg. It means, in your language—'

'I know what it means,' said Kernow, suddenly impatient. 'Shalamerg . . . Shawl Meadow. Because of the pattern of the flowers.'

'That is so,' said Mohammad. 'It is a good name.'

'No doubt,' said Kernow drily. 'But it doesn't seem to have much to do with Bulbul.'

'Before it was called Shalamerg,' said Mohammad, 'it was known as Wonmuhnoemerg.'

Kernow was startled. 'But that means—'

'Yes,' said Mohammad, faintly triumphant. 'It means Wild Man Meadow.'

'What do you know about it?'

Mohammad rose. 'I have much work this morning, *sahib*. I must arrange to buy another pony. And I know little—I am not a tribesman, I am a modern man.'

His voice was becoming a little shrill, and his normally careful English began to slip.

'I go to cinema in Srinagar. Last month I see *Saturday Night Fever*—very good. I drive car. I take but one wife.'

'But you know . . . something?'

Mohammad turned before he left the tent. 'There were stories, *sahib*. In my grandfather's time. Few people would come to this place—they believed it to be the home of a wild god. There was much superstition then, *sahib*.'

'But nothing since?'

'Once . . . my grandfather . . . he found a bear . . . dead. Its neck was broken.'

'And?'

A trace of irony had crept into Mohammad's voice.

'What animal do you know that can break the neck of a bear, *sahib*?'

He turned and vanished through the flap of the tent.

Harry Kernow sat on his camp-bed, thinking. What could kill a Himalayan bear in such a way—or, for that matter, a Himalayan pony? A tiger, perhaps. But there simply were no tigers in the mountains of Kashmir. Tigers belonged further east, in the jungle areas of Nepal. A snow leopard, possibly? It was a rare animal up here, but there were certainly some in these mountains. But no . . . if a snow leopard had killed Bulbul, there would have been noise—snarling, screaming, neighing. And yet whatever had happened, had happened silently. And I very much doubt, he thought, if the snow leopard exists that would tackle a Himalayan bear.

So could it really be an unknown creature, the so-called wild man of—what had he called it?—Wonmuhnoemerg? The wild man legend, in various forms, was common enough in the Himalayas, though it was much stronger in the eastern Himalayas, far away from here.

He went out across the *merg* to Meachem's tent. The American was seated at his small trestle table, writing notes. He looked up as Harry appeared at the tent-flap.

'Tom,' said Harry abruptly, 'there's something damned funny about how that pony died.'

'I know,' Meachem said soberly. 'We all know, Harry. Liliane . . . Mohammad . . . Prakash . . . Judy, too. Especially Judy.'

'Why especially Judy?'

'Have you seen her this morning?'

Harry shook his head.

'She's changed,' said Meachem. 'She's not tired and listless any more. She's scared, really scared. And she won't say why.'

Harry made an impatient gesture. 'Well, I'll have a look at her later, though I'm running out of tranquillisers. But first —will you come down and look at what's left of Bulbul?'

As they emerged from the tent together Liliane came across the short turf towards them. Her face was a little pale, but determined.

'Are you going down to the pony again?'

Harry nodded.

'Then I'm coming too.'

'Better not, Liliane. No need to upset yourself unnecessarily.'

She whirled on him, her eyes alight with anger. 'What do you mean, "unnecessarily"? She was my pony, I'm the leader of this expedition, and I want to know what's going on. There's nothing "unnecessary" about that. Do you think because I'm a woman I can't bear the sight of a dead pony?'

Harry answered her steadily. 'You didn't seem too eager to look over the edge at her last night,' he said.

Liliane shrugged, her face composed again. 'I was quite fond

47

of her. But I'm through that now. I want to know what happened.'

'Wouldn't we all?' Meachem said drily.

Silent and subdued, Chowdhuri joined them as they picked their way carefully down the stony pony-trail which led to the bottom of the bluff. Judy Agar had come to the entrance of her tent as they left the *merg*, but had turned away without speaking when Liliane called a greeting. Even before they came round the corner of the bluff beside the jumble of rocks where Bulbul lay, Harry could hear a faint pervasive sound becoming more and more insistent in his ears. There was a gasp of astonishment from Meachem, walking a few yards ahead. As Harry came up beside him the reason was clear. Around the corpse of the pony buzzed a great swarm of flies.

'What's happening?' Harry exclaimed angrily. 'She's only been dead twelve hours—there shouldn't be anything like—'

Meachem walked forward and peered at the pony.

'My God,' he said quietly. Harry turned swiftly. Liliane was beside him, her face appalled. Bulbul lay on her back, not as Harry remembered her lying, but with her head towards them. Except that Bulbul no longer had a head. Over the raw red stump of her neck crawled hundreds of eager insects.

'You didn't say,' said Liliane. 'You didn't say she was like this.'

'She wasn't like this,' Harry said gently. 'When I was down before she was five yards away from here. And she had a head.'

'How long ago was that?' Meachem asked.

'About an hour.'

'Then,' said the American, 'whatever did this can't be far away.'

Harry knelt beside the pony, while Chowdhuri took off his light twill jacket and flapped it up and down in a vain effort to drive away the flies. Harry examined the neck thoroughly. The head had not been severed cleanly. Nerve and muscle ends projected from the body in a ragged circle, and a strip of flesh from the vanished head still remained. He looked up at Meachem, who came forward and made his own examination. Liliane, clearly forcing herself, knelt beside him. At last the American looked up, his face expressionless.

48

'Do you think what I think, Harry?'

'I imagine so. That head wasn't cut off, was it?'

'It sure wasn't.'

Beside them, Liliane got stiffly to her feet.

'If you two know something, then tell me,' she said crisply.

'We don't know anything,' Harry answered. 'But you've looked at the . . . neck. There's nothing resembling a clean cut.'

'So?'

'So,' said Meachem, interrupting, 'the head was pulled off. Dragged off, by the look of that neck. Maybe only a few minutes ago. But what the hell would have that kind of strength . . . your guess is as good as mine.'

They stared around them, across the piled rocks in the mountain's overhang. The shadow of a cloud moved majestically across the green-brown slopes across the valley. The world seemed, all at once, very silent. Very faintly came the murmur of the stream, fifty yards away. Suddenly there was a harsh cry as a crow got up from the long scrubby grass beyond the stream. The shock of the sudden sound froze them for a second or two, but nothing else moved. Never in his life had Harry experienced such a feeling of primitive dread as the one that gripped him now. He cursed himself, and almost without realising it, spoke his thoughts aloud.

'I'm an incompetent fool. I should have brought the rifle.'

From somewhere above them, where the mountain bulged out, supporting the plateau of the *merg* where the camp was set, a pebble rolled, gathering speed as it ricocheted off the almost vertical rock wall until it fell at their feet. Liliane looked at them, her eyes wide.

'Judy's up there,' she said. 'And she's alone.'

'She's not alone,' said Harry. 'The Kashmiris are there—and they know where the rifle is. Still, we'll go straight back.'

Afterwards Harry could not remember the exact moment when his sensation of tingling apprehension had begun . . . whether it was before or after the pebble rolled. He felt as he imagined a trapped animal might feel—every sense alert and yet a creeping paralysis of will. And there was something else, too . . . a sense of presence. For a moment, inconsequentially, there flashed into his mind the memory that long, long ago, men had believed that each stream and mountain and wood and glade had its own spirit, its attendant god. He correctly identified now the feeling he was experiencing. It was awe.

'Come on.' He forced out the words. 'Let's hurry.'

Ten minutes later they were back on the *merg*. All was exactly as they had left it—Mohammad and Zareer and the boy Jinni patching an old tarpaulin sometimes used as a shelter over Bed Four. Mohammad watched them curiously as they came up to the tents, but said nothing. Judy Agar was still in her tent, lying on her camp-bed, and disinclined to talk. Liliane went to join Chowdhuri, walking over to the specimen hut. Meachem and Harry were left alone. Meachem faced him squarely.

'You felt it, too, didn't you, Harry? I saw your face. Christ, I was cold. Really cold.'

Harry nodded, and after a second Meachem went on, a little doubt creeping into his voice.

'A shock, of course, finding the head gone. What do you think . . . a leopard?'

'It wasn't a leopard. The leopard doesn't live that could or would tear the head off a horse in that way. Or that could have killed Bulbul so silently in the first place.'

Meachem met Harry's eyes.

'What are we going to do?'

'I think we ought to have a little conference, Tom. All of us—including Judy. But not the five Kashmiris—not yet. I'll speak to Liliane.

6

Liliane watched the others as they crowded round the trestle table in the specimen hut. Tom's face was filled with eager curiosity, Harry's was as impassive as ever, Chowdhuri seemed worried, and Judy . . . well, it was difficult to analyse Judy's expression. Part sulky, part frightened . . . with, Liliane thought suddenly, an extraordinary flicker, every so often, of something like triumph. Perhaps Judy ought to be replaced. She'd done little enough work for the past fortnight, and she didn't really seem suited for the party any more. There was no room for passengers at Shalamerg. An immense amount of work remained to be done, and they could never be certain that Delhi wouldn't decide abruptly to withdraw their work permits. The dig was so close to the Indo-Pakistan ceasefire line that permission could easily be cancelled on security grounds. So time was precious . . . but Harry was speaking. She jerked her mind back to the meeting.

'What do you think, Liliane?'

She tried hard to keep the impatience from her voice.

'The trouble is that there are no facts. The strange death of a pony, the even stranger removal of its head, Mohammad's story that Shalamerg was once called something which means Wild Man Meadow, and that his grandfather once found a dead bear, and that local people thought the hill was haunted. They probably think half the hills in the Himalaya are haunted. Everything's so insubstantial. I agree it's all rather mysterious —and, like you, I did feel frightened down there. But we probably communicated our fear to each other. Somebody was walking over our graves.'

'There's something different,' Harry insisted. 'Something wrong. I don't give a damn about facts. I don't want to play the Old Kashmir Hand, but I've been around these parts for the last four years, and I've learned to trust my instinct. Up on Everest, once, it was a fact that the area where we were climbing was clear of avalanches. Much too early in the season. Even Tensing Ponay said so. But my gut told me something

51

about avalanches, and my gut was right. That's why I'm here today.'

He paused for a moment, and Liliane realised he was more disturbed, more emphatic, than she had ever seen him. Then he went on.

'In any case, there *are* one or two facts. It's a fact that no leopard could have done that to Bulbul. It's a fact that it would have been behaviour totally alien to a bear—and in any case I doubt a bear could have done it. The only animal I can imagine with that kind of strength would be a gorilla, and there are no gorillas in the Great Himalaya, or anywhere else in Asia for that matter. And there are no great apes up here—no *known* great apes, I mean—with anything like that strength.'

'I suppose a group of human beings could have done it, working together,' said Meachem slowly.

'Possibly they could have, but they didn't,' said Harry. 'The first time I went down, Bulbul was still in one piece. I looked down the trail along the stream—you know, where the spur comes down from the old glacier bed, and the trail goes out of sight?'

Meachem nodded.

'Well, that trail was empty. To get from that point to where Bulbul lay would take forty minutes by pony, and about an hour on foot. I don't think any group of human beings could have got up to Bulbul, wrenched off her head, and disappeared in the space of a single hour. In fact, I'm absolutely certain they couldn't. In any case, why would a group of human beings want to do it?'

Wearily, Liliane pushed the heavy dark hair back from her forehead. Once more, absurdly at this moment, Harry felt an irrepressible quiver of desire.

'Riddles, riddles,' she sighed. 'The Himalaya is full of riddles, it seems.'

'Including,' said Harry deliberately, 'the one about the Abominable Snowman.'

There was a giggle, half-stifled, from Chowdhuri. Judy, who had seemed half-asleep, lifted her head and looked at Harry for the first time. Liliane gave a little groan. Meachem was the first to speak.

'It's not such a joke as all that,' he said sharply. 'There've been footprints found for more than a hundred years, and a lot have been photographed. British parties on Everest have spotted footprints over the past half century—people have argued endlessly that they were made by bears. The British Everest guy—what's his name?'

'John Hunt,' said Harry. 'Lord Hunt.'

'That's the man. He and his wife saw prints only a year or two ago. He thinks there's a case for investigation. Mind, there have been expeditions. But they found nothing. And most of the reports come from further east, in Nepal.'

'You seem to know a lot about it, Tom.' Liliane sounded slightly resentful.

He shrugged. 'Like you, I began with anthropology, and I was once invited to join a Washington State University team looking into the *susquatch*—you know, the North American Bigfoot. Kind of an Alaskan Snowman.'

'Why didn't you join?'

He smiled, slightly sheepish. 'I guess I thought the *susquatch* was a lot of hooey. But I did a little work on the problem before I decided it wasn't for me, so I did look at some of the Asian reports of similar sightings.'

He leaned forward.

'I'll tell you something, though. The Russians take it seriously, though they keep their research under wraps. They call their beast the *alma*, and they've got full-time research teams working on it. Not so long ago they put an expedition through the Pamirs—north of the Karakoram, not such a hell of a long way from here. Found nothing, though. But there's supposed to have been an *alma*, some kind of ape-man, killed by a sentry at the end of the Second World War, at Khulm, up on the Soviet-Afghan border. And that's not so very far from here, either.'

'An American party did bring back some hair said to have belonged to a . . . a creature,' said Chowdhuri, who was obviously regretting his giggle. 'The Department of Anthropology at Delhi University examined it—I saw a report in a scientific journal. I forget all the details, but I remember they said it came from some sort of ape. Not a bear. But there have been many fakes, many fakes. There was a scalp, from a village up in Nepal, not far from Mount Everest—'

'Khumjung,' said Harry. As though his mind was a camera, he remembered the blaze of yellow bell-like flowers across the green valley from Khumbul Yul Lha mountain, with the puffs of white cloud drifting above the long, low houses. God, he thought with sudden despair, I suppose I'll never climb on Everest again.

'Yes,' said Chowdhuri. 'The scalp was from Khumjung. I saw photographs of it. It looked very strange, that scalp. A pronounced sagittal crest, front to back. But when they took the scalp for examination, it turned out to be goatskin.'

'Well, that's a fact, at any rate,' said Liliane. 'But it's a negative fact. There's absolutely no scientific case to be made—'

'I don't give a damn what scientific case can be made,' interrupted Harry brusquely. 'If John Hunt says it's worth a thought, then it's worth a thought. He knows the Himalayas —and I don't just mean climbing Everest. I'd back his opinion against any scientist who hasn't spent a quarter of a century up and down these valleys. And which of you has done that?'

He paused, and went on more quietly. 'Besides, Liliane, you have got what seems to me to be a scientific case. You've got that second skull.'

Liliane sighed, and Harry continued relentlessly.

'According to the tests you place confidence in, that skull was still attached to its living owner between about 1750 and 1850. And it's the same as the one that was tested as being about a million years old, isn't it?'

Liliane nodded.

'Then,' Harry went on, 'if a species can survive for a million years, what's to stop members of the same species being alive today?'

'We would need proof,' Chowdhuri began angrily, but Harry interrupted.

'I know what the trouble is. It's outside your chosen field, isn't it? None of you seems able to adapt to inconvenient facts. You've come here as palaeontologists. You're skull merchants —you don't want living heads. I'll bet every one of you really wishes it hadn't all happened this way. You don't want facts you can't understand. You'd be happier with just that one million-year-old skull, because then you could slot it into your time-scale for Adam and Eve, name it, classify it, argue about it, and get a lot of scientific mileage out of it. And it would only raise the kind of questions you feel able to answer. Well, think again, all of you. Because something's telling me loud and clear that there's something out there that killed Bulbul, that tore her head off only a couple of hours ago, and it isn't a million years old and it isn't a fossil. And it knows these mountains far, far better than I do, and about a million times better than you. So you'd better start accommodating that into your thinking.'

'Yes,' Harry,' said Liliane. She was ironically meek, and Harry grinned. She spoke to Meachem.

'What do you think, Tom?'

He hesitated. 'Well, it would have to be a remarkable species—a relict fauna which survived, unchanged, in a tiny population, and undetected, for a million years.'

Harry stirred. 'What's a relict fauna?' ˉ

'The distribution of an animal into small localised communities, such as mountain tops, as survivors of a distribution which was once much wider,' said Liliane. 'But—on what you said a moment ago—you're right, Harry, at least as far as I'm concerned. I didn't want that second skull—it messes everything up. And, of course, up until some time between 1750 and 1850, it *was* a relict fauna—it must have been. But not now . . . surely?'

'Why not?'

'These mountains have been climbed over for the past century. There've been planes over them, helicopters, men with cameras, tourists even. No ape-man, no man-ape, could live here undetected. Not now.'

Harry was astonished. 'Is that what you believe? Then you simply don't grasp the sheer . . . immensity . . . of the Himalayas. There are valleys above here, and further north, in the Karakoram, where no European has been for a thousand years—maybe where no human being of any race has ever been. This is the wildest mountain country on earth. Some of it is inaccessible in any weather, at any time of year. If your . . . your relict fauna could take care of itself, then there's no place on earth where it would stand a better chance of surviving undetected.'

55

He turned to Meachem. 'Tom, you made those models. Supposing the owner of either of those skulls was around today—what would it look like? I mean in terms of height . . . that sort of thing.'

Meachem pursed his lips. 'Well, it's all palaeontological and anatomical guesswork, but we've reconstructed species on a lot less evidence that this. In simple terms, I would say first of all that it was definitely hominid—man-like, ape-like— probably very much nearer to what we accept as man than what we classify as ape.'

'How do you know that?'

'The dentition—the teeth. Size, arrangement, all very like man. And strong evidence that he—or she—' he glanced for a moment at Liliane—'was neotenic. That means,' he went on hastily, 'that the creature had the kind of milk teeth that humans have, and that, like human babies, it was born "early" —in a helpless, undeveloped state. As a matter of fact, it's physically impossible for a human female to give birth to a baby with a fully-developed head. The head and brain grow after birth—that's what makes us such clever little people. The owners of both these skulls were born in the same way. That's why they're nearer man than ape. As to size, judging from the measurements of the skull and jaws, and the kind of muscles that would have had to support them, the creature was bipedal —I mean it walked upright on two feet—and it was probably between six and seven feet tall. Nearer six than seven, I'd say, because it was probably also pretty thick in the body. Yes, it would be around, say, six feet four inches, and very strong indeed. It certainly wasn't *Gigantopithecus*—that's a great ancestral ape which lived in the Middle Pleistocene, also around a million years ago. We only know him for his jaws, but we reckon he was more than ten feet tall, and probably went on four feet for a least part of the time. This skull wouldn't fit a creature like that. No, I'm afraid we haven't found King Kong—not even a mini-Kong.'

Liliane rose. 'That seems an appropriate note to finish on, Tom. I agree with your model of the species, as it must have existed . . . well, unless the dating is wrong, until compara- tively recent times. But I'm sorry, Harry. I find it very difficult to accept that it's still wandering around Shalamerg. There may be valleys where no European has been in a thousand years, but this isn't one of them, is it? I think we're all over-reacting—it may be the height that affects us, because, after all, we're more than 10,000 feet up. Everything that has happened can be more reasonably explained in some other way.'

'What way?' Harry asked quietly.

She answered sharply. 'I don't know . . . I don't know. But I don't think it's an Abominable Snowman. That's all I need now—an Abominable Snowman. What a stupid name, anyway.'

'It's simply a literal translation of the original Tibetan, *metoh kangmi*. Means "terrible creature of the snows".'

Liliane held up her hand. 'One thing is very important. Please, I beg you, do not talk about this in Srinagar or Chandigarh or anywhere else outside our own party. I'm already accused of being a fraud—a lot of nonsense about Snowmen will only add fuel to the flames.'

She turned to Chowdhuri.

'You don't need to put this in your reports to Chandigarh, do you, Prakash?'

He shook his head. She smiled at him, a little palely, as she left. Meachem tapped him on the shoulder.

'Prakash, you were talking about that fake scalp, the goat-skin one with the sagittal crest.'

'Yes?'

'I wonder why whoever faked it thought to fake a sagittal crest. Almost as though it was modelled on the two skulls we found, wasn't it?'

Chowdhuri shrugged. From where she still sat beside the trestle table, Judy Agar spoke. With a shock, Harry realised they were the first words she had uttered throughout. Her eyes seemed very bright.

'You talk and talk,' she said scornfully. 'And you miss the point, all of you. You understand nothing.'

'But you do know something, Judy?'

It was Tom's voice, but Judy Agar's eyes were fixed on Harry. She was, he thought, totally unlike the merry, hard-working girl she had first seemed to him when he joined the party.

'You're not quite as stupid as the rest,' she said. 'Surely you can see?'

He said nothing, waiting.

'The heads,' she said. 'You've found two heads. Nothing else, was there? Just two heads?'

'Yes.'

'And what happened to Bulbul? She lost her head. That's three heads. Perhaps . . . perhaps there'll be more.'

She laughed.

7

The General who was the latest President of Pakistan sat at his desk in a small office high in his official residence in Islamabad, and absently fingered the little silver polo trophy he had won at Simla when he was a young man . . . how long ago? He narrowed his eyes as he peered at the inscription, because there were two army brigadiers in the room, and it was his practice never to allow them to see him wearing spectacles. Yes . . . there it was . . . 'Simla District Championship: 1st Marri Lancers (Queen Mary's Own) 23rd August 1938.'

Another world . . . another time . . . and another man, he conceded ruefully to himself. The young man who had won a cup on that summer's day would soon be seventy: And Simla was far away and in another country . . . a rival country, India. As for himself . . . once he had been a subaltern, now he ruled a hundred million people. There was Bhutto—look what happened to him!—and there was Zia and now it's my turn, he thought. And for how long? For a moment he remembered that regiment of the old Indian Army, long ago destroyed by the partition of the British Raj, which had left him on the Pakistan side of the divide, and Indian friends whom he had respected on the other. There was the long, familiar walk down the shop-lined Mall of the Indian hill-station . . . the British ladies in their big hats and white dresses, the portrait of the King-Emperor in the officers' mess. It had all seemed fine and elegant to an innocent subaltern *subadar* in a crack Indian cavalry regiment. But all that was over. The King-Emperor had been dead for more than thirty years, and his Empire—good riddance to it—for longer still. History was history, but the realities of power were here and now. In Pakistan, the army was power. Unconsciously he squared his shoulders as he looked across the desk at the two officers seated facing him.

'Then what the devil is she playing at, this damned Mantis?'

The younger of the two brigadiers, a swarthy man with a single line of medal ribbons, tapped the map which lay between them on the desk. It was the big, green-and-brown contoured air operational map of Kashmir, the Western Himalaya and Western China, Sheet ONC G-7. Marked on it, in grey hatched lines, were the boundaries of the air defence interception zones between India and Pakistan. They followed, almost exactly, the old ceasefire truce line established after the inconclusive struggle between the two nations thirty years previously—and stamped along them, at intervals, were the words 'Warning: Aircraft infringing upon Non-Free Flying Territory may be fired on without warning.' The young brigadier was the chief army intelligence officer for the Pakistan-protected area of Kashmir diplomatically known as Azad, or Free Kashmir. His headquarters was near Gilgit, almost in the shadow of the stupendous range of the Karakoram. He knew ONC G-7 like the back of his well-manicured hand, and his finger slowly traced the ceasefire line.

'You see, sir, that Shalamerg is no more than a mile south of the line, on the Indian side—indeed, to get to it by road it is necessary to go within about four hundred metres of Azad territory.'

The General bent over the map. 'Technically speaking, some of it is a demilitarised zone,' he said, his voice neutral.

'Perhaps we could call it territory in which we have an interest,' said the intelligence officer. 'And it's also an area we might expect the Indians to be sensitive about. Yet they have this mixed party of Indians and Americans excavating bones almost right on the line. I ask myself why, sir.'

The General considered for a few moments. 'It could be legitimate, you know, Magib. There is an Indian university representative?'

The brigadier nodded. 'A Dr Chowdhuri. He's not on our lists, but, of course, that's not necessarily conclusive. No, sir, what attracted my attention was that it doesn't seem to be a genuine scientific party.'

'Why not?'

'They seem to have made some rather ridiculous discoveries —skulls that shouldn't be there, impossible datings, that sort of thing. I asked some of our own university people in Karachi. They say the claims are absurd.'

'So you think they may be a front for something else. But what else? I know the Mantis is a clever woman, but I can't

60

imagine that she's really going to start anything in Kashmir. Not with Afghanistan always on the boil.'

'And yet,' said the brigadier softly, 'when her own minister urged her to withdraw permission for the dig, she personally overruled him.'

'How do you know that?'

'I had a report from Central Intelligence.'

The General kept his face impassive. He was careful not to know too much about how Central Intelligence worked. Let's just remember, he thought, that its information from inside the Indian Government is usually reliable. He turned to the other brigadier, an infantryman.

'Which is the nearest battalion?' he asked.

'The 8th Hunza Rifles,' said the brigadier. 'They're at Shirma, just over the line from Shalamerg. No more than four miles away.'

'Who commands them?'

'Azraf Khan, sir.'

The General looked up sharply. 'A Pathan, eh? Yes, I knew his father. What's he like, this Azraf Khan?'

The infantry brigadier, who thought all Pathans were mountain savages, kept his voice as neutral as possible. 'He is . . . a very active officer, sir.'

'Well, he'd better be active round Shalamerg, then. A little company exercise, perhaps. But discreetly. Just a very small patrol . . . something that might have lost its way, if explanations become necessary. But—' the General's voice hardened —'I trust that Azraf Khan will handle it so that explanations do not become necessary. Do I make myself clear?'

'Perfectly, sir.'

The infantry brigadier stood, saluted, and marched from the room. The other brigadier made as though to get to his feet, but the General waved him back to his chair.

'The 8th are a good battalion, I'm told. And, possibly, they might spot something. But I wouldn't be happy if that was the only card we had.'

The intelligence brigadier swallowed. 'No, sir.'

The General's tone was becoming impatient. 'Magib, I know you don't like talking, even to me, about the people you recruit. But . . . I hope there's another card in our hand.'

'There is, sir. We have a man . . . in the party digging at Shalamerg.'

'Ah.'

The General waited.

'He's a Kashmiri, sir. Mohammad Pingnoo. He superintends the camp.'

'Reliable?'

The other hesitated. 'Well, sir, as I said, he's a Kashmiri. You know what they're like—no love for India, and not much for us, either. And they tend to work for the highest bidder. We've used him in the past, but on pretty minor stuff—just local situation reports, that kind of thing. He tells us which unit is moving into the barracks at Pahlmarg, where the Indian patrols will be operating . . . nothing very important. We pay him, but I doubt if we've bought him. We've had no report from him yet—there could be a hundred reasons for that. But at least he's there.'

'There used to be a saying, up on the Frontier, when I was a young man,' said the General reminiscently. 'The local people said, "If the world is coming to an end, do not choose either a Pathan or a Kashmiri as father of a new race. They are disastrous men." And now we'll have both at Shalamerg . . . a Pathan *and* a Kashmiri.'

'Frankly, Kim, the trouble is that Erckmann's not popular.'

Richard Kimbell looked across angrily at the pink cherubic face of the University's Administrator of Scientific Research, shadowed by the early Californian twilight where he sat in the deep armchair opposite.

'What the hell does that matter, Sam? She's not trying for Miss America.'

'It does matter, Kim. If she rides right over everybody who gets in her way—' he held up a restraining hand—'and, after all, she usually does just that, then she can't complain if people are less than sympathetic when she gets herself into a mess. I'm under pressure from Paris. They want to withdraw her grant—jointly, with us.'

God, how often do I have to go on trying to get the point across? thought Kimbell wearily. He tried again.

'Sam, it doesn't matter whether she's entitled to complain or not. It doesn't matter whether she's the scientific equivalent of Attila the Hun or whether she's the Goody Two-Shoes of palaeontology. What does matter is that she's come up with something we don't understand—something that might change our thinking. She needs our support. She's our baby —at least, mostly our baby, because we supply the bulk of the cash. We can't just turn and run. You say Liliane's getting herself into a mess. Maybe it's we who're in the mess. We and every other palaeontology department in the western world.'

The Administrator did not miss the adjective. 'Why the *western* world?'

Ho, ho, thought Kimbell. Maybe I've found the key to the cash-box.

'I've been reading back, Sam. It seems to me that the Soviets take this general area of research a lot more seriously then we do. One of these days they're going to come up with something really big.'

The Administrator stirred uneasily, his face visited by doubt. But his voice was sceptical.

'What . . . a relict hominid fauna, surviving unchanged from a million years Before Present until a couple of centuries ago? Do you really believe that?'

'There's the coelacanth,' said Kimbell. 'As I recall, that's survived for around three hundred million years. Unchanged. And it may have been the grand-daddy of us all.'

The other waved a hand. 'A primitive fish, Kim. Not an advanced ape. And in the Indian Ocean. We don't know much about the bottom of the Indian Ocean.'

'I've been talking to our geography people,' said Kimbell. 'It seems we don't know much about the Himalayas, either. Nor the Karakoram. Nor the Pamirs—where the Soviet Academy of Sciences have just put through a full-scale expedition with the sort of budget that would give you a major cardiac arrest.'

'An expedition . . . looking for what?'

'Looking,' said Kimbell soberly, 'for what Liliane's two skulls may represent.'

The Administrator was silent, thinking.

'I have to think about the Press,' he said at last. 'You know that. The popular dailies aren't really on to it yet—it's a bit abstruse for them, and the only thing anybody seems to want to write about in that area is Afghanistan, thank God. But the scientific journals . . . well, you know as well as I do. They're publishing an article here and there, and correspondence —nearly all of it hostile. There's not enough cash to fund all the projects we're asked to back—and people are already asking how long we're going to go on funding Erckmann to make a fool of herself and us. But . . .'

'But?' said Kimbell softly.

The Administrator swallowed. 'Could you let me have a rundown on that Soviet stuff, Kim?'

Kimbell nodded.

'Because you're right about one thing,' said the Administrator. 'It would be something of a classic boo-boo if we withdrew Erckmann's grant, and then the Soviets published something really big. The popular papers would really have a peg to hang us on.'

'I never said that,' said Kimbell.

'No, but you came through in your own way,' said the Administrator, smiling for the first time. 'Erckmann could learn a lot from you.'

Down beside the great artificial lake of the Ob Sea, the last leaves swirled from the silver birches as a freezing wind drove in across the slate-grey water. From the crest of the rise where the couple walked they could just see the tops of the buildings of Akademgorodok, the Soviet science-city set a few miles from the great industrial complex of Novosibirsk, two thousand miles east of Moscow, in the heart of Siberia.

'Another week and the ice will be here,' said the woman, shivering and tucking her gloved hand into the arm of her companion. He nodded absently, and she pushed her short sturdy body round to face him, bringing them both to a momentary halt.

'I don't understand the details of what happened—after all, I'm a catalyst chemist, not an anthropologist. But you're still worried about Mustagh Ata, aren't you, Nikolai? Surely it wasn't your fault? It was a bad time of year for an expedition —everybody says so. They should have waited. And after all, it was your first.'

Dr Nikolai Plekhanov laughed shortly. 'It was the only

64

possible time this year, Arina. Mustagh Ata is high country . . . seven thousand metres, more in places. By the time we got back to camp at the lake it would have been impossible to go again. But I was so frustrated. So much evidence . . . and then . . . nothing.'

'You found footprints.'

He shrugged. 'Footprints, yes. The travel books are full of footprint-pictures, from Lenin Peak to Everest. We can argue forever over footprints. I wanted a . . . a man.'

'You're still sure it *is* a man?'

He laughed again. 'I'm not sure of anything, except that the Academy of Sciences is not very pleased. Three months' work for six scientists, an expedition that needed thirty porters. You know the kind of money that was spent—and nothing to show for it. And now there is this Liliane Erckmann.'

'Who is she?'

'An American, inevitably. At least, half American. The other half is French, I'm told. She's digging . . . Americans are always digging. And she's found something in Kashmir—a modern skull. I think it fits what I'm looking for, though we haven't got all the details. The Americans are keeping it all very quiet. The Academy knows she's found it, of course—it's been reported in half-a-dozen digests of foreign journals.'

'Will she publish?'

He leaned forward and kissed her lightly on her cold cheek, where a little curl of brown hair escaped from the brown-and-white foxskin hat.

'Of course she'll publish, my little squirrel. Who wouldn't, with a chance like that? And she'll draw the correct conclusions. I've had a look at her track record—it's very, very good. No, what puzzles me is that the Americans are keeping it so quiet. Nothing official from them at Berkeley, or from the Paris museum, for that matter. It's not like them. I have an uneasy feeling that they're sitting on something big . . . something very big indeed. They're getting a real blockbuster together—and suddenly, when they're ready, they'll publish. Then I—and the Academy—will look as though we're limping behind. As we shall be. We'll have Moscow on our backs —there'll be political implications. I shan't be popular.'

'Well, you're popular with me, Niki,' said the woman. 'I'm

glad you're here, not thousands of metres up in the Pamirs. Let's go back—we're going to the concert tonight. It's getting colder every minute.'

Rifleman Gundar Ali shivered in spite of himself, angry at the reflex weakness which had caused even so tiny a movement. He was wedged in a small overhang of boulders above Shala-merg, a pair of army binoculars beside him, and his loaded carbine within easy reach of his right hand. Infinitely slowly, he picked up the binoculars once more. A freezing wind, laced with a little driven snow, was cutting into the rock-tumbled corrie where he lay, but he was determined that he would not again give the least sign of his presence. The camp and the diggers were 200 feet below him. One of the diggers, a dark-haired woman, came out of the little hut at the side, followed by a short, plump Indian who was talking volubly. The tall man was still in the tent he had entered twenty minutes ago. Gundar Ali raised the binoculars a trifle. The five Kashmiris were busy round a small fire from which curled a thin column of blue smoke. They were making coffee.

High above them Gundar Ali's stomach contracted with longing for that hot coffee. He had been in the corrie for two hours, and there was another hour yet to go before he could slide down the mountain to rejoin his officer and the two other soldiers of the patrol who waited, hidden, below. The Hunza Rifles patrol was roughly a mile over the wrong side of the old truce line, and Gundar Ali had been told by his young platoon commander exactly what to say if he was caught.

'Colonel-*sahib* was very insistent,' the *subadar* had said to him. 'If they find you, say you have lost your way. If necessary, say you are a deserter. You can always make your way back to us later.'

There was not the least likelihood that Gundar Ali would be caught. His home was in the frontier mountains of Waziristan, now part of Pakistan, a bleak geological jumble of towering, razor-edged peaks where a human being had to be something between a leopard and a goat to survive. Gundar Ali was a tribesman, almost illiterate, but he knew the mountains as comprehensively as any western scientist knew his own research field. No movement in the rocks, no change in the wind, no cloud formation escaped him. The exact nature of the bending of a primrose in a crevice could tell Gundar Ali what animal had passed that way . . . and when. And he could lie as motionless as a leopard waiting to kill. This, he knew, was why he had been chosen for this particular task. Another hour . . . Once more he steadied the binoculars on the tall man's tent.

Something hit him in a blur of movement at the exact moment that his fingers made a minute adjustment on the focussing screw. The driving force of the impact was tremendous. His head and face were smashed into the rock in front of him, shattering his jaw in that first half-second. For another half-second his wide, astonished eyes saw a redness, a bulk, a shape above him, and then his head was wrenched round on his neck, severing the connection between his spinal cord and his brain. Gundar Ali twitched once, twice, and was dead.

Six hundred feet below him, the *subadar* and the other two soldiers waited an extra hour. Then, puzzled and anxious, the young officer took his patrol back to Shirma and Lieutenant-Colonel Azraf Khan.

8

Harry Kernow opened his eyes and was at once fully awake, listening. It was a characteristic he had developed long ago in the army, where some devotee of Rider Haggard's novels had nicknamed him Macumazahn—a Zulu word meaning He Who Sleeps With One Eye Open—after the Zulu name given to Allan Quatermain, hero of *King Solomon's Mines*. His whole being now was flooded with a sense of unease. A little wind was shaking the tent, gusting across the breadth of the *merg* and coming, he knew, from the Karakoram and the Indus River, north of Shalamerg. Had the rattling of the tent-flaps disturbed him? His hand went out to the .30 Winchester hunting rifle that, since Bulbul's death, he kept loaded beside his sleeping bag. He listened again for a few moments, and then, cursing, wriggled from his sleeping bag and went to the entrance of the tent, the rifle in his hand.

The night was clear and cold, though a few flags of cloud still clung round the peak high above Shalamerg. The clusters of stars which had earlier sprinkled the night were vanishing even as he watched, paling rapidly at the faint prophetic glow of the arriving dawn. He glanced at the luminous dial of his watch. It would be first light in about twenty minutes. The other tents were silent . . . no one else seemed to have been disturbed. Nevertheless, he stood at the tent-flap for a couple of minutes longer before he turned back to his sleeping bag. At the same instant, a sound he would never afterwards forget cut through the night.

It was a deep rising roar . . . a fierce cry of over-mastering rage and despair. The sound was not recognisably human, but no animal known to Kernow had ever made it. As he stood at the entrance to the tent it came again. He collected his wits at the second roar, and listened carefully to locate its source. The sound was coming from above the camp . . . from Bed Four. He ran across the *merg* to Meachem's tent, but the American, zipping his anorak, was outside before he reached it.

'What in hell's name was that? I wish we had two rifles. Wait a minute, though . . .'

He turned back into the tent and emerged almost immediately with the squat, double-barrelled flare pistol that was kept as emergency mountain rescue equipment.

As they ran together to the path leading up the mountainside to Bed Four Liliane came out of her tent, stooping to fasten her boots, her dark hair streaming over her shoulders. From above them the roar came again, primitive and desolate. Torches began to flash in the other tents.

'What do you think . . .' panted Liliane as she scrambled up the path beside the other two. Harry did not answer, but put out a restraining hand as they came up to the jumble of rocks which fringed Bed Four.

'We'll have a look,' he said. 'But don't go any closer for the moment. We can see from here.'

He peered into the white ground mist which swirled round the overhang where they had found the skulls. At first he thought there was no sound at all, but then, very faintly, he heard the tiniest rasp of indrawn breath. He took Tom by the wrist, and whispered.

'Is that thing loaded?'

Against the paling sky, he saw Tom nod.

'Put up a flare, then. Above the overhang.'

There was a dull thud from the flare pistol. Harry pulled back the bolt of his rifle and eased a round into the breech. High above them, seconds later, the flare burst, casting a blue-green light on Bed Four, ten yards to their front. Beside him, Tom stood rigid. Liliane gasped.

Turned towards them, seen more and more clearly as the flare sank towards the ground, was a face. In the bluish light the teeth seemed to be bared. The face was broad and hairy, with a flattened nose, and heavy brow-ridges. The reddish hair which fringed it grew thickly round the large ears and head. As the light from the slowly sinking flare became more intense Harry saw that the desperate eyes were fixed on his. For a moment an extraordinary sense of urgent communication filled his mind. Then the flare died in a sputter of bright sparks. He turned to Meachem, who was gazing transfixed.

'The other flare, quickly.'

Meachem fired the second barrel. As the flare burst high above them he could see more clearly what had happened. The creature, whatever it was, was trapped. It had apparently reached in under the overhang from which they had taken the two skulls. Perhaps it had pulled at one of Tom Meachem's supporting metal struts: possibly the strut had simply been nudged out of position by the massive shoulder. At any rate, it had given way, and the overhang had collapsed, pinning the creature by the left arm and shoulder. Probably half a ton of rock was now holding the arm, and though it struggled silently, fiercely, it had not yet managed to free itself. But what in the name of God was it?

Harry walked forward and looked more closely. The eyes under those great brow-ridges glared into his face. He felt a strong impulse to help it. With an effort he turned from its gaze and looked at the rest of the powerful body. It was something like a gorilla, something like a man . . . covered in hair. It was hard to estimate height while the creature was still crouched in the shadows, but it was probably around six feet. The body was barrel-shaped, squat and obviously powerful. With every tug it made the rock-fall from the overhang stirred.

'It's like my model,' breathed Meachem beside him. 'My God, I never dreamed I'd see anything like it.'

Liliane put her hand on Harry's shoulder, leaning forward to peer at the contorted face beside the overhang. Her lips were parted, and she was breathing quickly, trembling. But her words were practical, and jerked the other two out of the trance into which they seemed to have fallen.

'It's going to get away,' she said sharply. 'Harry . . . how can we . . . secure it?'

'Secure it?' he echoed stupidly.

'Of course. God, don't let it get away. Harry, Harry, it's knowledge undreamed of. Look at it . . . it's something unknown. It mustn't escape.'

He looked at the struggling body. The second flare had now died, but in the last minute the sun had touched the eastern mountain crest, bathing the whole of Bed Four in orange light, growing stronger every second, though the white mist still clung to the ground.

'It's no use trying to tie it,' he said at last. 'None of us could get within reach of that free arm.'

'We have chloroform,' said Chowdhuri softly, from the path behind them. He, too, was trembling, with cold or excitement or both.

'Harry, in your medical kit . . . you have a bottle . . . I remember. And it's never been used.'

Harry thought quickly. 'A cotton wool pad—a big one and well-soaked. On the end of a pole. It might work.'

In front of them a little fall of pebbles rattled from the collapsed overhang as the creature pulled silently at the rock. Liliane flinched involuntarily, and then asked Harry, her face doubtful, 'Could it harm . . .? I mean, we simply don't know exactly what . . .'

'You can chloroform a tiger,' said Harry quickly. 'I've seen it done, by the conservation people in Nepal. So I don't see why it should harm this . . . this thing.'

It was a second or two before Liliane nodded. At once, Chowdhuri turned down the path back to the camp. With a half-bitten-off curse, Tom Meachem jumped to his feet.

'I must be mad . . . the camera. At the very least, we can get some shots.'

He ran off down the path behind Chowdhuri. Harry and Liliane were left alone. The sky was now rapidly brightening towards full daylight, and a little black-and-white flycatcher perched on top of the overhang, looking for early insects, curiously oblivious to the creature struggling below it. Liliane touched Harry's arm, though she did not take her gaze from the overhang.

'You were right, Harry. Look at it . . . I think it's the creature of the skulls. The head . . . it fits our models exactly.'

Harry circled round the overhang, careful to keep clear of the free, powerful right arm.

'What are we going to do if we manage to chloroform it?' he said. 'We aren't equipped for this sort of thing.'

'We'll just have to take a chance,' said Liliane. 'As soon as we get word to Chandigarh and Delhi, there ought to be some action. Meanwhile, we have to keep it here. Somehow . . .'

The creature had now turned its head away from them, and seemed to be concentrating on moving a rock to the side of its trapped arm. Harry watched, feeling helpless.

'Keep it?' he said. 'You mean dead or alive?'

'I don't want it to die, but even dead it would be a fantastic discovery,' said Liliane.

He tried to keep his voice expressionless. 'You'd better not talk like that. Are you sure what this is?'

She shook her head. 'Not exactly, no. Obviously I can't be.'

'Could it be classified as man?'

Liliane hesitated. 'I don't know . . . it would need a lot of anatomical examination. Maybe eventually it will be classified as *Homo*. Maybe not.'

Harry laughed shortly. 'And maybe, if it is, we could be classified as murderers. That's what they usually call people who knowingly take the lives of creatures classified as *Homo*, outside war.'

Chowdhuri came panting back up the path, carrying Harry's metal medicine box and one of the spare tent poles, about eight feet long. Behind him came Tom Meachem with the camera, and the five Kashmiris. Mohammad was carrying a coil of rope. Tom began to circle the rock-fall, steadily taking pictures. The creature raised its head and roared once more. At close range the sound was infinitely disturbing. Fearfully, the Kashmiris chattered among themselves. The creature struggled frantically.

Harry took the bottle of chloroform from the box, pulled off his shirt, and soaked it thoroughly. With adhesive medical tape he tied the rolled shirt to the end of the tent pole. The sweet sickly scent of the chloroform was making him feel slightly dizzy, but he went forward, held out the pole, and thrust the package under the flared nostrils. His heart leaped for a moment as the creature stopped struggling and bit savagely at the package dangled in front of its face. Then, with a roar, it tore the chloroform-soaked cloth from the pole and flung it away. Yet it seemed to stagger as it turned back to struggle against the rockface.

Sweating with effort and excitement, Harry poked the package clear, and refixed it to the pole. Again he pushed it under the great head. Immediately it was flung away once more. The operation was desperately difficult, and he had to try again and again, while he saw with despair that the level of chloroform in the bottle was dropping steadily. But at last the creature seemed to falter.

Harry went forward a couple of paces, trying to hold the package-laden pole more firmly against the creature's face. For a moment it stopped struggling, watching him. Then, with almost inconceivable speed, its free arm lashed down within inches of his head, a blow that might well have snapped his spine. Shocked, he stumbled back, realising that if the creature's reactions had not already been at least marginally slowed by the chloroform, he would probably be dead. Now, however, it made a fatal change of tactics. Instead of flinging the package from the pole, it once more sank its teeth into it, worrying it as a dog might shake a rabbit. Within a few seconds the deep-sunk eyes clouded. It tore weakly at the sodden cloth, but the teeth could get no grip. The massive head fell forward to the chest, and the body slumped from the overhang, pinned there only by its trapped left arm.

His legs suddenly weak, Harry sat down on the cold ground. For the first time he was aware of the freezing wind sweeping up the valley, chilling the sweat on his naked chest. Meachem made as though to go forward, but Harry checked him, holding the chloroform under the creature's nostrils for another half-minute.

'Better safe than sorry,' he said, and swung sharply on Mohammad.

'Give me the rope.'

The Kashmiri, staring as though hypnotised at the huddled body, seemed not to hear. With an exclamation Chowdhuri took the rope from Mohammad's hand and gave it to Harry. As Kernow went forward to begin securing the creature, he smelt its pervasive odour . . . rank, alien, but not wholly unpleasant. He looped the rope around the legs, drawing it tight with mountaineer's knots.

'Will it hold?' whispered Liliane.

'This is eight-millimetre Braidline,' he said. 'We used it on Everest.'

She knelt beside him. For the past few minutes she had felt helpless, out of her depth, but her frustration was giving way to a sense of wonder as she looked more closely at what they had found. Her heart was thudding. She turned to Harry as he worked on at her side.

'How long will the chloroform last?'

73

He shrugged, tying another knot. 'This thing, whatever it is, is around the weight of a very big man, I'd guess. If it got a good dose, and I think it did . . . well, about an hour. We have to get it free of the overhang by then, and fully tied.'

Above him Tom Meachem was already wedging in another metal strut before starting to clear the debris of the fall. Chowdhuri toiled at his side, struggling to clear large rocks, the spectacles above his round, sweating face misted with effort. All five Kashmiris refused to come forward. They watched, talking excitedly among themselves, from several yards away.

Within half an hour the unconscious creature was free of the rock-fall. Occasionally it grunted, and once made a high whinnying sound in its drugged sleep, but it did not struggle. Mohammad was at last persuaded to go down to the camp to fetch two more metal tent poles. Harry tied these in the form of a cross. The effort of getting the creature into position above them, unaided by the Kashmiris, was almost more than even the four of them could manage. When they had finished, Chowdhuri—the oldest among them—was breathing unevenly.

Harry tied the creature's arms and legs to the points of the cross. The left arm was bleeding a little, the blood clotting amongst the reddish hair, but the arm did not seem to be broken. He stood back and looked critically at his work before he went over to Chowdhuri, who was sitting on the ground, his head between his hands.

'Prakash,' he said. 'We've got to get this thing down the path to the camp. The Kashmiris won't help. I wouldn't ask you, but it's going to take four of us—one at each corner.'

Chowdhuri looked up at him and nodded. Panting, he scrambled to his feet. 'Of course,' he said. 'My word, my word, Liliane. What are they going to say at Chandigarh? What are they going to say . . . now?'

Strapped to the poles, the creature looked disconcertingly helpless. It was unmistakably a male—the large genitals half-buried in the red, hairy thickets round its groin. Indeed, the whole body was hairy, especially down the neck from the back of the skull, where the hair grew like a mane. Before they set off down the path, Liliane parted the thick hairy scalp, and for the first time they could see the line of the raised sagittal crest running front to rear. She nodded to herself before picking up her end of one of the poles.

It took twenty minutes to get down the quarter-mile of path to the camp, and the operation proved a little easier than Harry had imagined. Liliane was strong and determined, though Chowdhuri had had to rest twice on the way down, and all of them were drained, exhausted when they reached the *merg*. At last, strapped to its cross, the creature lay there, on its back and between the tents. It was beginning to stir, and its black eyes opened. Liliane looked down at it, and then across to Harry.

'But why . . . why in Heaven did it come to Shalamerg? Especially with all of us camped here. Why did it go to the overhang on Bed Four? It doesn't make sense . . . you've never heard any recent reports of anything like this round here?'

He shook his head. 'Not since Mohammad's grandfather and the bear. And that must have been fifty years ago. And it's a pretty circumstantial story, at that. Nobody actually saw anything like this.'

'The coincidence is indeed remarkable,' said Chowdhuri, from behind them. He seemed recovered, though his face was still drawn.

'We come here as palaeontologists, investigating the remote past,' he said. 'We find bones . . . an ancient skull . . . and a new one. And then, suddenly, it is here . . . the creature itself.'

He turned to Liliane. 'It is very like Tom's models, is it not?'

'Yes. I can't believe it's coincidence . . . I simply don't understand how . . . unless—'

There was a burst of laughter from the others as Chowdhuri, beaming all over his round, bespectacled face, began once more to execute the little hopping dance of triumph which he had shown them on the morning—it seemed so long ago —when they had found the original skulls. With a whoop, Tom Meachem joined in, capering beside the Indian. At once they were all laughing, tired but exultant. Below them, the creature on the cross flexed the muscles of its right arm, tugging against the bonds. Liliane, suddenly grave, spoke nervously to Harry.

'You're sure about those ropes?'

'Yes. Strapped like that, it can't get any leverage. In any

case, even a tiger couldn't break eight-millimetre Braidline.'

'This isn't a tiger,' said Judy's voice behind them. For the first time, Liliane realised that Judy had not been in the group up at Bed Four.

'So you've brought him home,' Judy said almost dreamily. She smiled, and Liliane looked at her sharply. The sullen, brooding look which had become so familiar in the past fortnight was gone from Judy's face. And Judy alone had called the creature 'him'. Liliane herself, Harry, Tom, Chowdhuri . . . all the others had so far used the word 'it'.

Judy spoke again. 'I saw you carrying him down the path. I thought for a moment . . . you know . . . with the cross and all . . .'

'What?' said Liliane.

Judy smiled again. 'It was quite weird. He looked as though he was crucified.'

FLASH . . . FLASH . . . FLASH
RUSHFALL SNOWMAN
CHANDIGARH, INDIA, TUESDAY

AN APELIKE CREATURE CAPTURED IN THE
HIMALAYAS OF NORTH KASHMIR, AND
THOUGHT TO RESEMBLE THE LEGENDARY
ABOMINABLE SNOWMAN, MAY BE THE
LONG-AWAITED MISSING LINK BETWEEN MAN
AND APE, SCIENTISTS HERE BELIEVE. THE
CREATURE WAS FOUND BY A PARTY LED BY DR
LILIANE ERCKMANN, OF CALIFORNIA, AND DR
PRAKASH CHOWDHURI, OF CHANDIGARH. IT
WAS SLIGHTLY INJURED BUT IS ALIVE AND
WELL.
    END RUSHFULL
    MORE FOLLOWS LATER

REUTER 1345

9

'And how are they feeding it?'

The Prime Minister's tone was mild, but once more Amrit Singh felt out of his depth. He was Minister for Science, he thought resentfully, not a damned expert on fossil men. Or fossil apes, as the case might well turn out to be. He spread his hands wide.

'I do not know, Prime Minister. I have not had the report from Chandigarh. The University sent a nutrition expert up to

Shalamerg to help Dr Chowdhuri, but I do not know what they decided. The academic side is being most unhelpful in declining to give us proper information, even though it is the Army—with Government money, Prime Minister—that has built the temporary compound for the . . . the discovery. Built it on the spot at Shalamerg.'

'I know,' said the Prime Minister. 'I ordered it.'

Thoughtfully, she began to light a cheroot, but then abandoned it, seeing the Sikh's mouth tighten puritanically. What a very adaptable lot we politicians are, she thought. Not long ago Amrit Singh had wanted to throw Erckmann out of India. Now he was furious because Erckmann did not take him into her confidence.

'We are not getting a proper propaganda return from this, Prime Minister,' he persisted. 'The whole world is interested. I had the Soviet cultural attaché at my office this morning, asking for a permit to go to the temporary compound at Shalamerg.'

'You did not grant it?' she said, her voice sharp. He shook his head and she relaxed.

'I am sticking to your instructions, of course, Prime Minister. I have given orders that access to Shalamerg shall be very strictly limited. But—'he leaned forward in his chair—'I am convinced that we should bring this ape, this apeman, whatever it is, down to Delhi, and let the world see exactly what an Indian scientist has discovered, here in India.'

'You mean Dr Chowdhuri?'

'Of course,' said Amrit Singh. He sounded defensive. 'He found the original skulls—Dr Erckmann does not deny it. And he played a great part in the capture of this creature. It is an Indian triumph.'

'But it is not Indian money,' said the Prime Minister.

Amrit Singh waved a hand. 'We shall not be short of funds if we ask for them. We could have as much as we wished, from half-a-dozen countries. But I emphasise that we are missing a great opportunity. We should make this creature an Indian responsibility. The cost need not be so great.'

'Dr Erckmann and Dr Chowdhuri believe that the creature should not yet be brought from Kashmir,' said the Prime

Minister. 'They think the change of altitude would not be beneficial.'

She paused for a moment, watching him, and then went on. 'You know that we have received an outline proposal of considerable funds from her University of California to set up a full research centre near Srinagar in Kashmir for the study of the discovery. And that this would be supported by funds from France—these being the two countries, apart from us, originally involved?'

He nodded. 'But we should not accept such an offer, Prime Minister. Or, at least, not yet. The Americans will pay the cash and take the credit—they always do.'

'But suppose,' said the Prime Minister softly, 'that there is more blame than credit. Whoever takes the responsibility, takes also the blame.'

'I do not understand you.'

Foolish little man, thought the Prime Minister. She explained politely.

'It seems to me, Amrit Singh, that the problems of keeping this creature alive will be considerable, quite probably insurmountable. Not all animals thrive in captivity. If Indian scientists take the responsibility—and I agree with you that to do so would be entirely within our rights—then they must also be prepared to suffer the howls of execration, the eternal inquest, that will begin when it dies . . . as it probably will. There may, indeed, be credit. I think, however, there is more likely to be blame. Perhaps the Americans should be allowed to set up their centre in Kashmir. If there is credit, we will keep a close eye on it. If there is blame . . . then how unfortunate. But at least it will not be our fault. And meanwhile, we will not allow hundreds of inquirers after truth to trudge up to Shalamerg. Just a very few. Dr Erckmann is right. Shalamerg is not a zoo.'

After Amrit Singh, shaking his head, had left the room, the red telephone on the Prime Minister's desk buzzed once. The voice at the other end was that of her Foreign Minister. He chuckled.

'There is a somewhat unexpected development regarding that extraordinary discovery in Kashmir, Prime Minister.'

'Oh?'

'You know that Shalamerg is very close to the truce line?'

'Yes.'

The Foreign Minister chuckled again.

'I had a note from Islamabad an hour ago. Well, not exactly a formal note—more of an *aide-mémoire*. They say that detailed examination of the map reveals that the creature in question can only have reached Shalamerg from the other side of the truce line. That is Pakistan territory, of course. And they say further that since this is thus clearly a Pakistani citizen that has by accident lost his way, it would be courteous of us to return him to them as soon as possible.'

The Prime Minister laughed harshly. 'Is this the General's idea of a joke?'

'The General,' said the Indian Foreign Minister, suddenly grave, 'has never been celebrated for a sense of humour.'

'Well, do you accept or don't you?' said the Administrator, walking briskly beside Kimbell over the newly-cut grass of the Berkeley campus. The California sun warmed them both, even now, in winter. Kimbell looked up at the blue sky for a moment, and the Administrator followed his glance.

'Mind, you'll miss this sunshine, Kim. I'm told it's chilly in the Himalayas this time of year, even down at Srinagar. But I hope you'll go. It would be a big thing for this campus. In any case, I think you're the only one Erckmann intends to accept as head of that centre. And we have to go along with Erckmann, because it seems she's got the Indian Prime Minister in her pocket. And that's one lady whose support we need.'

I wish he'd stop calling her Erckmann, thought Kimbell irritably. I get tired of some of these Women's Lib conventions. Though I guess Liliane herself would be the last to agree with me. Aloud he said, 'Why does she want me? I'm no big wheel in research. There are half-a-dozen better people for the job.'

'She trusts you,' said the Administrator. 'You backed her. And why? Well, I imagine you know better than I do.'

Kimbell glanced quickly at his face, but the Administrator seemed as bland as usual. He laid a hand on Kimbell's arm, stopping in the shade of a silver-grey eucalyptus. Nearby on the grass a couple were locked in each other's arms, the boy's blond hair as long as the girl's. They looked up incuriously for a moment, and then resumed love-making.

'Like baboons in a zoo, aren't they?' said the Administrator softly.

'What about the funding?' Kimbell asked.

'Don't worry about the budget,' said the Administrator. 'We'll see to that—and the French are putting in, as well. There's a man from the Musée in Paris coming over next week to hassle with me about the details. They want to be in on the act. There'll be money and to spare.'

'Things have changed.'

The other's voice was comfortable. 'Sure have. Well, we wiped the Soviet eye, didn't we?'

'*We* did?' said Kimbell.

'This university put up most of the money in the first place,' said the Administrator. 'Oh, I admit I had my doubts, at one point. Anybody can have doubts. But you convinced me, Kim. So it's sort of natural justice that you should be head of the investigation team.'

'If I've learned one truth from thirty years of primate anatomy,' said Kimbell, 'it's that there's no such thing as natural justice. But yes, I'll go. I can't pass up a chance like that.'

'Besides,' said the Administrator, 'you'll be seeing Erckmann again.'

Father Glory stood on the roof of his gold-painted camper outside the little Colorado township of Weems, and tossed back his head so that his long white hair streamed in the wind. He had been baptised, long ago, as Bruce Sidney Hatcher and he had been, successively, a bank teller, a travelling salesman and a circus astrologer before becoming Father Glory twenty years before.

Father Glory had been fortunate. Soon after he had discovered that he was, in fact, a divine representative on Earth to bear witness to the glory of Creation, the great bandwagon of the conservation movement had begun to roll in America. No respectable conservationist, of course, would have touched Father Glory with a ten-foot pole, but he had a curious habit of saying in simple, scriptural terms what they were saying in scientific jargon. Across the Bible-belt of North America,

Father Glory could gather men, women, and dollars. The men and women, he knew, were often unsophisticated. The dollars were dollars. Now, in the field outside Weems, he prepared to give value for money. Below him nearly a thousand people waited . . . old and young, men and women, even a fair sprinkling of teenagers. An assistant adjusted his microphone, and nodded. Father Glory lifted up his voice.

'Behold,' he boomed, against the wind that blew down from the Flatirons, bulking dark against the evening horizon. '"Behold, Esau my brother is a hairy man, and I am a smooth man." That's what Jacob said . . . Genesis 27, verse 11. My friends, the Bible speaks to us each day. And each day the Book speaks true. You will have heard, most of you, that far away in the mountains of India, a woman of science has found a hairy man. A hairy man like unto no man we have known. For, my friends, we are smooth men, are we not?'

A subdued murmur of assent came from the crowd. Sitting on the step of the camper, the tall thin youth who was the reporter for the Weems *Bugle-Sentinel* wrote industriously.

'We are smooth men,' Father Glory shouted. 'We are the seed of Jacob. And what did Jacob do?'

The crowd below the camper murmured again.

'Jacob tricked Esau,' roared Father Glory, thrusting the microphone from him. 'Jacob frauded Esau of his birthright for a mess of pottage. Jacob frauded Isaac, their own father. Truly Jacob was, indeed, a smooth man.'

Somebody in the audience gave a loud laugh, but subsided quickly amid angry shouts from the crowd. Father Glory held up his hand, speaking once more into the microphone.

'In those mountains far away, Esau has returned. I fear for Esau once more, my friends. For we are smooth men, deceivers, tricksters, spoilers.'

He pointed over to the west, where the twin towers of a new nuclear power station thrust into the reddening sky.

'See there what the seed of Jacob build, in mockery of the glory of God's creation. Has God, then, sent Esau again to lead us from the evil we have made? Yet when God sent Christ, what did we do? We killed him, my friends. That's what we did to Christ. I tell you, I fear for Esau in the hands of the men and women of science . . .'

'Anything much?' the man at the city desk asked the young reporter when he got back to the *Bugle-Sentinel*.

'It's not great,' said the reporter. 'Just that old ham tearing off about the Himalayan ape.'

'Oh, it's a quiet night,' said the man at the desk. 'Not much else around. You'd better put it out over the wire . . .'

'He doesn't look too good this morning, Liliane,' said Tom Meachem from where he squatted beside the steel-meshed fence of the temporary compound at Shalamerg. Through the gap between the tents he could see the four distant dots that were the latest two scientific visitors and their guides riding away down the valley, down to the road far below which led back to Srinagar. A few weeks ago virtually nobody came to Shalamerg. And hardly anybody had ever heard of it. Now it sometimes seemed that half the anthropologists and palaeontologists in the world wanted to make the 10,000-foot prilgrimage up to the high mountain meadow. Thank God, the Indian Government was restricting permits—allowing only one or two at a time to visit the compound. Compound? He was touched by an unexpected sense of guilt—not an emotion he would ever have thought he would feel in a matter of science. We may try to comfort ourselves, he thought, by calling it a compound, but it's really a cage. Twelve feet by twelve—that was the exact amount of eight-inch steel mesh that the squad from the Indian Corps of Engineers had brought up to Shalamerg. Within those limits, the soldiers, he conceded, had done a good job. The creature inside could not get out— though it had so threatened to injure itself by trying that, at last, it had been chained . . . hobbled rather, by a chain connecting its feet, so that it could do no more than shuffle round its prison. Soon, though, it would be confined in better conditions, at the new prefabricated research centre now being set up outside Srinagar.

'You're following Judy,' said Liliane. 'She always calls it "he". And I'm beginning to do it myself.'

'Anybody who watches that cage for a half-hour will always think of what's inside as "he",' said Meachem. 'He's not *Homo sapiens*, I know that well enough, but he's *Homo* something, all right.'

She nodded. 'Well, we must wait for the detailed tests. But I agree. There's something indefinable, but unmistakable.'

The creature, which was half-sitting, half-lying in the corner of the cage beside the pile of sacks and branches where it slept, opened its eyes and looked directly at her. Its stare was disconcerting, unfathomable. After a moment it extended a long hairy arm to touch its genitals. For once, she saw, this was not followed by the usual massive erection. Instead, it reached into the sacks and pulled out one of the legs of goat—raw meat—which was all it had so far been persuaded to eat. It bit at the leg, and then thrust it away again. Its eyelids closed, and its head sank back on its chest. At intervals the deep-sunk eyes opened very slightly, glittering in the bush of hair above the great brow-ridge. It was not asleep.

'Yes,' Liliane said again. 'I'm sure he's hominid, man-like. We'll know more when we get the results of the first DNA checks—we got enough blood for a double test.'

Meachem tried to repress a shudder. The process of getting the blood from the creature, small and presumably harmless though the amount had been, was one that he could not forget. Meachem had achieved a doctorate in anthropology before specialising in palaeontology, and his parallel training in primate anatomy had begun with the dissection of a newt and had ended with the vivisection of a chimpanzee. He still, sometimes, uneasily remembered the chimpanzee, but he had never felt the overmastering sense of shame that had burned inside him at the simple act of transfusion from the struggling creature of Shalamerg.

'You worked at Trinil in Java,' said Liliane. 'Does that—'she nodded towards the cage—'stir any thoughts?'

'We're both thinking the same thing, aren't we?' said Meachem soberly. Into his memory came the shallow, stony stretch of the Solo River, the bulk of the old Lawu volcano quivering in the heat of the day, the brilliant green-and-black birdwing butterflies which cruised above the spiky plants growing out of the lava deposits of ancient Java eruptions. There had been those bones . . . a femur . . . and the top of that skull.

'*Homo erectus*,' said Liliane. '*Pithecanthropus*, we used to call him.'

'The dating isn't quite right, of course,' said Meachem. 'We got a potassium-argon date of around 700,000 years Before Present from what we found in the Kabuh Beds. That was in freshwater sandstone, down beside the river. Good material for dating.'

She nodded.

'So,' said Meachem, 'if this creature is the creature of the skulls—our Shalamerg skulls, I mean—then the date should be more like a million years. It doesn't really match.'

She got to her feet, making a half-contemptuous gesture. 'Match—how can it match? We're playing a guessing game, Tom—our whole careers have been one long guessing game. What do we really know about the descent of man? Nothing, absolutely nothing, that we can regard as certain. There just isn't the evidence. You could take every ancient hominid bone that's ever been found—every bit of skull, thigh, vertebra, the lot—and pile it comfortably on to one family dining table. And you could put all the teeth into a . . . an opera hat.'

'Sometimes,' said Meachem, 'I wish somebody would.'

'We work on reasonable theories, not on indisputable facts,' said Liliane. She began to tick off her points didactically, tapping the forefinger of her right hand into the palm of her left. Meachem glanced at the compound. Under the shaggy brows, the creature's eyes were open, watching.

'So what do we really have? We have *Ramapithecus*, a ten-million-year-old ape-like creature with certain man-like characteristics found in the Siwalik Hills in India and in Africa and in Europe. *Ramapithecus* was one of the clues that brought me here, to the Himalayas. Mind you, all we have of him is jaws—but from this we work out, reasonably enough, that he could walk upright. And we theorise, Tom—I emphasise the word *theorise*—that *Ramapithecus* may be the ancestral stock of both men and apes. And then what do we have?'

She was speaking more and more quickly.

'We have a few inconclusive bones, followed by a five million year fossil gap. We don't have any hominid, man-like fossils over all that colossal stretch of time. We simply don't know what was happening to our ancestral stock, nor the processes by which it developed. Then, suddenly, we get the Leakey finds in Tanzania. They're three million years old, and they're pretty mysterious, too. Because the Leakeys found not one descendant type of ape-like man or man-like ape, but three kinds . . . *Australopithecus boisei*, *Australopithecus africanus*, and *Homo habilis*. All with man-like characteristics, all roughly contemporary, and all different. And then we jump forward to around a million years Before Present, and hey presto, here's *Homo erectus*, the proto-man you helped to dig up in Java, and who spread, as far as we can see, from Asia into Europe. Was it a direct line of descent? Well, all we can say is that it could have been—because after *erectus* came Neanderthal Man and our own forebears, *Homo sapiens*. And the modern consensus is that we and Neanderthal were different branches from the same tree—although later we absorbed Neanderthal into *sapiens* by conquest and interbreeding. And all of it, Tom, is theory. Nothing is certain.'

'We all know this, Liliane. I don't see where it gets us.'

'It gets us thinking again,' she said. 'It was Harry, of all people, who started me off . . . Harry and that creature there. If *Homo erectus* was alive 700,000 years ago—according to the Trinil finds—then he may well have been alive a million years ago. Or more. After all, that wouldn't be a tenth as surprising as finding something not very unlike him alive today. And that's what we're both beginning to think, isn't it?'

'On the basis of *erectus*, the cranial capacity doesn't fit,' said Meachem, his voice stubborn. '*Erectus*, on the basis of all pre-Shalamerg fossils, was a pretty early form of man. He had a brain size of around . . . well, at most 1000 c.c. Those Shalamerg skulls were around 1400 c.c. And one was very, very old and one was very new. What happened to evolution in the intervening million years? Why are the skulls the same? And apparently no Broca's Region in the forebrain—a big brain but no speech.'

Liliane shrugged. 'What happened to evolution in the chimpanzee, Tom? A chimp's genetic material is 99 per cent the same as ours. Chimps ought to be much nearer to us in appearance and other features than in fact they are. We've still got a lot of questions to answer.'

And about you, too, Liliane, he thought, looking at her in admiration as she stood facing him, her hands on her hips.

'There are some other questions,' he said quietly, 'which

have nothing to do—that I can see, at any rate—with evolution. How the hell does a modern skull come to be side by side with one from a million years BP? And what happened to Bulbul's head? And, for the jackpot, why did that thing—'he jerked his head at the cage—'come to Shalamerg?'

'Ritual?' she said. Her doubt showed in her voice. 'I suppose the heads might represent some sort of ritual behaviour. That would argue that it . . . the creature we found . . . would have a position fairly far up the evolutionary scale. As you might expect, with a 1400 c.c. cranium.'

'A ritual that goes back a million years?' said Meachem. 'Unchanged? That won't wash, and you know it.'

She sounded resigned. 'Yes, Tom, I agree. It won't wash, as you say. But I still fancy *erectus*—or something close to *erectus*—as the candidate for what we found. Be honest, now . . . if you were reconstructing *Homo erectus* from those two skulls, and from what you know of earlier fossils, he might very well look quite a lot like that.'

She nodded towards the cage. The creature got to its feet and hobbled towards them, its chain clinking.

'He might,' agreed Meachem. He went towards the cage. The creature stood by the mesh, watching him.

'I'll be relieved when they build the proper centre outside Srinagar,' said Liliane.

He laughed. 'Well, it will be easier access for elderly researchers. Some of them are puffing a bit by the time they get up here. But I guess it will bring the usual bunch of scientific bureaucrats with it. Those who can, work. Those who can't, tell the rest of us what to do.'

'Richard Kimbell's going to run it,' she said. A faint inflexion in her voice did not escape him.

'You'll like him,' she went on. 'He's not like that.'

She joined him beside the cage, where the creature stood beside the mesh.

'Look, Tom, I know you hate it . . . his being like this. I hate it, too. I couldn't sleep properly last night. But what else can we do?'

Several seconds passed before Meachem replied.

'Let him go?'

She swung on him angrily. 'Don't be ridiculous—you know

we can't do that. If he goes, he'll vanish. No, we'll take him to the new centre at Srinagar, as soon as it's ready. He'll be better there.'

Meachem did not answer her directly, but watched the cage. 'You remember the doctor—the Canadian—who came over to get the blood sample?'

'Yes.'

'You know what he said to me? He said, "Well, I'll do the best I can with this. But blood's not the best stuff for testing DNA. I'd rather have meat. Any chance of meat?" That's what the bastard said.'

She did not reply, and he went closer to the mesh.

'*Homo erectus*,' he said slowly. 'Or *Pithecantropus*. Or something that isn't quite either of those . . . I don't suppose you care. Are you really the same sort of creature that could kill a stegodon elephant, three-quarters of a million years ago? We found their bones with bones like yours, down by the Solo River. So you're our brother in terms of species . . . maybe. First you, then something else, and now us. I guess we haven't made you feel at home.'

In a movement so fast that Liliane's eyes could hardly absorb it, the creature's hand and arm shot through an eight-inch square slot of the mesh. Meachem was a bare half-inch beyond its reach, though he felt the brush of the stiff hair on the hand as it smashed down fractionally short of his face. Trembling in spite of himself, he stepped back. The creature stood by the mesh, watching.

'Better give it some more goat,' said Meachem shakily. Liliane, looking into his face with concern, noted that for the moment he had dropped the 'he'.

'I reckon,' he said, 'old brother there is trying to tell us something.'

Extract from a letter from Dr Richard Kimbell, head of the Primate Research Centre at Srinagar, Kashmir (Indian Zone) to the Directeur of the Musée de l'Homme Primitif, Paris, France.

. . . the new Centre here at Srinagar is now working well, though by no means all the equipment is yet installed. On the medical side, we've been doing the best we can without full laboratory facilities. There's no chance yet of anything down at the molecular level, but the basic tests show some intriguing differences both from ourselves and from the African apes. Some of the metabolic processes of the Esau (I am afraid that for convenience we have adopted the name for our study-creature which was coined by the popular Press a few weeks ago) seem to be more efficient than our own. His haemoglobin is better at carrying oxygen, and the white blood cells are turned over much more rapidly in his blood. These white cells don't seem to last very long, but the bone marrow must be producing them in quantities all the time. Dr James T. Davies, of the Sandell Institute for Medical Research in Illinois, became very excited about this when he visited here two weeks ago, and I shall be interested to know if his views are shared by Dr Gustave Vachée, of the Sorbonne, when he arrives next week. Dr Davies holds the opinion that the white blood cell factor, when combined with the findings of his other tests on the immune-system of the Esau, show the creature to be exceptionally resistant to disease, including cancer. The Esau would also probably be much less affected than human beings (I mean *Homo sapiens*!) by radiation.

I think you will agree, Directeur, that something of the kind might be expected. After all, if these creatures have been living in the Great Himalaya for a million years, they have been exposed to more background radiation from space than creatures which live at sea-level, and which are thus better protected by the Earth's blanket of atmosphere. The ones which were not resistant to radiation must have been disposed of by natural selection a long time ago. I must say, however, that I feel uncomfortable about the suggestion made by medical researchers in both our countries that we should attempt to extract interferon from the Esau's blood. It's a wild idea, and you can imagine what the newspapers and television will make of it if word gets out. I feel that we should be thinking strongly in terms of a big effort to acquire another Esau, preferably female, and to know much more about each of them before we undertake any such project. We know that the Esau must be a member of a surviving relict fauna: we have no idea of how many members might make up the total population. My own guess is that it will prove to be surprisingly small.

I share your desire that at least one French scientist (apart, of course, from Dr Erckmann herself) should be stationed here at the Centre, especially in view of your generous financial committment. We have made representations to the Government of India, but these have so far been unsuccessful. The Indian Government, at present, is insistent that only the present scientific staff of Dr Erckmann, Dr Chowdhuri, Dr Meachem, and myself should be permitted to stay here semi-permanently—though limited access, as you know, is granted to other scientists for short periods for specific research. The Englishman, Colonel Kernow, remains in administrative charge of the Centre. He knows the area well, and is most useful. An opportunity to bring in another French scientist may occur when Dr Erckmann's assistant, Mlle. Agar, leaves for California, where she has decided to return in two weeks' time. I shall not fail to urge such a replacement on the Indian authorities.

> Acceptez, mon cher Directeur,
> l'assurance profonde de mon amitié . . .

10

With a flourish, Richard Kimbell signed the letter. He was rather proud of the final phrase that he'd culled from a book of French memoirs. The rest of the letter was in English, because his French was at best uncertain—and in any case the Directeur wrote excellent English. Well, that should hold Paris for a while, he thought. Though, no doubt, they'd try again. They were putting up twenty per cent of the funding, and they wanted fifty per cent of the action. That was fairly typical French accounting. And, anyway, they did have the biggest wheel, Liliane, though it was still hard to think of her as French. American mother, French father . . . she could have gone either way, years ago, but she'd opted to stay European. Once he'd asked her why—because, after all, she did two-thirds of her work for Berkeley, and her home, when she was in it, was in California. 'Oh, Kim,' she'd said. 'There's more than an ocean and a continent between Berkeley and Paris. Berkeley is good—maybe the best there is, in some ways. But Paris suits the way my mind words. I'm my father's daughter.' Kimbell had met her father, before he died five years ago. Étienne Erckmann had been a senior official at the French Embassy in Washington. Kimbell remembered him wryly as rather like a plastic construction kit of a French diplomat. That, maybe, was where Liliane got her conviction of intellectual divine right.

From across the Nagim Lake came the long wailing sales-call of the flower-seller, known to Kashmiri travellers for a genera-tion as Mr Wonderful, approaching in his flower-laden *shi-kara*-canoe. Kimbell went out from the cool saloon to the stern-deck of the houseboat, ornately carved in teak and cedar wood. White wisps of cloud, almost stationary, clung to the mountains across the glittering water. Far away on the oppo-site shore a bus sounded its horn, and a *shikara* taking tourists back to a houseboat for an after-lunch sleep paddled slowly out from the bank. Below the houseboat, close in to the edge of the lake, an old woman in a battered wooden *shikara* was steadily cutting weed for cattle-food. A couple of jewel-like kingfishers flashed across the decks, diving into the shoal of little silver fish which played about the sides.

Richard Kimbell took a deep breath. Even here on the lake, a few miles from the city, he fancied he could sniff the exciting spicy smell of Srinagar. He sat on the cushioned bench under the stern-awning, watching as Mr Wonderful's *shikara* splashed nearer with its owner's usual invincible optimism. Kimbell enjoyed the houseboat . . . falling asleep to the lapping of the lake, waking in the morning to the faint shouts and calls from *shikaras* crossing the water, the boy Jinni waiting with their own private *shikara* to take them wherever they wished, and the little formal dinner in the evening, when Zareer or Mohammad would spread a white cloth on the table in the saloon, and serve curried chicken or lamb or lake-trout.

Kimbell sighed. He was due back at the Centre tomorrow . . . it was his turn. The houseboat slept six, in three two-berth cabins. The living accommodation in the prefabricated Centre on the road north out of Srinagar was limited, hot and uncomfortable, and Liliane had eventually been persuaded that it was better that as many as practicable should sleep on the houseboat, and drive the four miles to the Centre in the Land-Rover each day. Kernow himself stayed more or less permanently at the Centre, and one scientist was always with him, with two Kashmiris.

In addition, the State Government of Jammu and Kashmir had arranged for a police guard—a sergeant and three constables—to be stationed at the entrance to the Centre. That was necessary. The reaction of ordinary Kashmiris to the presence of the Esau had varied from academic interest in the University of Kashmir, along the road at Srinagar, to wild rumour and something like fear among the rice and saffron growers who worked in the fields outside the town. In America and Europe, in Soviet Russia and Japan, active interest had so far been necessarily scientific—in terms of visitors, at least. Kashmir was a far and distant goal for any but very determined travellers and tourists. In the past two or three weeks, however, something rather more unsettling had developed. Srinagar had slowly become the camping-ground of a section of wandering western youth, some scores of them . . . American, British, German, French, Scandinavian.

Apparently rootless, penniless, ambition-less, they had drifted up from India, bringing with them their drug-culture and a strange multi-national jargon. They seemed interested in the Esau, lounging around the steel gates of the Centre, smoking and talking. 'We've drawn 'em here from Nepal,' Harry Kernow had told him. 'A couple of years ago, you could hardly cross the old parade ground at Tundikhei in Katmandu without getting a whiff of the hash smoked by western kids like these. The Nepalese didn't mind at first—they thought the kids would bring money. But they didn't . . .' Kimbell had manoeuvred the Land-Rover, morning after morning, through these bearded youths and dishevelled girls round the Centre gates. He had seen them, too, sprawled along the long road of the Bund, on the banks of the River Jhelum. They had looked at him incuriously, at either place. It was as though they were waiting for something.

He got to his feet and peered through the saloon towards the gangplank which connected the side of the boat to the bank. He could hear Liliane's voice out there, talking to Zareer, who was squatting in the reeds washing a pile of pans. On the other side of the houseboat there was a bump and judder as Mr Wonderful arrived, his professional smile appearing over the deck-rail a moment or two later. Kimbell turned to tell him to go away, and then changed his mind. He thrust a few rupees into Mr Wonderful's brown hand, and received in return an armful of blue and crimson flowers, knowing that he had paid too much, but unwilling to face the protracted bargaining that would otherwise be necessary.

As Liliane stepped down from the gangplank and came along the corridor into the saloon, Kimbell made her a half-mocking bow, and gave her the flowers. She took them with a smile, sniffed at them perfunctorily, and laid them on the table. In the last few days, he thought, she had completely lost the bubbling elation with which she had greeted him at the airport two weeks ago.

'Kim, I'm worried about the Esau. He's not eating, and he's very lethargic. This is the second day he's taken only water. I have a horrible feeling that . . .'

Her voice trailed away. Even Liliane, thought Kimbell, talked about 'the Esau'—never, interestingly enough, using just 'Esau' as a pet name. None of them did. It took only a few hours' study of the creature at the Centre for everybody to know that it was not a pet. No one had succeeded in establishing the slightest emotional contact. The creature's only easily recognisable behaviour came when—less and less often now—the raw meat and vegetables offered were seized and eaten. And yet, in spite of the repeated examinations and humiliations imposed in the name of science, the Esau had maintained a strange dignity. There was neither defeat nor resignation in the deep-set eyes that glowed under the brow-ridges of the flat, hairy face. Sometimes the stare of the Esau was remote, unfathomable. Sometimes the eyes showed rage. Occasionally they seemed to show desperation. But never despair. Or was this, now, the beginning of despair?

'Any idea what's wrong?'

'I don't know, Kim. We know so little about him. It could be the altitude—I have a feeling it is. Srinagar is 5,000 feet above sea-level, I know. It's as high as Denver. But he's probably used to at least 10,000, and he's almost certainly never been down to 5,000 before. And to think those Ministry idiots wanted to take him to Delhi. He'd have been dead weeks ago.'

'Shalamerg was 10,000 feet,' said Kimbell, musing.

She put her hand on his arm. 'Yes, and for all we know, even 10,000 might have been lower than he liked. We don't have any idea of why he came to Shalamerg, but his presence there can only have been . . . well, exceptional. There is no record of any kind of sighting over the last fifty years in the area. Suppose he's a creature that's fully adapted to living at, say, 15,000 or even 20,000 feet? Coming down to 5,000 feet for some weeks, and then being confined and messed about a lot—it's not surprising if he begins to have trouble.'

Her anxiety was beginning to be infectious.

'Maybe I'd better come out and look at him,' he said. 'I've been writing to France, and I was going to go over my notes. But I guess that can wait.'

'I've got the Land-Rover on the shore road, up over the bank. We'll drive round the lake—much quicker than going across with Jinni in the *shikara*.'

As she went out she brushed against the table and sprays of flowers fell to the floor of the saloon. She did not pause, but Kimbell, following her, picked them up. As he passed Zareer on the bank, he told him wryly to put them in water.

After a few minutes beside the lotus-patches of the lake the Land-Rover turned north, inland, along a narrow road lined with poplars and bordered by checkered rectangles of rice paddies and saffron fields, laced with dividing stone walls. So close in to the town there were many people—groups of women in baggy robes and bright kerchiefs, men in shabby western suits, waiting for the jammed twice-daily bus into Srinagar. Old men sat talking outside the wooden houses. Tiny children played in the dust. When the road had thrust further away from the city, near the little hamlet of Dragri-yung, Liliane swung the Land-Rover off the highway and they jolted the last three-quarters of a mile up the dusty track to the Centre. The usual knot of grubby western youths and girls clustered round the mesh fence, watching as the police sergeant came slowly out, opened the steel gate, and closed it with a crashing clang behind them.

Kimbell had been up to Shalamerg several times before the Centre had been hurriedly made ready. The Centre down here was another world. It was undeniably ugly—prefabricated in plastic and breeze-block, raw and without grace. The three administration huts, in one of which Kernow and the duty scientist had their rooms, were positioned on the south side of the little complex. The windows of all the huts were arranged so that, in the compound thirty yards beyond, the Esau was always within easy view. The compound here was much larger than the virtual cage in which the creature had been confined at Shalamerg, yet perhaps Liliane was right. It might well be that, even after a few relatively trouble-free weeks, altitude might yet prove to be a problem. But if it was, how were they going to solve it? To go back to Shalamerg was hardly a serious option—tens of thousands of dollars had been spent here, and in any case, there would be a flood of protests from researchers who would find Shalamerg far too remote and inaccessible. Maybe, he thought, we shouldn't worry about researchers. Maybe we should be thinking of halting research . . . for the moment.

They walked up to the steel mesh fence. It was taller than the one at Shalamerg, but with the same size of mesh. Liliane stopped two yards short—since Meachem's near-disaster at Shalamerg, this was now a strict rule. Kimbell looked for the Esau. A small cave had been built for him, inside the compound, from rocks and timber. It was constructed so that the interior was always visible from outside the compound. The Esau was not inside—hardly surprising, because Kimbell knew that the creature had never set foot in it since being introduced to the compound. Kimbell looked at the pile of rocks and sacks and drooping cedar branches which was where the Esau was usually found. He was not there, either. Perplexed for a moment, he turned to Liliane.

'Where . . .?'

She pointed to the centre of the rocks. At once he saw the Esau. He was in his usual posture, half-sitting, half-lying. The reddish, hairy body was not even the same colour as the sacks, yet the Esau had in some way blended against the background so that for those few seconds, Kimbell could have sworn he wasn't there.

Liliane laughed. 'He's good at that—it's one of his most interesting characteristics. He seems to be able to arrange himself, intuitively, so that he looks like part of the landscape. He knows the precise angles at which to position his body and limbs—rather like a stick insect. You know what I mean—you can look at a patch of grass without knowing it's there, but the moment somebody points it out, you wonder why you couldn't see it in the first place. Sometimes, when I come out in the morning, he can make me think for a minute that he's gone. I wouldn't have thought any creature as big as he is could do it.'

'Tigers do it,' said a voice behind them. Kimbell turned, holding out his hand. He liked Harry Kernow, except for an occasional prickle of jealousy on the occasions when he saw Harry, imagining he was unobserved, look in a certain way at Liliane.

'Hi, Harry,' he said. 'You're always quoting tigers at us.'

'You can learn a lot from tigers,' said Harry. 'A tiger has to work hard for its dinner.'

'Don't we all?' said Kimbell, but Harry was looking over towards the Esau, and was speaking as though half to himself.

'I've been thinking a lot about tigers—and the Esau—just lately. A tiger has to know everything about its territory—the pattern of daily activity of every animal within it. It has to know exactly how the animal it stalks will react to certain kinds of movement, certain kinds of noise. A tiger can take half an hour to cover eight yards of ground. It can put its foot so carefully on a dead teak leaf that it crushes it very, very slowly into dust without the slightest sound. At Chitawan in Nepal I once spent four hours watching a tiger approach a herd of spotted chital deer—some of the most wary animals in the world—across open country. In that time it covered about a hundred yards. And it got its chital. It knew exactly how to move, and how to wait. But there's something else, too, about tigers.'

'What do you mean?' said Liliane. She felt impatient, eager to talk to Kimbell about the Esau.

Harry smiled. 'I don't think you'd accept it as scientific evidence,' he said. 'Tigers sometimes "pook"—they make a sound like the call of a prey deer, especially a sambar. Some people think that a tiger can convince a sambar deer that the tiger itself is a sambar. That it's able to deceive the sambar into believing that there isn't a tiger there.'

'Do you believe that?' said Liliane, interested in spite of herself.

The Englishman shrugged. 'I've never seen it myself. Once I had a Gurkha *shikar* who swore it was true. But the idea of it made me wonder about him over there.'

He pointed towards the sacks.

'No human being, even the wildest aborigine, hunts like a tiger, armed with just brain and teeth and claws. Human beings have learned about weapons. A blowpipe or a bow and arrow give a man a percentage. A rifle gives him a bigger one. He doesn't have to close with his prey, or approach it within easy reach. That made me think about the Esau. You reckon he's some kind of man, don't you?'

'Well,' began Liliane in a doubtful voice, but Kimbell interrupted her, speaking to Harry.

'Yes, you could say that. Perhaps an earlier type of human, or something very, very close.'

'Exactly,' said Harry. 'Not *quite* like us. Now suppose that the Esau was a creature that had no feeling whatever for technology. Like a tiger, he's never made a tool or a weapon. But, for a million years, he and his kind have had to hunt. And he's got a brain bigger than a tiger's hasn't he?'

'His brain is probably as big as yours,' said Liliane. 'Or mine,' she added hastily, seeing his face.

'Then,' said Harry, 'if generation after generation of his kind have applied that big brain to the techniques of bare-hands-hunting over a million years, they're probably pretty good by now. I'd be interested to see him tackle a tiger. But I don't think I'd put my money on the tiger.'

He watched Liliane's face, and grinned. ' "And Esau was a cunning hunter, a man of the field . . ." '

'You religious?' said Kimbell.

'Oh, we Old Kashmir Hands,' said Harry easily. 'We always carry a Bible.'

He walked off to where Mohammad was supervising the unloading of jerricans of diesel for the generator which provided the Centre's power. Thoughtfully, Kimbell watched him go.

'Interesting man, isn't he?'

Liliane's reply seemed unnecessarily tart.

'Sometimes,' she said, 'I get the impression that he thinks he owns the Himalayas.'

'But you couldn't have done without him, when the Esau came to Shalamerg, could you?'

There was only a moment's hesitation before she replied.

'No. He knows how to deal with a problem. Some problems, at any rate.'

Together, they walked round to the point outside the mesh-fence that was nearest to the place where the Esau sat. The creature's eyes were closed. Ten yards away lay a dead goat. It seemed to be untouched. Kimbell looked at Liliane, a question in his eyes.

'Tom thought maybe he wasn't adapting too well to the single haunches of goat we've been giving him,' she said. 'So we thought if he got a whole goat, he might feel more at home. But he didn't.'

'Did he kill it himself?'

She gave a little involuntary shiver.

'No, we tried that. We put the goat into the compound alive, but he just ignored it. So this morning Mohammad managed to rope it and get it out, and then killed it and put it back in. But so far, he hasn't shown the slightest interest. It's curious, because he ate the haunches at first. What do you think?'

'I'd like to have a good look at him.'

Her face was troubled. 'Kim, I'd be very unhappy about having to drug him again. He's had a remarkable lot of pressure on him lately—people measuring everything in sight, length of leg, hip to knee, knee to ankle, foot bones, toes, arms, hands, the lot. I think some of the researchers who come here would be delighted if he died, so they could quarrel over his liver and his kidneys. I don't know—I have a feeling it's all getting to him in a way we can't really understand. Not many human beings could have stood up to it, even if they'd known why it was being done. And he doesn't, poor devil. I had a talk with Prakash Chowdhuri this morning, and he agrees with me. What we'd do without Prakash standing between us and all that Indian bureaucracy, I can't imagine. He's got so much common sense. He told me . . . well, suggested to me, I suppose—you know how diffident Prakash is—that I should send a personal memorandum to the Prime Minister herself, summarising what we've found so far, and some of what we theorise, as soon as we get the preliminary report from the DNA tests. He thinks it will help, coming from one woman to another. And in any case he's unhappy about the material she's getting from her own Ministry people —some of them are hostile, apparently. Incidentally, he agrees with me, and I hope you will, too. We should stop further scientific visits, indefinitely. Otherwise we're going to lose the Esau.'

'I wouldn't dream of drugging him again, except as a last resort,' said Kimbell. 'I'll do what I can with the binoculars.'

He walked across to the little administration hut where Tom Meachem was working. The young American took the binoculars from the hook where they hung, beside the special rifle loaded with an anaesthetic dart, which was kept as an ultimate precautionary measure.

'Want to look at the patient, do you, Kim?'

'Is that how you think of him . . . as a patient?'

'Take a look. When you have, I guess you'll think that way, too.'

In the powerful lenses the Esau was a disturbing sight. The massive head was low on the chest, eyes closed. At intervals a series of little shudders shook the powerful body. The reddish hair seemed limper, less wiry, than it had been before. Kimbell lowered the glasses.

'I don't like the look of him at all.'

Meachem picked up the binoculars and focussed them.

'Have you noticed that he occasionally rubs that big brow-ridge, like a man worried about something?'

'No—let me see.'

Kimbell raised the glasses just as the Esau repeated the action.

'Yes . . . they're certainly massive ridges.'

Liliane picked up the binoculars and gazed at the Esau.

'I must say, Tom, you made a good job of those clay models, from the original skulls. The moment I saw him alive, I knew that was what the skulls had once been.'

Tom crossed to the locked chest beneath the window, and rummaged amongst its books and papers.

'I made a few minor corrections I'd like to show you—based on him outside,' he said, nodding towards the compound. 'I put the two models in here—where the hell are they?'

'Judy was looking at them yesterday—where is she, anyway?' asked Liliane.

'Probably down at the gate, talking to the kids. She goes down there sometimes—I must say that a conversation with that crowd wouldn't be my personal bag. But they're more her age group, I guess. One good thing—she's really pretty well back to normal, as far as I can see.'

'Only "pretty well"?'

Meachem went out and into the small adjoining office, talking over his shoulder. 'Well, at any rate she communicates again—no more of those sulky silences. And she works hard and is cheerful enough, most of the time. Just once in a while she seems to brood. It's usually then she goes down to the gate . . . Here they are. She'd put them on the shelf above the filing cabinet.'

He came out holding the two clay skull models. It was the first time Kimbell had seen them, and he examined them with interest.

'Come outside,' said Meachem. 'If we look at the Esau from the end of the compound, you can see where I was slightly wrong in my original guesswork. But I was pleased with them, if I say it myself.'

The three of them walked out together to the far end of the compound, looking back along it to where the creature was slumped. Tom held out one of the clay models.

100

'If you look here, Kim, you'll see that in comparison with the Esau himself, I'd slightly distorted the occipital ridges—only by a few millimetres, but it affected the—oh, Jesus Christ!'

With unbelievable speed, the Esau was standing in front of them on the other side of the mesh, clinging to the fence. Once more came the deep roar they had last heard in the dawn beside Bed Four. The eyes, glittering under the brow-ridges, looked down at the models, and then straight at Liliane. They seemed to hold a frantic question. She felt a strange wave of feeling, but she forced herself to be calm.

'I think he wants the models,' she said. 'Tom—what do you—'

'Put them over the fence,' said Meachem. 'I can make new models in a few hours.'

He ran over to the hut and returned with the basket and rope which were used to drop food—sometimes drugged food —into the Esau's compound. Standing beside the mesh the creature waited, looking upward as the basket was slowly lowered. With infinite care the hairy hands took the models from the straw in which they lay. Then, with one model incongruously in each hand, the Esau went straight across to the cave and in the shadowy interior positioned the two clay skulls side by side.

'That's the first time he's ever been inside,' whispered Liliane, entranced. 'And look at him now . . . look . . . look.'

The Esau left the cave, crossed to the dead goat, put a foot on its body, and with a single long pull tore off its head. Holding the blood-soaked object in one hand the creature went back to the sacks, turned away from the watchers, and began steadily to eat.

'He was a good soldier?'

It was a statement rather than a question. The second-in-command of the 8th Hunza Rifles smoothed the thin black line of his moustache before he replied. From outside the regimental office at Shirma came crashes of leather and metal as an infantry company drilled on the sun-baked earth of the barrack square.

'Of course, Colonel. His company commander gives him an excellent report.'

101

Lieutenant-Colonel Azraf Khan grunted, rubbing his beaky nose. He looks like a bird of prey, thought the second-in-command. He himself came from the coast, and he was wary of Pathans, especially the one who was his commanding officer. Azraf Khan had been trained, under an exchange scheme, at Sandhurst in England, but sometimes it was hard to remember it. Not that he was a poor soldier—far from it. A glance at his medal ribbons revealed that he had fought twice against India—and if the campaigns had been unsuccessful it was not the fault of battalion commanders of the quality of Azraf Khan. But he was a man who liked independent command to the point of obsession. It's never possible to forget, reflected the second-in-command, that he's a Pathan.

'Not likely to have deserted, then,' said Azraf Khan. 'That leaves three possibilities, as I see it. First, Gundar Ali was captured and taken into Indian Kashmir. I think, though, that if that had happened we should have had news by now. Second, he had some kind of accident. It's been several weeks since that patrol, and in that event he must long have been dead. Third, this . . . this animal the Indians say they've discovered . . . this ape-man killed him. His company commander says he was last seen very near the position where the thing is said to have been found.'

'We can only guess, Colonel,' said the second-in-command uncomfortably.

Azraf Khan nodded. 'I'm told Shalamerg is still guarded, even though they've taken the ape-man, whatever it is, down to Srinagar. I know it won't be easy, but I want another patrol out there. I want Gundar Ali's body, if it's there. And I think it is.'

'Yes, sir. I'll see to it.'

'Then,' said Azraf Khan, 'we'll know how he died.' He looked up from his desk at the other man. 'They claim this Indian thing's some kind of man, don't they?'

'So I understand, sir.'

The second-in-command watched fascinated as the colonel's mouth tightened beneath the bushy black Pathan moustache. Azraf Khan's voice, though, was almost gentle.

'Gundar Ali was from the hills, Zulfikar. Many of us in this battalion are from the hills. We should want blood for blood.'

·

Memorandum from Dr Liliane Erckmann at Srinagar, State of Jammu and Kashmir, to the Prime Minister of the Republic of India.

SUBJECT: A PRELIMINARY ASSESSMENT OF THE SPECIES OF *HOMO* DISCOVERED AT SHALAMERG IN INDIAN KASHMIR

We have now received the results of the first set of DNA tests. These are sufficiently startling for me to believe that you would wish me to bring them to your personal attention, before we meet next week. It is not too much to say that it seems likely that India holds a creature which may revolutionise our thinking about the nature of the human race.

Note: Perhaps an explanation, in lay terms, of the nature and purpose of DNA tests would be helpful.

1. DNA (deoxyribonucleic acid) is the major constituent of the chromosomes in our cells, and is the hereditary material of the majority of living organisms.

2. It is a long double molecule (the double helix) with strands twisted round each other. On these strands information is stored in genetic codes by a pattern of chemicals.

3. With modern biochemical techniques it is possible to unravel a strand. When this strand is combined with a similar strand from a closely related species, the two strands try to link up wherever the genetic codes carry the same message.

4. This was done with strands from the Shalamerg 'Esau' and from a human being. The results are as follows:

FIRST: Earlier DNA tests some years ago showed that man and chimpanzee and man and gorilla each share 99 per cent of their genetic material. The tests on man and Esau are beginning to show that the two may be much more closely linked than man and chimpanzee.

103

SECOND: In general, the longer it is since two species shared a common ancestor, the more different their DNA will be. Pioneer work by the American molecular biologists Dr Vincent Sarich and Dr Allan Wilson has established that, according to this molecular clock, men, chimpanzees and gorillas split from the same ancestral stock no more than four million years ago. The DNA results on the Esau thus indicate that man and Esau split from a common stock more recently than that.

THIRD: The most likely cause for the split is climatic change—probably that which led up to the recent Great Ice Age. Isolated populations became separated and went down their separate evolutionary paths. Man became what he is today: and a small relict Esau population has survived, astonishingly, in the remote Himalayas.

FOURTH: We now have to accept the fact that for some millions of years we have shared the Earth with a brother hominid almost identical with us, descended from the same ancestral line.

FIFTH: The moral and religious implications of this can hardly be over-emphasised, as you will certainly realise . . .

11

'Sure you won't take a hit?'

Judy Agar shook her head. The other girl shrugged, lighting her own cigarette so that the sweet-sour smell of marijuana drifted around them.

'You don't know what you're missing,' she said.

Judy Agar shifted uncomfortably where she sat in the strong Kashmir sun among the handful of youths and girls around the steel gates. With her clean hair and neater clothes, she knew she was the target for fairly good-natured contempt from some of the group, but she felt that, in an indefinable way, she needed them. At twenty-three, she was by far the youngest of the original Shalamerg party. Sometimes, she thought defiantly, I need to talk to people my own age.

The girl who was smoking beside her called out derisively as a youth a few yards away got to his feet and shambled off to urinate. Ellie Hayne was also in her early twenties, a sociology drop-out from a mid-western university. She wore a faded embroidered shirt-top and a long red cotton skirt, filthy and frayed at the bottom where it brushed her open-toed sandals. Her fingernails and toenails were broken and dirty, and her blonde hair was long, dirty and dishevelled. She had wandered the East with a succession of groups. In Bangkok she had born an illegitimate child, later adopted by a childless German couple. From there she had drifted to Katmandu, and now here to Srinagar. She lived mainly on what she could beg—from western tourists, of course, because by eastern standards her possession of objects like a wristwatch and a transistor radio made her relatively wealthy. At intervals Ellie attached herself briefly to one or other of the men in her group of the moment.

'What really bugs me,' said Ellie, 'is that I can't get up to see him. Sweet Jesus, you've got him in a cage up there, and all you can do is stop us seeing him, while you measure his God-damned penis. Maybe he'd like to see somebody who aimed to be just friendly.'

Within herself Judy smiled, though she was careful not to let this appear on her face. She could imagine Liliane's reaction —and Harry's too—if she appeared at the Centre with Ellie. Harry had already described white people who begged in a country as poor as India as 'obscene'. Yet Ellie had much more going for her than either Harry or Liliane would imagine. She was generous and easy-going. She could be funny—she had a sharp sense of the ridiculous. Behind the fashionably vague theories of life to which she clung, she had a surprisingly shrewd mind. And she's got something I haven't got, thought Judy. She's free. If she decided to go back to Katmandu or Singapore—or Oklahoma City, for that matter—tomorrow . . . well, she'd just get up and start moving out. She does what she likes and when she likes. When I get back to California I'll take a long look round before I decide what to do next . . . Because palaeontology didn't work out, that's for sure. I don't have the academic qualifications for the real, heavy science, so all I get is the maid's job, scientifically speaking. It sounds great, an expedition to Kashmir, but it gets oppressive after a few months. And then there was that time I felt so low . . . as though I'd lost somebody I loved, and there was no more reason for living. And I dreamed and dreamed about those skulls. Well, that's over. And maybe Ellie would come back with me—I could get my father to cable the air-fare. Ellie could teach me things.

'Nobody's seeing the Esau now,' she said. 'He's a little sick.'

'Why do you call him "the Esau"?' asked the other girl curiously. 'His name's just Esau.'

Judy laughed. 'Nobody knows what his name is,' she said. 'He can't speak. Anyway, he may be far too primitive to have a name.'

'Why can't he speak?'

'He hasn't got that kind of brain,' said Judy.

Ellie sounded shocked. 'You mean you've been looking into his brain?'

'No, no. You can find out with measurements. The part of his brain that would let him speak just isn't there.'

Ellie took a long drag at the cigarette before she spoke again, softly. 'Everything else is there, though, isn't it?'

'What do you mean?'

Ellie giggled, looking suddenly younger and more vulnerable. 'Well, I guess he's missing his sex, wouldn't you think? Jesus, I know men who'd freak out if they didn't get it two-three times a week. And your Esau is a big strong guy . . .'

'He's not my Esau,' Judy said.

'Who's is he, then . . . that Lib-love Frenchwoman's?'

'No, of course not. We hope one of these days we'll find him a mate.'

'Jesus, I wonder what she'll look like,' said Ellie reflectively.

'So, in a sense, this is a man from the past?'

The Prime Minister delicately stirred her tea, looking across the desk at Liliane, who sipped at her own cup before replying.

'Yes . . . you could say that. It is likely that the Esau—'the

106

Prime Minister smiled faintly at the name—'has changed very little over some hundreds of thousands of years, while we, his near-relatives, have developed from something which was much like he is now, to . . . well, to what *we* are now.'

'You do not think that we are, so to speak, his descendants?'

'I don't know, Prime Minister. None of us can be certain yet. But I think it unlikely. I think he is a brother . . . a brother under the skin.'

'How is this?'

'Can I put a hypothesis to you?'

The Prime Minister laughed. It was an unaffected laugh, yet in some indefinable way it seemed to enhance her formidable qualities.

'I spend my days having hypotheses put to me, Dr Erckmann. About everything from nuclear power to next year's maize crop. One more hypothesis I can take in my stride.'

Liliane paused to marshal her thoughts, while the other woman waited. At last she spoke again.

'I think we are seeing in the Esau an illustration of—amongst other things—parallel evolution. We're pretty sure that parallel evolution is a valid biological hypothesis because of what happened to monkeys in the past forty million years.'

'What do you mean?'

'A hundred million years ago,' said Liliane, 'South America and Africa were physically connected—before the present phase of continental drift began. The ancestors of monkeys —and of us, too—were tree-dwelling creatures. Their fossil remains have been found in both continents. The earliest monkeys appear as fossils about forty million years ago—but by that time South America and Africa were separated by the slowly-widening gap of the Atlantic Ocean. Completely independently, monkeys evolved in the Old World of Africa and the New World of South America. To a casual eye today they seem identical—though in fact there are important differences —in the nature and use of their tails, for example. But it's as though nature, through natural selection, beginning with the one common stock of more than forty million years ago, had been faced with the problem of designing a primate well able to cope with tree life in a tropical jungle, whether in Africa or America. Thousands of miles apart, with no possible physical

107

evolutionary connection, nature produced only one answer —the body type we call "monkey".'

'I see,' said the Prime Minister slowly. 'And you think . . .?' She waited.

'I . . . we . . . believe,' said Liliane, 'that the same thing happened with the Esau. The design pattern, for a successful ground-dwelling ape, was a product of the same evolutionary pressures at work on a very close relative of *Australopithecus* —the man-ape the Leakeys discovered in Tanzania. But then part of the population of this design-pattern got cut off, in the Himalayas, most probably by climatic intervention, and possibly an Ice Age. It was a small population, and it became a relict fauna. Isolated, interbreeding, unique. Meanwhile we ourselves—a very similar design pattern—spread and flourished.'

She leaned forward, while the other woman watched her curiously. I had that kind of eagerness once, thought the Prime Minister . . . exactly that kind of happiness in facing a challenge. What happened to it?

'People often imagine,' said Liliane, 'that continued inter-breeding produces a degenerate race. That doesn't always happen, as any pedigree animal breeder will tell you. Small, inbred populations don't necessarily produce weak individuals. Any recessive genes producing weakness are quickly bred out of the population, because the carriers of those genes die. What happens, however, is that the variability provided by a large population of different individuals is lost. Generation follows generation, and the individual members of the inbred population become more and more like clones of each other. The other Esaus—and, of course, there must be other Esaus—almost certainly look like twins of ours.'

'When I lived in England for two years, after I left Oxford,' said the Prime Minister absently, 'I had a boxer dog. He was killed by a car, and for months afterwards I would see other boxer dogs and my heart would seem to stop. So often, they looked exactly like him.'

'Of course,' said Liliane, 'if something happened to expand an inbred population, to give it a chance to spread, then the Esaus—and boxer dogs, too—would become as diverse and variable as we are ourselves.'

The Prime Minister got up from her chair and moved rest-
lessly to the window, looking out to the broad lawn where two
gardeners had harnessed a buffalo-bullock to a mowing
machine to cut the grass.

'He's like us in many ways, but he's very, very primitive,'
said Liliane. 'His brain capacity is almost identical with ours,
but it doesn't seem to have developed in at all the same way as
Homo sapiens—he can't speak, for instance. That alone rules
out much of our own type of progress for him.'

The Prime Minister watched the buffalo pull the machine
across the grass.

'I wonder,' she said at last, turning to look at Liliane. 'I have
an idea that if you and I could climb into a time-machine, and
go back unimaginable millions of years to watch the behaviour
of those tree-dwelling creatures you tell me of . . . well, would
we have imagined that they would one day rule the earth?'

'Perhaps not,' said Liliane.

'And if we had looked at the great dinosaurs, the terrible,
powerful, apparently invincible creatures that *did* rule the
earth . . . if we had compared them, Dr Erckmann, would we
have imagined that the tree-creatures would eventually write
Hamlet and Beethoven's Fifth Symphony and the Declaration
of Independence and the poetry of Tagore, and would one day
paint like Rembrandt and Cézanne and Monet . . . while the
terrible dinosaurs themselves would vanish from the world, to
become piles of bones in the tree-creatures' museums?'

'These are unknowable things,' said Liliane steadily. 'As a
scientist, I have to deal with what is knowable. And by our
existing standards, the Esau is very primitive. He's carnivorous—'

'So are we,' said the Prime Minister. 'Some of us, at any
rate.'

'Yes, but he eats his flesh raw. He cannot speak, as you
know. And so far none of us has managed to achieve any
contact with him—with what he thinks, or even with what he
wants.'

The Prime Minister sat in her chair again. Her voice was
unexpectedly bitter. 'You call your Esau primitive. Do you
know how many people there were in India, at the last count?'

Liliane shook her head, catching the bright glitter in the

other woman's eyes. The Prime Minister's question seemed strangely inconsequential.

'Well, I'll tell you, Dr Erckmann. There are around seven hundred millions of us—we can't be sure to a precise million because there are more and more of us every hour. We've doubled our population in twenty years. We have fourteen languages in this country, and around three hundred dialects, most of them mutually incomprehensible. We have seven major religions, and people in various parts of the country who worship animals. Almost all Indians live in poverty—some in poverty so excruciating that you in the West simply have no conception of it. In some of our cities people die in the streets each night that passes. And yet in your western world—which is the only tiny economic hope we have—I sense a slackening of will, a lack of impetus, a cynical despair about the future of human life. In the civilised West, there is even the beginning of a fall in population.'

'It will change, eventually,' said Liliane, regretting the foolish, anodyne words as soon as she had said them.

'You are far from a fool, Dr Erckmann,' said the Prime Minister softly, 'so do not talk like one. It will not change. It never changes. There are corners of the world—perhaps like your own in California—where life can be comfortable. Even in such corners it is not now entirely safe on the streets, is it?'

Liliane shook her head.

'In my own lifetime,' said the Prime Minister, 'I have seen an aircraft set out from a great civilised nation and drop bombs which extinguished two hundred thousand human lives at a single blow. I have seen another great civilised nation, following barbaric superstition, attempt to extinguish an entire culture in gas-chambers. I have seen yet another great civilised nation oppress and absorb nations on its boundaries, purely to use them as a defensive belt in time of war. And, speaking of war, I see the great nations, without exception, arming themselves with weapons of inconceivable barbarity, moving steadily towards a conflict which could well wipe out the *Homo sapiens* whose descent from the trees you are so eager to trace.'

The Prime Minister stopped speaking, and looked at the notes on the desk in front of her.

'Something occurs to me. Wasn't there somewhere a note

saying that this creature, this primitive Esau, as you call it, is resistant to radiation?'

'To a great extent . . . yes,' said Liliane.

The other chuckled. It was not a reassuring sound.

'The final irony, perhaps. Will Esau survive, after we are all gone? Are we the dinosaurs, while he is the Shakespeare of the future? Perhaps an Esau will sit in Delhi, in a hundred thousand years, ruling over seven hundred million other Esaus. I wish him luck of it—or perhaps it will be a she-Esau.'

'If you feel so . . . so without hope,' said Liliane, 'why do you trouble yourself with the kind of life you lead? Why struggle to keep all this?'

She waved a hand at the Prime Minister's room and the garden outside, where just above the flowering hedge could be glimpsed the military turban of a Sikh sentry, patrolling steadily to and fro. For a moment she wondered if she had been impertinent, but the Prime Minister stared at her, and then laughed, sounding more relaxed.

'Not because I have any intellectual conviction of a better human future, Dr Erckmann, in or out of India. But I myself am *Homo sapiens*, after all. So far, it has always been our nature to try, to fail, and to continue to hope. And, more personally speaking, when I was young, in my father's house we had a *sayce*, a sort of servant, who had once been a fisherman in the Bay of Bengal. That is a sea where a storm blows up very quickly, I am told. And the *sayce* told me that when a storm was at its fiercest, the men in his boat sang. You must always sing on a tilting deck, he said. It helps to drive away fear.'

'Why did you ask me to come?' said Liliane quietly.

'Ah, back to business,' said the Prime Minister. 'Well, frankly, I was curious. I have looked at your career, Dr Erckmann. You are a rather unusual woman. I myself am a woman in what is still rather an unusual position. I thought perhaps there would be some fellow-feeling between us. I always like to meet a kindred spirit. In my life, I have not found so many. And—'

She paused, and turned back to the window, while the long-cased clock in the corner of the room, a relic of long-ago vice-regal days, ticked steadily on.

'And?' said Liliane at last. She felt strangely moved.

111

The other woman smiled at her. 'And I think perhaps I have,' said the Prime Minister. 'I will do what I can to help you. You will need help . . . more, perhaps, than you now realise. In a sense, this . . . creature . . . that you keep at Srinagar is a man. Or if not a man, a brother.'

Liliane nodded.

'Then,' said the Prime Minister, 'if it is a man, or what can be called a man, there will be problems. Not all the conundrums which face us in the world are stricly scientific. There are other areas of conflict. You are returning to Kashmir at once?'

'Yes.'

'Go in peace,' said the Prime Minister. 'And enjoy it while you can. Peace of any kind—of mind, of heart, of nations—is a fragile commodity.'

She placed her hands palm to palm in courteous dismissal.

12

'Well, Harry, it was your Kipling who said that "East is East and West is West, and never the twain shall meet" . . . but he seems to have been wrong. That woman and I really got through to each other. She's still going to back us. It will make a tremendous difference.'

'I'm glad to hear it,' said Harry Kernow. 'But you're a bit hard on poor Kipling. He did write "East is East and West is West," but nobody ever seems to quote the rest of the verse.'

'And what's that?'

She smiled at him. He watched her with admiration. She was happy this morning, and she looked magnificent . . . blue eyes, tanned cheeks, black hair. Suddenly he felt he could eat her alive. What a woman she could be, if only she'd drop that guard for an hour or two.

'My goodness me, Liliane,' he said mildy, 'there are days when you make even this old heart go pit-a-pat. I've never seen you look better.'

For once, the familiar put-down did not come. Instead, Liliane smiled again.

'Thank you, Harry. But you still haven't told me the rest of that verse.'

'As I remember it,' said Harry, 'Kipling goes on to say "But there is neither East nor West, border, nor breed, nor birth, When two strong men stand face to face, though they come from the ends of the earth . . ." '

'Ah,' said Liliane.

Harry grinned. 'I imagine the old boy had never thought of two strong women standing face to face. But I expect the effect is much the same.'

'How is the Esau?' Liliane asked abruptly. 'And where are the others?'

'Tom's in Srinagar—he spent last night on the houseboat. Fair enough—he's been here every night for a week, and he could do with a couple of days off. Prakash also went into Srinagar, to get his typewriter repaired. He'll be back late tonight. Richard Kimbell's gone to Chandigarh. And Judy —she's around somewhere. I saw her at the gate about an hour ago, talking again to that girl in the red skirt—the one with the dirty toenails.'

'I wish she wouldn't go down there,' said Liliane. 'They really aren't a very attractive group.'

Harry laughed. 'The old Maharajah wouldn't have put up with them. Hari Singh would have had them out of Kashmir before you could say "cannabis". But they're young, Liliane . . . very young compared with me, and even quite young compared with you and Tom. Youth speaks to youth, you know. Anyway, she's going back to California soon, isn't she?'

'Next week,' said Liliane. 'But, Harry, that means there's been no scientist here today.'

'Until you came, no. Just me, the Old Kashmir Hand. I don't expect it made any difference to him out there.'

He nodded towards the compound. From the window of the administration hut the shadowy form of the Esau could just be seen. He seemed to be squatting inside his cave.

'How has he been while I've been away?'

'Not good,' said Harry, with a grimace. 'The little boost, whatever it was, that Tom's two model heads gave him seems to have faded. He's eating very little, and he seems to mope a lot.'

He hesitated for a moment, and then plunged on.

'Liliane . . . have you really thought this through?'

Her heart sank, but she turned her eyes to his.

'What do you mean?'

'You know what I mean,' he said. 'How long can we keep him here? He's going to die . . . next week, next month, sometime soon. He hasn't got a chance. We're destroying him, and he's a man. A sort of man. A brother.'

Impulsively, and quite unexpectedly, she placed her hand on his arm.

'That's exactly how the Prime Minister thinks of him. But thank you for saying "we", Harry. You could easily have blamed me. And you'd have been right. It's my responsibility.'

'We're all in it together,' he said awkwardly. 'That's why I felt I could put my feelings to you.'

114

She sighed. 'I said it was my responsibility, Harry, but that's not really true, perhaps, any more. The Esau has become a scientific property, I suppose. Scientists are examining Esau material all over the world. There's a lot of money involved. French money, American money. There are research projects planned . . . research budgets being worked out. Dead or alive—and even dead, he would have tremendous potential for research—the Esau now belongs to the scientific community. It's only because the Indian Prime Minister insists that I stay in charge that he's not been moved elsewhere—to Delhi, or even to California.'

'Quite a few of the people who come here try to sound me out about getting another Esau or two—preferably a female,' said Harry.

'What do you tell them?'

'The truth—that it's virtually out of the question. We don't know where he came from, or where his home is. And the whole area in question is right on the ceasefire line—territory permanently in dispute between India and Pakistan. They've already fought one war over it. It's not out of the question that there'll be another, some time in the future.'

He stood there, strong, neat, compact, reliable. For the first time, she felt a personal comfort in his presence.

'Pakistan has already claimed the Esau,' she said. 'I was told in Delhi. They say he came from their side of the line.'

Harry whistled. 'Do they, indeed? That might be complicated.'

She looked at him sharply. 'You don't mean . . . they wouldn't start fighting?'

He laughed. 'No, not for the Esau. Not a chance. But the General's no fool. He might try to use the whole thing to . . . well, to adjust the border a bit more in his favour. And to give the Indians something to think about. And, of course, he's probably right.'

'How do you mean?'

'Well, I've always thought that the Esau probably did come in from north of the ceasefire line, from the Pakistan end. It's wilder country up there, around Gilgit and up towards the Karakoram. The Esau's strong, active, and probably pretty tireless when he's fit. That sort of country is the area where I'd expect him to live. With the rest of his kind. How many other Esaus would there be likely to be?'

She shrugged. 'It's anybody's guess. It could be as few as fifty. That's enough to keep a relict population alive, in exactly the right circumstances. Perhaps there are only a few males, and, relatively, a lot of females. That's a possible ecological pattern.'

'Then he could be pretty important to them . . . all by himself?'

'Yes. It's something that keeps coming back to me. Have we disturbed the Esau balance? Did we just tip the scales against him and his kind when we captured him at Shalamerg? In a way, it's a good thing that any project to acquire more Esaus seems so impossible. To find them might be to doom them.'

'Well, I wouldn't worry about that,' said Harry. 'It would take a couple of brigades of mountain infantry to stand even the faintest chance of finding them in that kind of wild country —and even then, capturing them would be very, very difficult. And I can't see India or Pakistan allowing a couple of brigades of infantry to wander to and fro across the ceasefire line. The other Esaus are safe. At least, they are for the moment.'

'What do you mean?'

'We used to have a saying in my old regiment,' said Harry. 'Always make room for the unexpected, because it's the unexpected that always happens.'

'Where's the Frenchwoman?' Ellie asked, standing beside the table in the administration hut, looking at photographs of the Esau.

'She's asleep in the accommodation hut,' Judy said nervously.

'Already?' said Ellie. 'Who's she with—the Englishman? I'll bet he gets a piece in the sack with her, for all her high and mightiness.'

'Of course she's not with Harry. She's tired—she's been down in Delhi, seeing the Government. Look, Ellie, I shouldn't have brought you here at all. And we can't see the Esau, anyway. He's in his cave. I keep telling you he's sick.'

'You certainly do that,' said Ellie. 'Jesus, kid, what can you possibly be scared of?'

She crossed to the window. Already the blue-grey Kashmir twilight was deepening into night.

'I wish I could lay eyes on him, just once. I guess I'll never get another chance.'

She looked at the other girl. 'I won't, will I?'

'Maybe not,' Judy said. 'You saw how difficult it was with the gate-guard. It's only because he knows I work up here that he let me bring you in. I hope he doesn't think to mention it to Liliane.'

'She really bugs you, doesn't she?' Ellie's voice was spiteful. 'Jesus, I hope that never happens to me . . . being bugged by somebody, I mean. Especially another woman.'

Angrily, Judy got to her feet, sweeping the Esau photographs back into the folder, wondering why she had been persuaded to bring Ellie into the Centre.

'Come on, Ellie. You have to go back to the gate. Harry will be here in a few minutes—he's only over at the vehicle park. I don't want him to see you.'

'All right, all right.'

Judy slipped out of the door, stood for a moment outside, and then spoke again.

'I don't think he's coming yet, but I want to make sure. Listen . . . if he *is* coming, I'll stop him and make some excuse to talk. And you go straight back to the gate—they won't make any problem about letting you out. It's getting *in* that's difficult.'

'OK.'

As Judy disappeared into the darkness beyond the door Ellie moved surprisingly swiftly, belying her casual and relaxed manner of the past few minutes. She went straight to the steel hook on which she had seen a bunch of keys as soon as she entered the hut a few minutes before. They must be the keys to the Esau, she thought. They must be . . . there's nothing else important to lock up around here. She went outside and peered into the darkness. There was no sign of Judy. Silently, in her scuffed sandals, Ellie ran to the compound. A faint early starlight now gleamed on the metal fence. She stood beside the locked steel gate, where the fence soared into the darkness above her, and tried all three keys on the bunch. With an excited lurch of the heart, she realised that the last one fitted. For a moment she hesitated, listening.

Very faintly, from the direction of the vehicle park nearly a quarter of a mile away, she could hear two voices, a man's and a woman's. Down the hill, on the road to Srinagar, a pair of car headlights flared, then waned. The voices, she knew, would be Judy and the Englishman, talking. And now she sensed, rather than heard, another infinitesimal sound . . . the Esau, breathing inside his cave. Her mind was made up. She put the key in the lock and turned it. The gate slid sideways under her gentle pressure, and she slipped quickly into the Esau's compound, crossing immediately to the cave.

Five yards away she stopped again to listen. Now she could hear no sound of breathing. Silently, her heart thudding, she tiptoed to the entrance. There was still no sound from inside. It was, she thought inconsequentially, more like a tunnel than a cave, open at both ends. She squatted on her heels and peered in, smelling the strong, rank scent of its inhabitant. With a little involuntary shiver she glimpsed, a few feet away, the white shapes of the two clay heads Judy had told her about. But there was nothing else. In the glow of the stars the cave was empty. Puzzled, she got back to her feet, and turned. She gasped, her body rigid with shock. Six feet behind her, massive against the night sky, the Esau stood watching.

For a few seconds, while she held her breath, the great form opposite made no movement. Then, infinitely slowly, it stretched out a hand and grasped her long hair, giving it a little experimental tug. She gasped again, and the Esau instantly released her. They were standing so close now that it was almost as if they were dancing. She could feel the brush of the hair on the Esau's body. But still nothing happened, and she felt her confidence return. She moved slightly to the side, so that the starlight fell directly on the Esau's face.

'Jesus,' she whispered, 'you're something else, aren't you?'
She stood back, appraising him.

'You're so big . . . all of you is so big. Don't be scared of me, Esau. I'm your friend, and I'm not going to do anything bad to you. You're lovely.'

Tentatively, she put out a hand and gently stroked the hairy arm. It felt like bristly leather. She stood closer, almost touching.

'I guess you'd like . . . oh, OH . . . OH.'

118

The Esau stretched out his other arm and swept her against his body. With her face deep in the matted hair on the great chest she could make no sound. With his free hand he fingered her clothes, seeming puzzled. Then he grunted and pulled at the skirt, tearing it from her legs. She was being forced back, back into the cave. For a moment she saw the fierce eyes glowing above her. The hands grasped her thighs, pulling them apart. The weight of him was enormous, and there was a deep piercing pain. What was happening to her was totally out of her experience. She was now only part-conscious, almost smothered by the hairy body, able to breathe only with an occasional gasp. The bulk of him crushed her down. There was pain, terror, helplessness, and even stabs of almost unbearable pleasure. Then consciousness left her altogether, and she fell down a long red tunnel into oblivion.

Two hundred yards away Judy was walking beside Harry Kernow. She stopped and turned her head from side to side—exactly, he thought incongruously, like a pointing dog. Then, with a little cry, she began to run towards the compound. Bewildered, Harry stopped.

'Judy, what's wrong? What are you . . .?'

Cursing, he began to run after her. She had reached the steel fence, and was peering through it, her face pressed against the mesh. He pulled her back, while she fought him silently.

'Don't be a fool, Judy—it's asking for trouble to go so close.'

'Where is he?' she said fiercely.

Harry looked towards the cave. 'He's there, in the cave. I can see him. He's lying down.'

'He's not alone.'

Harry pulled her to face him. 'What do you mean?'

She shrieked at him suddenly, surprising him so much that he stepped back a pace.

'He's not alone you fool. He's not alone, not alone, not alone. What do you think I mean? He's got somebody in there with him. It's Ellie. Damn her, damn her.'

'Who in hell is Ellie?'

She made no answer, but ran again to the fence. Harry took the big rubber-covered torch he wore at his belt and shone it on the cave. The Esau was now standing in the entrance, and as

119

the light fell on him he gave once more the roar they had first heard at dawn on Shalamerg. Behind him, on the ground, there was a glimmer of a white form. Harry pointed the torch at it. He felt the sweat start on his forehead.

'God, it's a woman. But how . . .? Come back, you little fool.'

He seized Judy by the waist and hauled her from the fence. She was struggling vainly against the mesh, trying to climb over.

'Don't be an idiot, Judy, you can't help that way. Listen —let's check the gate. Then I'll run and get the anaesthetic rifle.'

Judy turned and spat at him before she began to run wildly towards the gate. He overtook her as she reached it. It was open, the keys still in the lock. Instantly he snapped shut the gate, and pocketed the keys. His heart pounding, he ran over to the hut, snatched the rifle from its wall-clip, and went back to the fence. Again Judy was clinging to the mesh, and again he had to haul her off. She scratched at his face, and with the flat of his hand he knocked her to the ground. Then he checked the anaesthetic dart in the breech, aimed and fired straight into the dark mass of the Esau's body, fifteen feet away. The Esau roared again. A hand was pulling at Harry's arm. He turned and saw Liliane beside him, half-dressed, still buttoning her clothes.

'What are you doing? What's happening?'

He pointed to the cave. 'He's got somebody in there—Judy says it's a woman. I've knocked him out—it's the only way to get in.'

The Esau sank to its knees beside the still white form.

'Is he going to do her any more harm?' said Liliane. 'How long is it since you used the rifle?'

'He'll be unconscious in thirty more seconds,' said Harry. 'But perhaps I should—'

'He doesn't want to hurt her,' said Judy's slow voice from where she sprawled, dazed, on the ground. 'Don't you see —he's guarding her. Damn her.'

With a grunt, the Esau fell forward, and lay motionless. Once or twice came the sound of a deep snore.

Harry went to the gate, unlocked it, and ran in. The woman's white body lay almost touching the fallen Esau. Harry knelt beside her, gently moving the long blonde hair from where it covered the face. She was completely naked except for a few rags of the embroidered blouse, and there was blood on her legs. He picked her up and carried her across the compound and out of the gate. Then he laid her on the ground beside Liliane.

'Is she . . . dead?' whispered Liliane.

He shook his head. 'No, but she's in a bad way, I think. Maybe her legs are broken.'

He bent over the huddled body.

'I'm afraid it's not too difficult to see what happened to her, Liliane. And—' he turned coldly towards Judy—'I could make a pretty accurate guess as to how she got up here in the first place. She's one of the crowd at the gate, isn't she?'

'She's Ellie,' said Judy. She was speaking now in an excited, almost giggling way, and seemed to have recovered from Harry's blow. 'She thinks she knows everything, but she doesn't, does she?'

They stared at her but she said no more, laughing occasionally as though to herself. Harry spoke quickly.

'I'll stay down here, Liliane. You go back and ring the hospital at Srinagar for an ambulance. I don't think we'd better move this one—' he nodded towards Ellie, now covered with his jacket—'until a doctor comes. And tell them there'll be two patients. This one . . . and Judy . . .'

Two hours later they sat together in the administration hut. The ambulance had been and gone, and they were left alone.

'How could it possibly happen?' said Liliane wearily. She sipped at the whisky Harry had poured for her—not a drink she'd ever liked, but one she needed now.

'Judy,' said Harry briefly. 'I thought she was better, but she's gone right over the edge now. It was Judy who did it, Liliane. I've seen her with that girl, at the gate.'

'Will . . . will the girl die, do you think?'

'Anybody's guess. Her legs are injured, as you know. But the shock . . . the sexual shock must have been terrific.'

She shuddered, but made herself think rationally. 'It's going to change everything, Harry. I don't know what will happen.

And there's Judy's father to be told, too. But we can tell him one good thing.'

'What's that?'

'Well, that she was brave, before she went out of her mind—temporarily, we pray. She tried to climb the fence itself, to save Ellie. You saw her do that.'

He shook his head. 'She tried to climb the fence all right, Liliane. But she wasn't trying to save Ellie. She seemed to hate Ellie.'

'Then what was she doing?'

'She was trying to climb in,' said Harry, 'because she wanted to be with the Esau.'

Memorandum from the Director-General, United Nations
Educational, Scientific and Cultural Organisation, Palais de
l'UNESCO, Paris, France.

COPIES TO: National Science Adviser to the President of the
    United States.
    Academy of Sciences of the Union of Soviet Socialist
    Republics.
    Ministry of Education and Science, United Kingdom.
    Ministry of Science, Republic of India.
    Ministry of Science, Republic of Pakistan.
    Ministry of Scientific Research, Republic of France.
SUBJECT: Recommendations for future policy regarding the
    living species of *Homo* found in Kashmir (Indian Zone),
    provisionally classified as *Homo kashmiriensis (chowdhuri)*.
PROPOSAL: A Special Committee of UNESCO, made up of
    two representatives delegated by each of the above
    addressees, will be held at the Palais de l'UNESCO at a date
    to be announced, but in not more than fourteen days' time.
PROCEDURE: The Director-General will take the chair. It
    would be his intention that any conclusions reached by the
    Special Committee would be reported to a full committee of
    UNESCO in due course.

13

The Director-General of UNESCO was Italian, a sophisticated
tactician on the rugged proving-ground of United Nations
politics. He sat at the centre of the gleaming committee table in
one of the largest of the six hundred offices of the Palais de
l'UNESCO. The eight-storey Palais was an extraordinary experiment in international decoration and design: ceramics by

Miro and Artigas, wall-paintings by Picasso, a figure by Henry Moore . . . an artistic and architectural *minestrone*, a bit of everything, the Director-General reflected moodily. He had no particular enthusiasm for *minestrone*, nor for the Palais building. But, in terms of national pride, it worked. The very table at which the Special Committee was now meeting was an illustration of the principle behind it . . . its makers, it was claimed, had used one piece of wood from every member-state at the time it was made. Privately, the Director-General doubted whether he would like to inquire too closely into its exact composition. And although internationalism surrounded them, UNESCO was rarely united. *Homo sapiens* was a difficult, suspicious creature. Yet perhaps today was a little different. The Esau in Kashmir had brought them together in common interest, common fascination. Only one invited delegation had declined to attend: that from Pakistan. The General would not send men to sit beside an Indian delegation, and in any case, it seemed, he claimed that the Esau was an inhabitant of Pakistan. Ah, the Soviet delegate was speaking. Surreptitiously, the Director-General looked at his table plan. Yes . . . Dr Nikolai Plekhanov . . .

'I think we will all agree that the tests have so far tended to corroborate each other. The first test we carried out at Akademgorodok, with material supplied from Srinagar, was a relatively simple comparison of DNA molecules. It showed, as we all know, that more than 99 per cent of DNA is the same in the Esau as in man—meaning, in crude terms, that the Esau is closer to us than we are to the chimpanzee. Of course, each of us here finds this fascinating—and yet, my colleagues, there has proved to be something even more interesting. At Akademgorodok we also carried out a second test—an inversion test on chromosomal DNA. Now forgive me if I remind you that on the measuring scale of such a test, man and gorilla differ by eight, man and chimpanzee by six. And with our second test—' he paused, momentarily anticipating the dramatic effect of his words—'man and the Esau differ by four.'

A little ripple of talk ran through the scientists grouped round the table.

'The Soviet delegation regrets,' Plekhanov went on, 'that

the results of the inversion tests came too late to be generally circulated until today, though I understand that similar tests have also been performed at Berkeley in California . . .'

He looked across to where Richard Kimbell sat with a Berkeley scientist beside him. Kimbell nodded.

'Berkeley did the same test, two weeks ago, with similar material. We got precisely the same findings. On the inversion tests, in fact, the result is clear-cut. The Esau is very closely related to us indeed—in fact, it is even just conceivable that the Esau male and a *Homo sapiens* female could produce fertile offspring.'

Dio mio, said the Director-General to himself, looking across to the Press table, there goes the cat among the pigeons. The British senior delegate, an elderly and famous scientist from London University's Department of Anthropology, cleared his throat. The Director-General tapped the table, and the buzz of discussion died down.

'Since we know,' said the Englishman, 'that copulation has already taken place, though in unfortunate circumstances, between the Esau and a human female, may one ask if there is any . . .?'

'The girl is not pregnant,' said Kimbell.

'Ah,' said the Englishman. 'In a way, of course, that is a pity. One does not wish to be callous, but a pregnancy in this relatively straightforward way would have helped us enormously. I foresee a somewhat debilitating moral argument ahead.'

The Director-General watched Liliane Erckmann tighten her lips as she sat opposite him. The French delegation, after all, was female. There might be difficulties. He rapped the table.

'I think,' he said, 'that now that we have had our preliminary discussion of the scientific data—of which you have copies in the folders before you—and have also heard the results of some of the latest tests, we might move on and listen to an analysis of the position from the scientist on the spot, Dr Liliane Erckmann. Dr Erckmann, ladies, gentlemen, I beg you to remember only one thing. I am a layman.'

He smiled, and a little ripple of laughter ran around the table. 'I'm the only layman here. The Director-General must be many things, but so far he has not needed to be an anthropologist or a palaeontologist. Yet I thought it best to take the chair myself. I have not, over the years—' he looked at them quizzically—'formed the opinion that scientists remain totally impartial in a situation of this nature. So perhaps you will remember that I *am* a layman, and will not take my comprehension for granted.'

Again there was a little moment of polite laughter, stilled when Liliane got to her feet. For a moment or two she passed a sheaf of notes from one hand to the other, and at last placed them face-downwards on the table. Plekhanov noted with admiration that she did not refer to them again.

'With my colleagues,' said Liliane, nodding first towards Kimbell and then to where Chowdhuri sat with the second Indian delegate, 'I have now observed the Esau for about four months. I—all of us—have come definitely to the conclusion, supported by the DNA tests, that the Esau is certainly a species of *Homo*, though he is not, of course, *Homo sapiens*. Regrettably, we have been able to establish remarkably little contact with his mind, with the exception of certain . . . personal . . . impressions of a purely subjective character which I certainly would not class as scientific evidence. For what they are worth, I have included them in an appendix to the notes which are in your folders.'

From his seat beside the Director-General, Kimbell interrupted briefly.

'You may not realise from these notes, ladies and gentlemen, something which Dr Erckmann modestly hesitates to tell you. Although the person most mentally affected by contact with the Esau was Miss Judy Agar, who became seriously ill as a result, nevertheless the only person who seems to have elicited anything approaching a reciprocal *response* from the Esau is Dr Erckmann herself. The sole other "human" contact achieved was the terrible episode with the girl Ellie Hayne, who, I am happy to say, is now making a good recovery. In each case, you may note, the other party to any significant interchange between our male Esau and *Homo sapiens* has been female.'

Unobtrusively, the Director-General's eyes rested upon Liliane. She was certainly female . . . very, very female. That superb high colour and that magnificent hair . . . even an Esau must look twice.

'I think,' said Liliane, 'we should return to basics. We cannot yet define the precise relationship of the Esau with ourselves. The Esau clearly belongs, of course, to the ape family, along with chimpanzee, gorilla, and man. In the past, DNA tests on all three of these have shown that man, chimpanzee and gorilla share a common ancestor around four and a half million years ago. I imagine that no one sitting at this table disagrees with that?'

She glanced along the line of listening scientists. There was a murmur of agreement.

'Then, on the basis of similar tests,' Liliane said, 'we must conclude that *Homo kashmiriensis*, the Esau, also shares this common ancestor. So when and why did the separate lines of man and Esau split away, each to go along its own evolutionary path?'

The Englishman cleared his throat. 'Is it possible that the Esau *is* the common ancestor—a member of a small relict poulation of common ancestral stock, which was cut off in some way and did not develop into *Homo sapiens*? Might the Esau be, for instance, a sub-species descendant of *Homo erectus*, our own ancestor who walked upright a million years ago? When we look at the Esau, are we looking back at our own past?'

Liliane shook her head. 'The same thought occurred to me, but I have since rejected it. I believe that the Esau, as a species, is certainly closely allied to *Homo erectus*—in fact, I believe that the man-Esau split may have taken place only a million years ago. One line became *Homo erectus*, developing eventually into *Homo sapiens* . . . into us. The other, I think, became the Esau, and developed into the creature we found in Kashmir.'

She paused, and turned to the English scientist.

'I say "developed" into the creature we found in Kashmir. In fact, the Esau appears to have developed relatively little over the past million years. That is evidenced by the remarkable similarity of the two skulls found at Shalamerg shortly before the appearance of the living Esau itself . . . the two skulls whose disparity in dating caused so many absurdly unjustified attacks to be made upon my colleagues and myself. One skull, as we know, is dated at a million years BP, and the other belongs to the very recent past. Now that we have a living —and identical—Esau, the conclusion seems clear. The Esau line has altered little since it split off from our joint ancestral stock. We are not, as you suggested a moment ago, looking at our own past, but we *are* looking at a "man" of a kind who lived at the same time as our own remote ancestors, and who has changed little since. For that, there is only one explanation I can see.'

'Punctuated equilibrium,' said the Englishman slowly. 'Whew . . .!'

'Precisely,' Liliane went on. The Director-General looked at her expectantly, and she smiled.

'Let me summarise. Since Darwin, the conventional wisdom about evolution has been that change is gradual. Small hereditary mutations—changes in the DNA of the chromosomes —apparently build up in certain populations of a species over millions of years. These changes are regarded as the raw material of evolution—because eventually the descendants of such mutations diverge so much from the common ancestral stock that they must now be regarded as different species, unable any longer even to breed together. An illustration of this process would be man and chimpanzee.'

Liliane stopped speaking for a moment and drank from the glass of Vichy water beside her. She certainly has their attention, the Director-General noted, watching the attentive faces turned towards her. And she's taking advantage of "explaining" it to me, a layman, to ram it home point by point. And, at last, to justify herself . . .

'Only a fool would now challenge the central idea of evolution,' Liliane continued. 'On the broad sweep of the idea, and in many of its details, Darwin was right. And yet the increasing wealth of fossils found over the past half-century shows a disturbing lack of evidence of the gradual evolution he imagined.

'What, in fact, do we see? We see species that, except perhaps for increases in size, stay the same for millions of years. Then, suddenly, they are replaced by other species . . . species clearly related to them, but also decisively different. And when we search the fossil record, in all but a very few cases we cannot find the so-called "missing links" between the ancestral stock and the new species.

'We know what absurdities this can lead to. We have "fundamentalists" seizing on these gaps in the fossil record, and the sudden appearance of new species, as evidence of "special creation". We do not need to waste time with such nonsense. Today, the inconsistencies of the fossil record can be explained by the concept of "punctuated equilibrium".'

The Indian beside Chowdhuri whispered urgently into his ear, but Chowdhuri shook his head. He was annoyed at the interruption, and his eyes were fixed on Liliane. She spoke now directly to the Director-General.

'A successful species, well adapted to its environment, will stay the same . . . in a state of evolutionary equilibrium. Its own mutations will usually be inferior and harmful, and will not survive to breed offspring and leave traces in the fossil record. Sometimes, however, the conditions in which the species live change sharply—and species that were previously well adapted are wiped out. Such a disappearnce can be on a global scale—as in the sudden disappearance of the great dinosaurs 65 million years ago. There may be many possible causes for such an ecological catastrophe . . . ice ages, meteor impacts, even the drift of continents leading to irreversible change. Whatever the reason, such extinctions have happened in the past, and will undoubtedly happen again in the future. They are the punctuation in the equilibrium of evolution.

'And, after them, we find new variations appearing in the fossil records. We all know that while mutations do not in general survive, they are always occurring. Sudden forms of change in the chromosomes—I will not bother you with the technical details, Director-General, except to say that they are known as "translocations"—can have an enormous effect from one generation to the next. In a sharply changed environment such mutations may suddenly prove to be better adapted than the parent stock. But there are two problems for the mutations. If they are monstrously different, they are likely to be killed or abandoned by the parent. And even if they survive, they may have difficulty in finding a similar mate, and breeding themselves.'

'I see what you're driving at,' the Englishman said slowly, as

Liliane paused. 'The best way for such mutations to survive —especially with social mammals like man and ape—is when they occur in relatively small, isolated populations.'

'We carried out some experiments with langur monkeys, in the Crimea, a couple of years ago,' said Plekhanov. 'We found the decisive factor was that there should be a harem-system in the community, so that one male carrying a mutant chromosome can produce a great many mutant offspring by a series of different mothers.'

'Exactly,' said Liliane. 'In an isolated population the offspring mutants, half-brothers and half-sisters, would in turn mate with each other. Gradually the mutation would become "normal". A new species would have appeared in a generation or so.'

The leader of the West German delegation was Hans-Joachim Stross, who had worked in the Fayum Depression south of Cairo on the oldest identifiable primate ancestor of man—the 28 million-year-old ape *Aegyptopithecus*. He spoke for the first time.

'The pieces of the jigsaw are beginning to fit. Because, as we all know, such a new species will not spread out from its isolated retreat unless one of two things happens. Either it is overwhelmingly more successful than any rival mutation, or some other catastrophe kills off the rivals, leaving the way open for the newcomers. Which means—'

'That possibly there were two mutations, or more. One became *Homo sapiens*,' said Liliane. To the Director-General, she sounded triumphant.

'And the other,' she went on, 'became the Esau, a totally effective hominid type inside its own restricted, inaccessible area, but unable to compete with man outside it. The Esau could survive only in an area where man—our form of man, that is—was not present to offer competition.'

'So we've found a brother,' said the Englishman. 'And what in Heaven's name are we going to do about that?'

For a moment Liliane's mind flicked back to the quiet room in Delhi, with the bullock-drawn grass-mower moving up and down the lawn outside, and a voice saying to her, ironically: 'Will an Esau rule in Delhi, in a hundred thousand years?'

'In the very long-term,' said Liliane steadily, 'the question may be the other way round. What is the Esau going to have to do about us?'

'I don't understand,' said the Englishman.

'Well, none of us has to look far in our contemporary world to imagine a sudden catastrophe that could kill off *Homo sapiens*, the Esau's rival. Nuclear war is the obvious possibility. Or it could be something undreamed of . . . global climatic change, or changes, which to us would be crucial, in the intensity of solar energy. The reason doesn't really matter, except in the short-term.'

She opened a briefcase beside her, and took from it a battered book with a red cover.

'This was written,' she said, 'by an old Scottish geologist in 1841. I think it is worth reading to you now. "As all the species of the past have died, so it is destined for all the species of the present to die. We now absolutely know, as geologists, not only that a beginning there was, but that the beginning was a comparatively recent event; and further, founding on the unvarying experience of the past, that the race, at least in its existing character and condition, is to have an end . . ." '

She looked down the table at them, remembering the Esau as she had left him in the compound at Srinagar, sometimes active, but often slumped, dulled, unresponsive. Hastily, the Director-General repressed a sudden impulse to put out a comforting hand, for he saw that her eyes held the glimmer of tears. But her voice was steady.

'Those words are as true today as they were in 1841. One day, our race of *Homo sapiens* will have an end. This happens to all species. It has happened before: it will happen again. One day something will replace us. It may be soon, and it may be the Esau. We owe to the Esau a colossal moral responsibility. He is the brother who may inherit.'

'But he's not *us*,' said the Englishman stubbornly. 'We owe him as much moral responsibility as we do to a chimpanzee or a gorilla. And don't—' he held up a hand—'misunderstand me. In my view, that is a *lot* of moral responsibility. It includes care, kindness, an attempt at understanding. I don't see what more is possible.'

Kimbell leaned forward. 'If I remember correctly, you haven't yet seen him?'

'That's true.'

'I think when you do—and I hope it will be soon—you will see what Dr Erckmann means. We all feel much the same way about this . . . those of us who are in daily contact with the Esau, that is.'

'That is certainly so,' said Chowdhuri, speaking for the first time. 'And it is interesting that, locally, around Srinagar, the Esau is not regarded as another ape, another form of animal. They see him quite differently . . . very differently indeed.'

'In what way?' the Englishman asked.

'These people see him as a rival. Perhaps . . . even as an enemy.'

Stross fingered absently through the typed pages inside his folder. 'It is interesting, is it not, that there should be this apparent resistance to radiation? And the blood analysis was fascinating—such a rapid turnover of white blood cells. Moreover, your observations have built up a picture of a big-brained, man-like creature superbly adapted to a wild and mountainous habitat, brilliant at camouflage, resistant to cold, undemanding—as far as we can see—of physical comfort, and almost certainly a silent and lethal hunter. It is almost—' he gave a little laugh—'as though the Esau was *designed* to survive a nuclear holocaust, and to live on at the edges of a broken world.'

'Oh, dear me,' said the Englishman, also laughing, 'don't tell me that you, of all people, are going to start believing in "special creation".'

'Ah, my friend, there is no fear of that.'

'The problem,' said Richard Kimbell, 'is not whether our Esau will survive a nuclear holocaust. It is whether he will survive the next six weeks.'

'He is as sick as that?'

'I'm afraid so. It's not surprising. We take a creature with the qualities Professor Stross had just listed, and confine him in a compound . . . a compound, incidentally, which is probably some thousands of feet lower than the habitat which the creature is genetically programmed to deal with. We remove him from his own kind, and expose him to what must be—in his own mind—bizarre and terrifying impressions. We can hardly expect him to thrive. He might do so more easily if he

132

were less intelligent. An antelope or a seal or even a chimpanzee might adapt. But the Esau has the potential mental power of any of us at this table. Though, of course, he does not organise his mental processes in the same way.'

'Not yet,' said Liliane.

The Englishman hesitated. 'I seem to be casting myself in the role of ruthless scientist in this discussion, and it isn't really one that's to my taste. But what do you mean by "not yet"?'

Liliane shrugged. 'Maybe the Esau will develop in a thousand years, or ten thousand, or a hundred thousand, or never. It's an unknowable chance. But it's not one we should be prepared to eliminate for purely selfish reasons.'

'You could say the same about the chimpanzee. Or the gorilla.'

'The chimpanzee and the gorilla aren't down to their last fifty representatives on this planet.'

The Englishman whistled. 'Is that the total population figure you estimate?'

'We think so,' said Liliane. 'It seems likely that they're confined to one mountain area. Even though the Himalaya is much less explored than I myself had earlier realised—' for a moment Harry's face came into her mind—'if there were a bigger population, spread over a wider area, other representatives would have been taken by now. The Esau is probably responsible for some, at least, of the Abominable Snowman legend. Much of that legend is demonstrably false. But on certain peaks, Esaus have probably hunted over thousands of years, and then moved on. An Esau is clearly a hunter-gatherer . . . probably more hunter than gatherer. As a hunter, he needs a territory. We estimate that the kind of territory he has available, and in which he could still remain unseen, would support about fifty of his kind. That's a bigger population than any other carnivorous creature could manage, but the Esau has the advantage of that big brain. He can really get the most out of his hunting.'

'Even so . . . would the loss of one Esau out of fifty be so disastrous? There are still enormous scientific returns to be gathered from this single specimen—especially if, as we're all beginning to realise, he embodies some kind of genetic blueprint for ultimate survival.'

'I think Dr Plekhanov gave us the best answer to that question. Almost certainly, the Esau population is organised on a harem system. That is the only way it could have survived.'

'Yes, I see. You mean . . .?'

'That there are probably no more than eight or ten male Esaus, and not all of those are necessarily of breeding age. The rest are females. In the Esau we have, we may hold as much as twenty per cent of Esau breeding capacity for the future. There is no practical way of obtaining a female Esau, and even if there were, I should now be against it. I, too, have dreamed of breeding Esaus, but I do not any longer think it possible. Our Esau is not the proud, fierce creature we took at Shalamerg. He is miserable, dejected, steadily failing, day by day. The girl Ellie Hayne was his last moment of dominance. Perhaps if she walked into his compound today, she would be safe.'

'You may be right,' said the English scientist. 'It doesn't always work . . . look at the trouble, all over the world, they've had trying to breed pandas. So we are rapidly arriving at the only possible conclusion?'

'Yes,' said Liliane. 'We should set the Esau free. Absolutely free. With no future interference.'

There was silence round the table. Then Plekhanov nodded, followed by Stross. The Director-General waited for a moment more, and then spoke swiftly.

'I think we should have time to digest what we have been told. I hardly need to inform you that nothing decided here has any power of law regarding the Esau, which is in the present custody of the Republic of India. Between you, those at this table represent some of the most advanced thinking on this subject available in the world. Your advice will carry weight. Very great weight. But let me, as a layman, remind you that there is a world outside. It is, ultimately, there that this question will be decided. If world opinion turns against any recommendation you make, that recommendation will be lost. We are talking about something which goes deep to the human heart, to human feeling, to human superstition, and even to human religion. These are matters that are notoriously unpredictable, as any novelist or politician will tell you. So discuss

what you have heard. Make your recommendation. And then
. . . we shall see.'

'I don't believe it,' said the television producer, standing at the
window of his fourth-floor office high above the River Thames.
Below him, the wet pavements of London shone in the spring
rain. He turned to face his assistant, who was sitting at the far
side of the desk.

'God knows,' he said again, 'I thought I'd learned not to be
surprised by anything in this game, but I find it damned hard
to believe *this*.'

'Well, it's true, James,' said the assistant patiently. 'The
programme didn't finish until midnight, so we only got about
twenty calls then. But there've been seventy-two calls this
morning. And that was an hour ago . . . probably been more
since.'

'And all from women wanting to sleep with this damned
ape?'

'Nearly all. Six, or it may have been seven, were from men
wanting to shoot it. But the women . . . well, yes, they want to
mate with it. It's been the same in San Francisco and various
parts of California. Their programme went out a bit earlier, and
they've had hundreds of calls. It'll probably be the same in
Paris after the French put theirs on the air tonight.'

'Not the French,' said the producer. 'The French have got
too much sense. Mind you, the moment that woman asked the
sixty-four thousand dollar question last night, I knew there'd
be trouble. "Can the panel tell us if there would be good results
from the interbreeding of an Esau and a human woman?" And
then, of course, they had to say that the outcome would be
fascinating. But I thought the uproar would be the other way
round—religious fury, that sort of thing. Has there been much
of that?'

'A few calls. But nothing like as many as the ones from the
ladies who want to help produce Superbaby.'

'Well, it beats me. You saw what this Esau thing did to the
only woman it got hold of . . . pretty well ripped her apart, as
far as I can gather. And this lot want to volunteer for something like that?'

'Oh, you know what a woman's like, sometimes,' said the

135

assistant. 'She always thinks she's the one who can straighten you out.'

The other laughed. 'You'd imagine with all this Women's Lib about, they'd think the Esau was a real male chauvinist pig. The scientists say it's probably got a harem up there in the Himalayas. But in any case, surely we aren't in the business of making lists of possible mates for an ape?'

'Of course not. The switchboard just takes their names and addresses. It keeps them quiet. Nothing'll be done about the list. Anyway, James, it's not an ape. The consensus is that it's a sort of man.'

'Stuff the consensus. It looks like an ape to me, and it looks like an ape on our film. But I'm just wondering . . .'

'What?'

'Well, we *have* got all these names and addresses. Is there a follow-up programme, do you think? You know . . . interviews . . . scientific speculation . . . "A Mate for Esau".'

'Could be.'

'I think it's worth a thought. Let's get it down on paper. Ask one of the girls from the typing pool to come up . . . the one with the red trousers and all the hair, if she's around. God, I wonder if she's volunteered? I wouldn't mind being in a cage with her for a few hours.'

'She'd eat you alive, James. You'll have to go into training if you want to be an Esau . . .'

The Collector for the newly-organised District of Srinagar, Sonamarg and Anantnag pursed his lips, while the three *tahsil* administrative officers waited for him to speak. A young, bespectacled Indian, thirty years old, the Collector was reckoned to have a brilliant future. He was a graduate of Bombay University and of London University, and he had passed out second in all the great list of successful examination candidates for the Civil Service of the Republic of India. The District over which, in effect, he now ruled was a new one, freshly and rawly carved from previous administrative divisions of the State of Jammu and Kashmir. It included three large *tahsils* —regional subdivisions, each of which was watched over by a subordinate officer. These men sat before him now in his office at Srinagar. The Collector had held his present position for less than three weeks. He scarcely yet knew the precise boundaries of his administrative kingdom, much less the mood and temper of its people. He needed time . . . and he could have done without this so-called 'wild man' at Srinagar.

'I do not understand exactly what they fear,' he said again. The *tahsil* officer for Anantnag, a rather superior Kashmiri Brahmin, had an annoying habit of wagging a fore-finger. He did it again now as he replied.

'They are ignorant persons, of course, Collector. But they know what happened to the American girl. And, of course, even in Kashmir, Anantnag is an exceptionally Muslim community . . . the woman are protected. Almost all of them wear the *bourka* . . . you can't tell whether a woman is mother or daughter, I sometimes think. The men are restive. They think what happened to the American girl could happen to their wives.'

'But the wild man is locked up behind a steel fence.'

'Yes, Collector. But they think that if a woman can get in to the wild man—and one did, after all—then the wild man can get out to the women. Then they would not know their own sons.'

The officer for Sonamarg spoke up. 'The fact is that there has long been irrational superstition about "wild men" in the hills. It has gone on for many, many years. I remember my mother telling me that if I was not a good boy, a wild man would get me. The *gujars* have a legend—'

'The *gujars*?'

'Hill people, Collector. They come down the passes in spring with goats and sheep. They live in tents. The *gujars* have a legend that one day a wild man will rule the mountains.'

'Perhaps I should hand over the *tahsil* to him,' said the Collector, laughing, but the other did not smile. The Collector turned to the man from Srinagar. 'You have said nothing yet.'

'I was about to tell you . . . there have been meetings in the city.'

The Collector was surprised. 'I should have thought they were more sophisticated in Srinagar.'

'Please do not forget that the wild man is much nearer to Srinagar than to Sonamarg or Anantnag.'

'What sort of meetings?'

'The largest was about two hundred men. They want the wild man taken away from the compound—they say he should be in a zoo at Bombay. Or—' He hesitated.

'Or what?'

'Or dead, Collector.'

The Collector rose, and the other three scrambled to their feet. 'Perhaps he will be dead soon enough, in any case—they say he is sick. But you think there could be trouble?'

'Perhaps.'

'In that case, the police guard should be strengthened. That should be done immediately.'

'But what will you do?' said the man from Sonamarg.

'I shall make my report,' said the Collector. 'It will go through channels but I shall try to expedite it. There is much to be done in this District, and this wild man is a stupid irrelevance. The sooner he is away from here the better . . .'

Mohammad Pingnoo stood in the warm spring sunlight beside a little shop on the riverside Bund in Srinagar. The dusty road of the Bund wound along the banks of the Jhelum: below him, at the water's edge, a wooden houseboat trailed a blue column of cooking smoke from its stovepipe funnel. The sound of chatter and laughter came from inside it as women prepared a meal. Two bar-headed geese cruised by, the black patches behind their eyes gleaming in the sun as they thrust their heads in and out of the water, looking for scraps.

The shop Pingnoo had just left was—in part, at least—a locksmith's. He fingered the two keys he had acquired. It had not been difficult to get them. Though the steel fence around the Esau compound was Indian Army issue made at some factory far in the south of the Indian sub-continent, the great padlocks which secured the gates had been bought in Srinagar. Locksmiths, like mountain guides, were a fraternity. And the locksmith at the little shop on the Bund was a cousin of his wife's father.

Mohammad Pingnoo was paid by Liliane Erckmann as compound superintendent and local guide . . . under Kernow-*sahib*, of course. He was also paid, from time to time, by an officer in Pakistan Military Intelligence, who made occasional secret trips into Indian Kashmir, hidden in a party of *gujars* coming down from the hills. And he had also a third source of income . . . he was not entirely sure what it was, but he believed that it was some agency of the Government in Delhi. Not one of these three paymasters had ever won a scrap of his genuine loyalty. His Muslim heart belonged elsewhere. He marched in spirit, like thousands of other young Kashmiris, with the old, independence-seeking Sheik . . . often arrested, always released . . . who was known in every peasant farm down the valley as the Lion of Kashmir. One day, Kashmir would stand free. Until then, Kashmiris must work and wait . . . and there was no reason why their enemies should not help them grow rich. He looked again at the shining steel keys in his brown hand. Exactly why he had troubled to get them, he did not yet know. He realised that the thing in the compound was already a source of dissension among his various masters. Each of them, for different reasons, had warned him to watch it closely. This was something he disliked doing. He was not, he boasted to himself, a superstitious man . . . but when he looked through the steel mesh at the thing in the compound, he felt a chill of fear. He would never wish to unlock those gates and go inside. And yet . . . some day soon, someone might want access. To be able to provide it, instantly, could be profitable. Mohammad Pingnoo was a man who believed in keeping his options open.

Extracts from leading articles in London, Washington and New York newspapers:

' . . . the responsibility for what is happening at Srinagar is shared by all of us, in the form of the scientific community, Indian, European and American, which is maintained by our taxes and by our moral support. This cannot be shrugged off on to the shoulders of Dr Erckmann and her party. It is on behalf of us all that the "Esau", this hapless hominid, is imprisoned for scientific purposes in Kashmir. Perhaps it is time for us to think again about our responsibilities to a brother creature . . .'

London

' . . . American dollars have been poured into this project, and, as often happens, they brought a mixed blessing with their golden shower. The man at Srinagar—if it is a "man" —has been transformed by dollars into a living research specimen, through which scientists hope to explore our own nature. Yet perhaps our own nature is more fully explored by the facts of what we do to the "Esau" . . . nothing tells us more about *Homo sapiens* than the way in which he treats *Homo kashmiriensis* . . .'

Washington

'Let him go! Decent folks across this country wouldn't treat a dog the way science handles the "Esau"! He should go back to his own kind . . . FREE. The American people do not support jailers—we can leave that to others . . .'

New York

14

The Esau looked down from his six feet three inches of height. He stood at the entrance to his artificial cave, where the two clay skulls still rested. He knelt and drew one out with elaborate care. Beneath their massive brow-ridges, his eyes were puzzled. Once or twice, he turned the model over in his hands. Then he replaced it in position, and walked to the fence, staring intently through the mesh. No one else was about. Narrowing his eyes, he could just glimpse a head through the open window of the administration hut. After a little he went over to the pile of sacks and rocks and branches where he usually sprawled. He moved a little more slowly than usual, though a hidden observer might have noted that he seemed rather more fit and active when alone than when he knew human beings were present. Once on the sacks, he raised a hand to scratch amongst the thick red hair on his barrel-like chest. The corner of a sack momentarily caressed his groin: a reflex of indiscriminate desire flooded into him, and his penis swelled, then subsided. Eyes half-closed, he continued to watch through the fence.

Inside the hut Liliane rose from her chair and crossed to the window. Shimmering in the heat of the morning sun the compound at first appeared empty. But by now she was used to the Esau's little trick, and after a few seconds she picked him out on his pile of sacks. His head was held low, as so often now. He had eaten little for the past two days. His condition seemed to waver between better and worse, his strength ebbing and flowing like a tide. Each time, though, he seemed to finish a little further from the high water mark of the time of his capture.

She looked down at the formal classification note pinned to the Esau file. Order: *Primate*. Sub-Order: *Anthropoidea*. Infra-order: *Catarrhini*. Superfamily: *Hominoidea*. Family: *Hominidae*. Genus: *Homo*. If some celestial scientist had ever classified Liliane Erckmann herself in the same zoological way, she knew that the sequence would be almost exactly the same.

Only one detail divided them: the Esau, at the end of that classified line, was *Homo kashmiriensis*. And Liliane was *Homo sapiens*. Each of them belonged to the great superfamily of the *Hominoidea* which included gibbons, gorillas, orang-utans, chimpanzees and men. Could one feel emotional loyalty to a superfamily of apes? The concept seemed ridiculous. And yet . . . All right, then, could one feel loyalty to the genus *Homo*, even if—unexpectedly—it was now found to contain two species?

Moodily, she went out into the sunlight, over to the compound. There would have to be decisions soon. Difficult decisions. She sighed. She was looking through a steel fence in Kashmir, but for a moment her mind was in Paris. There was a shop by the corner of the Rue d'Anjou, quite near the Madeleine. It sold what the French called *frivolités* . . . there had been a pair of gold and jade earrings. Liliane tucked her shirt more firmly into her trousers. The earrings were a piece of charming nonsense, eight thousand miles away. The Esau was a brooding presence, here and now. Well, the UNESCO Special Committee had backed her, unanimously. That had been the first surprise. And the second was that the Director-General—a typically chauvinist Italian, she'd thought, but very competent—had said he believed a full Committee would almost certainly do the same. Even the Soviet Union had raised no points of difference . . . though perhaps Plekhanov had something going of his own, way up there in the Pamirs, and wouldn't be exactly sorry to see the Indian Esau returned to the wild.

Nevertheless, a lot of general international opinion—newspapers, television, even religious leaders—was coming to one conclusion. Free the Esau. For the Christian churches, certainly, the absence of the Esau from constant speculation would perhaps come as a relief. It was hard for churchmen to preach that man is made in the image of God, and then to discover that God had made *two* images. Though, of course, they always had that remarkable chapter of Genesis to fall back on. From everybody's point of view, freeing the Esau was coming to be seen as an easy, conscience-saving 'solution' which would cost the world nothing, even if it did frustrate a few clinical scientists. But vague stirrings of world opinion were one thing. The realities of ground, of frontiers, of local national rivalries were another. *Homo kashmiriensis* had chosen to appear upon one of the most disputed borders of *Homo sapiens* in the world. If we free the Esau, thought Liliane, how will Pakistan react? There's no point in releasing him up in the Pir Panjal if he goes straight over the truce line, and ends up in a cage at Gilgit, or Islamabad.

She halted on the white warning line painted a few feet short of the mesh, and looked into the compound. As usual, the Esau seemed to be dozing, but she had learned over the past months that this was another of his little tricks. Seen more closely, he seemed to have lost a certain amount of weight . . . hardly surprising, since he now ate little. The chief warden of the Gir Forest game reserve, much further south in Gujarat, had warned that this sometimes happened to large mammals after some weeks of captivity. 'We occasionally take them into temporary confinement for what seems to us to be some good reason,' he said. 'Then, occasionally, appetite goes, weight loss begins. You go to them one morning, and they are dead. It can be very sudden.' That must not happen to the Esau.

The Esau got to his feet and moved across the compound until he was exactly opposite where she stood. He rested one hand on the steel mesh, and gazed at her steadily. For the moment his great head was held high, dominated by the beetling ridges above the eyes. The nostrils in the broad nose were flared as though he was following a scent. Beneath them the mouth was clamped shut like that of a stern man rather than a volatile ape. His lips opened, and she saw the gleam of the strong, yellow-white teeth. The Esau was no taller than a tall man, and yet he gave an overwhelming impression of sheer size. She felt a feeling of weakness go through her. He took his hand from the fence, and rubbed his arm, so that the russet hair which grew on it shone in the sunlight in a silken ripple.

Liliane could feel her heart thudding through the thin cotton of her shirt, like a young girl with her first love. Involuntarily, she stepped over the white safety line and up to the fence, but the Esau made no move, simply looking down at her from his commanding height. She could smell him now . . . it was sharp, unmistakable, disturbing. She was standing so close to

143

the mesh that she could see tiny prickles of sweat above the line of his mouth. His eyes were dark, unreadable. Infinitely slowly, he pushed his hand through the bars, and she felt the brush of its hairs upon her cheek. She felt melted, mesmerised, helpless, half-frightened, half . . . what was the other half? Deliberately, gently, he rolled a long curl of her hair through his square fingers. Then he released it, but his hand remained on her shoulder. She reached up and took it. It was warm, dry, firm. They stood together for two, three seconds . . . a lifetime. Then he withdrew his hand through the bars, and walked back to his resting place, sitting again in his usual way, eyes half-closed. A keen sense of pain swept through her . . . something akin to grief. The ridiculous impulse came into her head that she should open the gates and go into the compound, but she fought it back.

'How is he today?' said Harry's voice behind her. She turned, searching his face for any evidence that he had seen, but there was none.

'Hard to tell,' she said, trying to force normality into her voice. 'He doesn't seem to have eaten.'

'No . . . the last time he ate was two days ago. Mind you, he's gone four days without food before now.'

'Yes. We'll keep a special eye on him today, though.'

Thank God that Harry had noticed nothing.

'We are under very considerable pressure,' said the Indian Prime Minister. In the armchair opposite, her Minister for Science stirred impatiently, and opened his mouth to speak. The Prime Minister held up her hand. 'Bear with me a moment, Amrit Singh, because I think we are going to have to change our policy.' The Sikh, however, could contain himself no longer. He was angry.

'What, because a talking-shop in Paris delivers a few platitudes? Or because a foolish American girl allowed her whorish instincts to lead her to trouble? Yet she was raped, after all, Prime Minister. Is it really suggested that we should set this creature free, to be used no more for science—and, for all we know, to kill and rape again.'

'Kill? The girl Hayne is not dead.'

Amrit Singh swallowed. 'I was about to tell you, Prime

144

Minister. I had a memorandum from the Foreign Ministry this morning. Apparently the Pakistanis have found a dead soldier, up near Shalamerg.'

'On which side of the border?'

'The Foreign Ministry say that the Pakistanis are vague about that. The truce line runs through the whole area, as you know.'

'How do they know the solider was killed by the Esau creature?'

'There is no certainty, Prime Minister. But they think it likely.'

Behind the Prime Minister's smile her face was grim.

'Not much of a case, Amrit Singh.'

'Exactly, Prime Minister. Of course, they also want us to release the creature, because they say it comes from Pakistan. They believe it would return there. And, once it did, they themselves would seize it. And it would be theirs. Surely we do not want that to happen?'

'If I decide to release the creature,' said the Prime Minister slowly, 'it will not be to please the General, I assure you.'

'Why then?'

She tapped a pile of newspapers beside her desk. 'You have seen the American and European newspapers?'

Amrit Singh nodded. 'Yes . . . predictably irresponsible, moralising about a situation they do not have to deal with.'

'Perhaps,' said the Prime Minister, 'it is a situation we would be better not to be dealing with. The fancied gains from the possession of the Esau—oh, Amrit Singh, do not look at me like that, because I agree with you that I, too, thought there would be gains—these fancied gains are disappearing fast. The local administration in Kashmir longs to be rid of it. And the western world, on which we depend in so many ways, is changing its mind. It believes that the creature should be set free. Every newspaper, every television station in the West is saying so—and when the people turn over in bed, the scientists have to turn with them. Many scientists are now conceding that we have gone too far. There is even talk of withholding research funds.'

'The Soviet Union would replace those,' said the Minister. He sounded sullen.

'Do not be so sure, Amrit Singh. The international reputation of the Soviet Union is not so unsullied that it can afford to take on responsibility for yet another captive . . . and this one the most celebrated captive in the world. And Russian roubles come with strings attached. They . . . impede independent movement, those strings. In any case, at the moment the Soviet scientists appear to be taking the Western line.'

'We should not be bullied,' said Amrit Singh. 'Not by anyone.'

'I agree. In that respect, your attitude is commendable, and what I would have hoped from you. But there is another consideration which, to me, tips the balance.'

'You mean the health of the creature?'

She nodded. 'You realise it, too. Since the . . . episode . . . with that stupid girl, the creature's condition has once more deteriorated. I have had a message from Dr Erckmann—I sent you a copy.'

He nodded, watching her.

'Amrit Singh, it would have been bad enough if it had died before all this happened, but at least we could have put some of the blame on the Americans. But suppose it dies now, with half the world clamouring for us to set it free?'

She looked at him while he rubbed his hand gently over his beard. He was obstinate and vain, and he was a chauvinist Sikh who thought there were only two places for a woman to play her role. But he was not really a fool. He could add two and two, and come close enough to four.

'You have a point, Prime Minister,' he said at last. 'But what does Dr Chowdhuri think?'

She smiled, and put the words as tactfully as she could. 'I think Dr Chowdhuri will agree with whatever Dr Erckmann thinks. Frankly, I do not know what either of them wants to do. I suspect it is here, in this room, that the decision will have to be made. But . . . perhaps it would be a good thing if you, Amrit Singh, pursued the matter, in strict secrecy, with them. It would be better to do that than have the approach made by me.'

'I agree, Prime Minister.'

For a moment, she was unable to veil the surpise in her eyes. 'I am glad I have been able to convince you, Amrit Singh.

Approach the scientists, then, and let me know what happens. I think it should be done at once. We do not know how much time we have left.'

'Yes,' said Amrit Singh. 'And I have had an idea, something which may help to balance the . . . possible loss . . . of our creature.'

'What is that?'

It was the Sikh's turn to smile. His voice was smooth. 'It may not be technically feasible, Prime Minister,' he said. 'I will not waste your time with it until I have an accurate idea of whether it is or not . . .'

She considered him thoughtfully as he made his formal departure.

15

The rain swept in across the Nagim Lake, drumming on the teak deck of the long houseboat, lashing the stiff reeds beside the bank. Every so often, for a few seconds or a few minutes, the electric lights in the little saloon went out, while Harry, swearing softly, fumbled for candles. Richard Kimbell, more philosophical, ignored the waxing and waning of the lights, dozing in his chair. From where she sat opposite, a battered paperback from the houseboat bookshelf in her lap, Liliane watched the two men amusedly. Each was so different. Harry was never content unless he was getting something done: Richard was perfectly happy when apparently doing nothing.

'I wonder how the Esau's making out in this,' said Harry, as the lights came on again for the fourth time. 'If he's got any sense he's in that cave. Though, I must say, in general, weather doesn't seem to bother him. But it may bother your Delhi flight tomorrow. The airfield gets pretty muddy, and they don't like landing that little twin-engined HS 179 when there's a really strong crosswind blowing. You could be held up.'

Liliane shrugged. 'I hope not, Harry, because I haven't really got time to waste. But at least my appointment isn't with the Prime Minister. It's with the Minister of Science himself —and he's left the time open. So if I'm a day late, for a good enough reason, he'll understand. But you . . . what are you going to do?'

Harry glanced at his watch. 'It's nearly ten. If I'm going to get back, I ought to be starting. But I'm not too keen on turning out young Jinni with the *shikara*. There's quite a wind blowing, and the lake can be tricky when it's like this.'

'Stay here overnight,' said Kimbell, opening one eye sleepily. 'There's no hassle about getting back to the compound —Tom's on duty there. You can sleep in the stern-end stateroom. Jinni will soon make up a bed.'

'I like to be at the compound at night,' said Harry. 'Especially since that fool girl . . .'

The memory of Ellie came back into all their minds. Kimbell was the first to speak.

'I must say . . . the newspapers have been pretty good to us on the whole. They don't seem to blame us here in Srinagar —they blame something they vaguely call "science". And they're definitley on the side of him over there.' He nodded his head towards the window which gave out on to the lake.

'I agree, said Harry. 'I'm surprised—I really would have thought they'd have been shouting their heads off about the rape of poor innocent Ellie.'

'They know as well as you do that Ellie wasn't innocent—at least, not in the sense of being a random victim,' said Liliane. Although her face was pale, she seemed to be holding up well under the strain of the past few days, with its endless official inquiries, written reports, explanations. She spoke with a sort of confident defiance.

'What happened to her was brought on by herself alone, and, thank God, the Press and television realise it. And, Kim, it wasn't rape.'

Kimbell sounded dubious. 'Well, Liliane, I guess that if the Esau was one of us, any court would call it so—'

'But he isn't one of us—not quite. And in any case, I don't think he meant to force her. He thought she was . . . available . . . and he was far too strong, and too quick, for her to make any protest, even if he could have understood it was a protest.'

'I spoke again to the hospital this morning,' said Kimbell. 'Her condition is stable, and she's recovering steadily. Both legs broken, of course, but they say there's no crucial damage. And her mind . . . well, it's strong.'

Liliane looked at him with affection. Since the Ellie episode, Richard had shouldered a heavy burden of administrative detail, resolutely charting a way, with Chowdhuri's help, through the endless maze of Indian bureaucracy.

'Judy will be back in California by now,' he said.

Liliane nodded. The whole party had gone down to the little Kashmir airfield at Damodar Karawa to watch Judy fly off to Delhi, on the first leg of her journey back home with the nurse her father had sent. She had passed close by them as she

149

entered the departure lounge, a way cleared for her by the airport authorities. There had been no expression in the small white face, and no hint of recognition.

'What are her chances?' said Harry.

Kimbell spread his hands. 'Her father's wealthy, powerful,' he said. 'There'll be a team of shrinks working on her. Whether that's good or bad, I don't know. How do you balance a thing like that? Of course, looking back on it, you can see that what happened the other night was simply the trigger. The explosive charge, psychiatrically speaking, had been building up for weeks . . . all those strange mysterious references to things that she knew but we didn't, all that violent alternation of mood . . . I'm no psychiatrist but I'd have thought it was a classic schizophrenic pattern.'

'I'm not sure about that,' said Harry. Kimbell was surprised. Harry rarely ventured an opinion on anything remotely scientific . . . and when he did it was usually some practical, empirical conclusion about wild life or the local environment, based on years of non-academic field study.

'You remember—' he glanced at Liliane—'that we were talking, not long ago, about the Esau's ability to convince us, briefly, that he's not there, that he's part of the landscape, a rock, a tree, not a living, moving creature?'

'Yes,' said Liliane. 'But—'

'Well, I wondered . . . oh, come on, we've all felt it. I felt it the very first seconds we saw him, trapped up above Shalamerg. I wanted to help him. There's always been that strange feeling about him—that although he can't speak, he can sometimes communicate—tell you what he wants you to think. That he's not there, that he needs help, that he's angry—'

Almost as though he was touching her again, Liliane seemed to feel the dry, warm pressure of the Esau's fingers on hers.

'But supposing,' Harry went on, 'that he got through especially well, for some reason, to Judy? She'd start to feel everything that he feels . . . terror, desperation, perhaps desire. Liliane, you saw her try to get over that fence. She wanted him. It would explain her very curious behaviour over the past weeks.'

Liliane thought back for a moment, trying to remain detached. Then she shook her head.

'If you remember, Judy didn't behave strangely until we found the skulls. At that point, we had never seen the Esau, and we didn't even dream he existed. So he could hardly have dominated her mind then.'

'We don't know how near to us he was on that day,' said Harry softly. 'But those skulls certainly got through to Judy —she referred to them again and again. And we know how important they were—are—to the Esau. He was trapped with his hand in the overhang where we found them—and we saw how he behaved even with Tom's models. So if the Esau was nearby—unknown to us—and he was thinking about those skulls, couldn't all that have got through to Judy?'

Liliane laughed. 'My first impulse is to say "nonsense", but I'm not as quick to reject your theories as I was, Harry.'

He sketched her a mock salute, grinning. A sharp gust of wind struck the houseboat, and the teak timbers creaked.

'I think you're right,' said Harry. 'I'd better stay.'

He went from the saloon, and they could hear him shouting to Jinni, who slept in the little wooden house beside the bank. Kimbell yawned. 'God, I'm sleepy. I guess I'm going to hit that bed. Don't stay up too long, my dear. If you do fly tomorrow, you'll have a tiring day.'

On an impulse, he stooped and kissed her gently on the cheek.

'That was a sudden rush of blood,' she said, smiling.

He laughed. 'Oh, it happens, from time to time.'

When Harry came back, she tried to settle down to read for another half-hour. But Harry himself was restless, prowling up on deck at intervals, letting gusts of cold, wet air in through the companionway. At last he said goodnight and went down the long corridor to his own stateroom. Thankfully she closed the book, feeling the beginning of a headache. She pushed the hair from her brow, and went out on deck. There was still a fleck or two of rain in the wind, and it was chilly out under the stars, but the night was clearing fast and the storm had gone. Faintly in the starlight she could see the usual banner of cloud trailing from the mountain peaks across the lake. A light moved steadily along the far shore . . . some late vehicle going into Srinagar. Somewhere beyond that road was the Esau . . . even as her mind formulated the word she was flooded by his presence. It was as though she stood again face to face with him beside the steel fence . . . briefly, she imagined that she could smell him. She fought to stay detached, but again she found her heart beating faster. What on earth was wrong with her? She tried to analyse her feelings dispassionately. Was it desire? No . . . surely not. Well, not exactly desire . . . not as she had ever known it, anyway. But had she ever known it? Was this what true desire was . . . what it ought to be? Something like a longing for submission, a need to be taken, to be locked together, to make one person where before there had been two? The feeling mounted within her so strongly that she gave a little moan, staring out over the deck-rail towards where, four miles away, she knew the Esau to be. The half-stifled sound from her own throat jerked her back to reality. Could he really influence her thoughts, her wishes, her whole sexual nature? Perhaps he was thinking about her now. Or was it simply that he had powers of thought-transference rather like those possessed by many ordinary humans . . . that, perhaps even without knowing it, he infected her with his own longings and his own uncertainties? Whatever it was, it was terrifying when it happened. I'm not his damned mate, she told herself fiercely. I'm *Homo sapiens*, not a female Esau. When I make love, I do it with my own kind . . .

Almost without any rational volition she stumbled down the little companionway to her own stateroom and quickly undressed. She sat beside the mirror on the little dressing table, shook out her hair and brushed it impatiently. Then she slipped on her dressing-gown, and went down the passage to Kimbell's stateroom. Quietly, she opened the door. His light was out, but she could see him lying there, dimly lit by the glow from the open window.

'Kim . . . Kim, darling.' He did not move. She pushed gently at his shoulder, and he snored once, grumbling in his sleep. The ripped tinfoil of two sleeping tablets lay beside a half-empty glass of water beside the bed. Somehow he looked old, vulnerable, strangely defenceless. Oh, Richard Kimbell, she thought. You used to want me often enough. And now when I need you, you can't even wake. She went out into the passage.

There was a thin line of light under Harry's door. Harry . . . ten seconds later she was standing beside his bed. He stared at her in astonishment. The bedside lamp seemed terribly bright.

'Put that thing out, Harry . . . please.' He stretched out a hand, and the starlit darkness returned. Deliberately, she let the dressing-gown fall open so that her naked body could be seen in the faint light from the window. Harry sat up in bed. She could glimpse the thin white line of an old scar across his bare stomach. 'Harry, I want you.'

'But . . .'

She put a finger across his lips to silence him, and pushed at his brown muscular body. 'Let me get in, it's cold out here.' Almost unwillingly, it seemed, he moved over in the bed and she slid in beside him. Her arms went round his neck.

'I want you, Harry. Now. Do you want me? What's wrong with you?'

His hand came up behind her shoulder, and took hold of her hair. She tried desperately not to remember how the Esau had done much the same, beside the compound. Passionately, she kissed Harry until, soon, he responded with the same intensity. His hands were roaming over her body now, caressing her breasts, moving between her thighs.

'There's nothing wrong with me,' he said, his face buried in her shoulder as he levered himself above her. 'As you're about to find out . . .'

Harry was a hard, vigorous lovemaker, and twice she cried out before, expended, he lay quiet beside her. Gently, she stroked his damp body. This had been no ultimate experience, but it had done what she wanted. She felt reassured, happier, almost sexually content. And there was another feeling, too. She found, to her surprise, that it was a sort of defiance, a kind of triumph. Harry opened his eyes.

'What was all that about?'

'Are you sorry I came to you?'

He kissed her slowly, firmly. 'Of course not . . . it's just that I never dreamed . . .'

'Never?'

He laughed. 'Well, hardly ever . . . My God, I hope Richard Kimbell's deaf. We made enough noise to wake Srinagar.'

'It's all right. He's taken a couple of sleeping tablets. He's right out.'

Harry switched on the light, and raised himself on one elbow. 'How on earth do you know that?'

'Oh, he always does,' she replied, disconcerted, angry with herself for her carelessness. 'He told me—he can't sleep without.'

Harry looked at her without smiling. 'Is this going to happen again?'

'What?'

'This . . . you and me, in bed together.' His voice was unexpectedly bitter. 'Was I all right for you . . . did I do the job you fancied? Or am I supposed to say "wham-bam-thank you, ma'am" and bow out?'

'I don't know what you mean.'

He got out of bed and put on a shirt. 'You know perfectly well what I mean. It's pretty obvious—you tried Kimbell before you came to me, didn't you? Only he didn't—or couldn't—for some reason. You *used* me, didn't you, Liliane? I don't know why you were so hot for it. But I wasn't Harry to you, I was just a male. I'm surprised you didn't offer me a few rupees.'

'Don't be so ridiculous.'

He was fully dressed now, pulling on his canvas shoes. 'The storm's over. I'll take the *shikara* across myself. The Land-Rover will still be parked on the other side.'

She pulled at his arm. 'You can't go now, Harry. You don't understand . . .'

'No,' he said, going out into the companionway. 'If that's your idea of making love, it's not mine. If you look on a man as just a good meal, don't expect to find me on the menu next time. Goodnight.'

Four miles away, Tom Meachem woke, listening. There it was again . . . something he had first heard one dawn at Shalamerg. He got from his bed and went to the window. Outlined in the starlight, the bulky form of the Esau stood inside the steel fence. Puzzled, Meachem watched. The Esau threw back his head and roared again in overmastering rage.

*

Amrit Singh's young visitor, an Indian technologist from Bombay, gave a nervous little cough as the Minister for Science placed his fingertips together, rubbing his thumbs thoughtfully against his dark beard. Outside the open window of the Ministry office, on the broad avenue of Rajpath, the afternoon traffic panted through the Delhi heat. A flagged limousine, escorted by four motorcycle-police outriders, drove slowly towards Rashtrapati Bhawan, the Presidential Palace. The Minister spoke. 'You are sure the whole operation could be carried out so quickly?'

The technologist nodded. 'Provided we had access, and the creature was unconscious, there would be no problem. It would take five minutes, perhaps less.'

'Excellent. And the equipment could be expected to be completely reliable?'

'I do not see what could happen to prevent it working properly, within its technical limitations. It is well-proved technology . . . American equipment, of a very high standard.'

'Certainly,' said the Minister, smiling thinly, 'if it satisfies American standards in this respect, it should be acceptable to us.'

The technologist cleared his throat once more. 'I shall need, of course, a written permission, Minister-*sahib*. The authorities will not release it to me without proper sanction. They would question why I wanted it. As you know, it is not really my field.'

'Of course,' said the Minister. 'I shall give you what you need . . . but not at this moment. We do not yet know the date in question. That will be arranged—' he looked at his watch —'later today. You are staying in Delhi?'

'For tonight, Minister-*sahib*.'

'Good. Be sure to let my assistant in the outer office know where you can be contacted. He will be in touch with you. And—' he paused to let the words sink in—'if all goes well, I shall be grateful. You may be assured of that.'

The Minister did not trouble to rise as the young man left the room.

16

Liliane came down the steps from the Delhi plane, blinking in the hot, sun-blazed glare of Srinagar airport. She walked slowly to the barrier, shading her eyes to look along the line of the crowd which waited to greet arriving travellers. Always, Harry had been there. This time . . . yes, someone was waving. Her heart sank. It was Tom.

'Hi, Liliane. Good trip?'

'Yes. I got a firm agreement—and a definite date—out of the Minister.'

'That's good. When?'

'Eight days' time. I'll tell you the details when we're all together. Is . . . is everyone OK?'

She thought she had kept her voice carefully neutral, but Tom glanced at her, surprised. 'Why, sure. Chowdhuri's on compound duty, Richard's over at the University this morning, and Harry . . . well, I'm not sure about Harry. He took one of the horses and went up the valley a way. I shouldn't think he'll be out long, though. It's not much for riding, that piece of country.'

'No.'

'I think old Harry gets intimations of middle-age from time to time,' said Tom, grinning. 'He's looked a bit down this last couple of days—older and somehow less certain. He's not a man who lies down in front of worries and lets them pour over him—I guess he took that horse to try to ride it out of his system. How old is Harry, anyway?'

'Thirty-eight.'

Tom laughed. 'Well, it's not exactly the sere and yellow leaf, but that forty-frontier is coming up fast.'

'I suppose so. Not so very many more years, and I'll be there myself.'

'You, Liliane? You've never looked better. But, say . . . is something getting to you?'

He sounded unexpectedly concerned. The idea of Tom cast

as a mother hen was so bizarre that, in spite of herself, she smiled. 'No, of course not.'

'Good. Because come a few days more, Liliane, we'll be rid of a load of responsibility, and the Esau will be off our hands . . . free. Then we can settle down and write our books and make our fortunes. I've had a couple of publishers' offers you wouldn't believe . . .'

Kimbell was already back at the compound when they arrived, but an hour passed before they sat around the table in the administration hut to hear Liliane's report. She had spent part of the time at the fence, trying to check the Esau's condition. He had remained in his cave, ignoring her and apparently asleep. Chowdhuri told her he had eaten nothing since she left, which meant that he had now been five days without food. She knew that she had gone to see the Esau on the principle by which a rider who falls off a horse gets back into the saddle. She must not allow her strange emotions of the past few days to dominate her. She was a scientist, and she must behave like one. But where was Harry? Even after an hour, he was not back, and she could wait no longer before talking to the others.

'Tom tells me we have a definite date,' said Kimbell. 'How did you find the Minister . . . what was his name? . . . Amrit Singh?'

'We got a date, yes. Eight days from now. He seemed to think it was a tremendous rush, but I told him I couldn't answer for the Esau's condition if we waited much longer. And the Minister? Well, I didn't much like him. Altogether too self-satisfied, I thought. He seemed to be positively hugging himself. However, eight more days and we shan't have to bother too much about him any more.'

'What are the nuts and bolts of the whole operation?' said Tom. 'Obviously, we can't release the Esau here.'

'Shalamerg's the obvious place,' said Kimbell. 'There's no population up there, it's very isolated, and—best of all—it's country he's already travelled. He can hardly get lost, or become disorientated.'

Tom Meachem nodded. 'Somehow I don't see that old Esau becoming disorientated on any mountain, but you're right. Shalamerg's the place.'

'There's another reason for hurry,' said Liliane. 'Apparently the Pakistanis now say the Esau killed a Pakistani soldier, on their side of the truce line. They want . . . well, it's not entirely clear what they want, but I'm certain they wouldn't want the Esau to be released.'

Tom whistled. 'Killed a soldier, eh? I wonder if he really did—'

'He did,' said a voice at the door. Liliane's heart gave an unaccustomed little lurch. Harry came into the room and sat at the table, nodding to Liliane, his face back in its usual polite mask.

'He did,' Harry said again. 'It's hot news in the villages north of here, though whether it happened on the Pakistan side of the line is open to question. It seems to me that it was bang on the line itself. But the Pakistanis have been up there and taken away a body. Not exactly a pretty sight, I'm told.'

'Under the circumstances,' said Kimbell slowly, 'I'm surprised the Indian Prime Minister is willing to authorise Amrit Singh to release the Esau. You didn't have any contact with her in Delhi this time?'

'No,' said Liliane. 'But I thought . . . when I met her . . . that she wasn't someone who would hesitate to take a dangerous line, if it suited her.'

'But why should it suit her? It could mean a load of international trouble, and nothing—from her point of view—gained.'

Liliane shook her head. 'She seems used to trouble. No, I think I know why she's willing to let us release the Esau.'

'Why, then?'

'She sees no future for *Homo sapiens*. She believes we're doomed.'

Chowdhuri made as though to speak, but then changed his mind. There was a silence, broken at last by Tom Meachem.

'Well, be that as it may, there are one or two things we have to decide. I imagine it will be best to drug him so as to get him back up to Shalamerg?'

Liliane's face was worried. 'I'm not happy about that, Tom. I think he should be tranquillised, not knocked right out. He shows a lot of unexpected resilience from time to time, I know, but it would be horrible to lose him in the last few days.'

'Agreed,' said Meachem, and Kimbell nodded.

'I wonder why he killed,' said Liliane. 'Do you think the Pakistani attacked him?'

Harry was impatient. 'He killed because it's his nature to kill. Sometimes you people don't seem to grasp what's under your noses. He killed because he's a killer . . . as we are ourselves. He's an animal . . . also like us. Every hunting animal has a territory. That's how hunting animals survive. But this animal is like us in a third way—he takes his territory around with him. Wherever he is, he has to be top creature. Like us, he takes what he wants, and he eliminates every possible rival. He's made himself damned efficient at it.'

'My, my,' said Tom, as Harry went out into the compound. 'Something's sure getting to old Harry. Now I wonder just what it could be . . .'

He did not look at Liliane, but she felt his growing awareness of a situation he as yet only half-understood. She sensed suddenly that Kimbell, too, was looking at her speculatively. Hastily, she spoke to Chowdhuri.

'Will you liaise with the Army people, Prakash? We'll need a truck, as before, and a small squad.'

The Indian nodded. 'Of course. And I think perhaps some escort up to Shalamerg. The local people . . . they will not be happy if they think the Esau is being released. And you know how quickly word travels in Srinagar . . .'

Half an hour later Liliane stood again outside the Esau's steel fence, with Meachem beside her. She felt slightly ill at ease with the American, but he made no further reference, even obliquely, to Harry. He peered through the mesh to where the Esau stood beside his cave, looking towards them but coming no nearer.

'I'd like to know just what he thinks of us,' he said. Liliane stiffened, but Tom's face was concentrated on the Esau. He seemed not to have hidden a double meaning in the words.

'We've certainly been notably unsuccessful in establishing contact with him,' she replied.

Meachem hesitated. 'Well . . . I'm not so sure. Before the Ellie episode, I wasn't even sure that he recognised us as being something like his own kind. But, Liliane, you can't deny that Ellie was proof positive that he did. If we'd put a dog or a goat in there, he wouldn't have tried to have sex with it, would he?'

159

'No, I suppose not.'

'He sure knew what Ellie was, what he could do with her. It was the first time he ever really connected. I wonder exactly how well he communicates, back home.'

'Back home?'

'Wherever he comes from. We know there must be others. It can only be some sort of thought transference. Damn it, some of us have felt it more than others.'

She kept her face immobile. Was Tom trying to tell her that he knew just how well the Esau could get through to her? Or did he mean Judy? She stole another glance at him, but his expression still seemed innocent.

'I agree,' she said steadily. 'At first, when you think about it, his lack of a spoken language seems to be an almost insuperable obstacle to advanced, relatively sophisticated co-operation with his own kind. But we all know how animals adapt—and this one is like us, exceptionally intelligent. He couldn't have developed that kind of intelligence without communication. He's obviously able to transmit images to either friend or enemy. It's not such a way-out idea, after all. Quite a lot of us have it, to some degree—perhaps it's an echo from the days when we had no spoken language ourselves. Dreams of falling still stay in our minds from ten million years ago, when we lived in trees. There'll be other dreams, too.' And I know what some of them are, she thought.

'My God,' said Tom, 'here he comes.'

The Esau walked to the fence, staring through in their direction, though it was difficult to say if he was really looking at them. For a moment his eyes rested on Liliane, and she felt a second of contact, but then it was gone. In one great hand the Esau held one of Tom's model skulls. In a blur of movement, his other hand came round from behind his back, and he ripped the skull apart, flinging the shattered pieces savagely over the fence. Then, slowly, he walked back to the cave.

'At last he understands,' said Meachem admiringly.

'Understands what?'

'That the skull isn't a real one—that he's been conned. Look at him now.'

The Esau had brought the second model skull from the cave and was pounding it to fragments with his fist. They watched, fascinated, until he had finished. Then he went over to his pile of rocks and sacks, adopting his usual position, ignoring them, seemingly dozing with eyes half-closed. Kimbell's voice, from behind Liliane, made them both jump.

'You're right,' he said to Liliane. 'I don't think we've explored the Esau's inability to speak nearly as much as we could. For instance, we've all wondered about the importance he seems to attach to heads and skulls. Maybe there's a relatively simple answer.'

His voice was dry, precise. Oh God, was there pain in his face? Richard knew . . . somehow he knew. Quietly, academically, he went on speaking, as though to a seminar. She realised that he had now put a distance between them, and she felt a sense of loss. He stopped and picked up a broken clay fragment of model skull which lay beside the fence. Slowly, he turned it over in his hands.

'We've always assumed that we, *Homo sapiens*, were alone in the world in being able to understand, explain and even record our own past. We could do that because we developed language, a sort of memory code. It made us what we are. But, after all, language isn't the only code.'

'What do you mean?' Meachem asked.

'When I was in California,' Kimbell said, 'I was talking with Burdick. You know him . . . the lepidopterist.'

Meachem nodded. 'They call him the Butterfly Man on campus. He's been working on *Danaus plexippus*—the Monarch butterfly.'

'Exactly. Now the Monarch is a very remarkable insect. In summer it lives all over the North American continent, even as far north as the Hudson Bay. In the autumn it migrates south, to spend its winters in California, Florida, Louisiana, and in the spring the process begins again, with countless thousands of Monarchs flying north. But there's one vital factor in this migration.'

'Oh?'

'It's an obvious one, really. The Monarchs that leave in the spring are not the same butterflies that return in the autumn. They're the second, sometimes the third generation. Yet they return to the same trees—often exactly the same trees—that their parents or grandparents left. There's a place . . . fifty, sixty miles south of San Francisco . . . called Pacific Grove. They really cover the trees there, year after year—a famous sight, locally. There's a 500 dollar fine if you as much as throw a stone at them. So I asked Burdick just how the Monarch, with a head no bigger than a pin's, passed this very precise information on to its descendants. And he told me that, in one way, they were *not* its descendants. "In a very real sense," he said, "the Monarch that comes back to Pacific Grove is the same butterfly that left the previous spring, although—in conventional terms—it has died once or twice on the round trip. Because that's all the Monarch basically *is*—a vehicle for transmitting its species-past. You could call it a form of immortality." And then, a week or two ago, I got to thinking . . . suppose something of the sort, only much more sophisticated, operates with the Esau? Does his preoccupation with heads and skulls mean that he has some understanding of the nature of his brain? Is a skull a sort of key to a memory-bank through which he can gain access to the past of his own kind?'

'Going back a million years?' Tom said, his brow wrinkled. 'It would explain his super-efficiency at hunting, concealment, and his ability to withstand cold and hardship. But even so . . .'

'It seems fantastic, doesn't it?' Kimbell said. 'But is it really any more fantastic than the Monarch . . . an insect that can navigate its grandchildren precisely to its own point of departure, two lives ago?'

'And, of course,' Liliane said slowly, 'with a small inter-breeding population, the process for the Esau would be enhanced year by year, so that—my God, what's he doing?'

The Esau was standing at the fence, twenty yards away from them. He roared loudly, head thrust forward in aggression. Beside the administration hut, Harry appeared for a moment, looked towards them, and then disappeared from sight round the end of the block. The Esau watched for thirty seconds longer, but Harry did not reappear. Slowly the Esau walked back to its former position, and squatted back among the rocks.

'He doesn't like Harry any more,' Meachem said softly. 'I wonder why . . .'

'He's certainly disturbed today,' Kimbell said. 'First he

smashes the skulls, and now this. Sometimes he's very frightening. I hope we're doing the right thing in releasing him. The Pakistanis aren't going to be very happy if he goes straight into their area and kills somebody else.'

'He won't kill if he's not threatened,' said Liliane. 'Otherwise he'd have killed before, over the years. There'd be endless legends of killer-beasts. But one thing is important. The Pakistanis mustn't know that we're going to release him . . . not until long after he's gone. Then they won't be tempted to try to capture him themselves, because that's when he'd become dangerous. So they simply must not get an inkling of what we're doing. I impressed that on the Minister, and he agrees . . .'

'The creature from Shalamerg will be released in four days' time, at dawn,' said the Pakistani intelligence brigadier, sitting stiffly on the edge of his chair in the General's office at Islamabad. The General rested his chin on his hand, looking down at the map spread on the desk.

'Where will they do it?'

'At Shalamerg. I imagine they think it's appropriate to release him where he was found.'

The General gave a grim little chuckle. 'Appropriate, eh? I think we'd better show the Mantis what's appropriate and what isn't. This . . . thing . . . has killed a Pakistani soldier. We shall be a laughing stock if that woman lets it go, without investigation.'

The intelligence brigadier hesitated. 'Which woman, sir? The Indian Prime Minister or the scientist? It seems that—'

'Any woman,' the General said angrily. 'Either woman —neither of them knows what a woman should be. Magib, when I was a young man, women had influence. A lot of influence. But they found better, more agreeable places to acquire it than in Cabinet offices, or digging up bones.'

'Indeed, sir.'

The General's voice was calm again. 'Do you imagine it will come back into our area?'

The brigadier spread his hands. 'I think it may do so, sir. But clearly that can only be a guess. Obviously the creature has no

163

knowledge of frontiers or truce lines, and Shalamerg is very, very close.'

'You can track it?'

'That is being taken care of, sir.'

'Hm. It looks like another job for Azraf Khan, doesn't it? You'd better go and talk to him, tomorrow. Or better still, today. I want that creature, and I want it alive. Tell Azraf Khan I shan't censure him if he makes a little map-reading mistake on the truce line.'

'Yes, sir.' Again the brigadier hesitated. 'I wonder, sir . . . are 8th Hunza Rifles the best unit for the operation?'

'What's wrong with them? Azraf Khan is an excellent officer.'

'Well, they're mostly Pathans. Impulsive . . .'

'And they know the hills, Magib. Nobody better than a Pathan in the hills. Besides . . . what's the nearest unit, apart from them?'

'1st Ghujerab Lancers, sir.'

The General laughed. 'Tanks . . . they can't do much tracking in tanks, can they?'

'We could move up another infantry battalion. But I see the difficulty.'

'Precisely. The Indians would know. They have as much information about us as we have about them. They'd know something was afoot the instant we relieved Azraf Khan before his operational tour of duty was complete. No, it will have to be Azraf Khan. Don't worry about him—he'll find your creature . . .'

That, thought the intelligence brigadier, is exactly what I'm afraid of.

17

Harry came out of his tent and looked across the broad expanse of the *merg* to the mountains beyond. The clouds were piled above Shalamerg, though the steady spring rain had ceased half an hour ago. He walked to the edge of the drop into the valley. Below him threaded the silver line of the stream, its banks smudged in the evening light by the blue shadow of the violets which grew beside it. As he watched, over the mountains the thunder clouds parted, and for a few seconds a gleaming dome-shaped mass floated before him, far to the north, in the pink and primrose gap of evening sky. He caught his breath with pleasure . . . it was Nanga Parbat, towering five miles high like a Himalayan dream, and rarely seen from this part of the Pir Panjal. But then the purple-black thunderheads obliterated the gap once more, and the great mountain vanished, as though to emphasise the impermanence of dreams. Only a thin line of gold remained above the black cloud-wall, lit by the dying sun. Harry's dark mood returned.

He walked through the wet grass to the cage. How small it seemed after the compound at Srinagar. The Esau sat there, unresponsive, not giving even the show of hostility Harry had come to expect over the past few days. A small Gurkha soldier patrolling methodically in front of the cage slapped his carbine in salute. '*Salaam*, Colonel-*sahib*.'

Harry nodded. 'Ready for dawn, Rifleman Deobahadur Pun? And I am no longer a colonel.'

The rifleman's slanting brown eyes gleamed with pleasure at Harry's recollection of his name, and a white-toothed grin seemed to cover his broad face. 'I forget always, Colonel-*sahib*. Yes, we are ready. But is he?'

He jerked the muzzle of his carbine towards the Esau in the cage. The Esau squatted in a corner, eyes half-closed.

'He will die soon, Colonel-*sahib*.'

Harry was startled. 'What do you mean . . . surely he's not as bad as that? What have you seen?'

The Gurkha shrugged. 'He is sad, Colonel-*sahib*. He is like a man who has lost his woman. He does not wish to live.'

'He will recover when he is freed at dawn.'

'Perhaps. But the local people say he is marked for death.'

'Do they know what is to happen? Has there been talk?'

'No Gurkah will chatter to this Kashmiri trash, though the girls are pretty,' the soldier said comfortably. 'But they know. Srinagar is a parrots' cage. A man cannot hear himself pass wind for the clack of the voices.'

Harry rubbed his chin. 'Do they realise he's going to be free at dawn?'

'I think they do not know the hour, Colonel-*sahib*. But do not concern yourself. We shall allow no interference.' Another great grin transformed his face as he dropped a hand to the hilt of the wavy razor-sharp blade of the *kukri* strapped to his belt.

Watching from her tent, Liliane made herself go out to greet Harry as he walked back to the little encampment. It was never easy to talk to him nowadays—not because he was rude or surly, but because he had become so impenetrably polite. Sometimes, and partly with pleasure, she remembered the night on the houseboat, the hard strong body above her. But that was over and already it seemed long ago.

'How is he tonight, Harry?'

'Pretty down, I think. I have a feeling dawn won't be an hour too soon for him. Mind you, he's hard to assess—up one day and down the next. He's had a pretty rough time for the last few months.'

'Yes.' She gazed out across the valley. Far below them, it was already night and even as high as Shalamerg the twilight was deepening fast, though the western sky was still veined with purple and gold. A lamp came on in Chowdhuri's tent.

'What a magnificent evening,' Liliane said.

For a moment Harry seemed to relax.

'That's why some of us live here,' he said. 'And I'm glad to think he's going back where he belongs.' He nodded towards the cage. 'He'll be better out there. It's a rough world, even though it's beautiful. But it's his own.'

'What are you going to do . . . afterwards?'

He did not answer for a moment, but then said quietly, 'I'll find something—there's an expedition on Everest next year. It will need a lot of planning at base. I can probably get in on that.

It will have to be base, though.' He tapped his leg. 'This doesn't bother me much normally, but it would be a liability on Everest.'

She hesitated, slightly encouraged by the moment of shared confidence. 'You could always stay on with us . . . I know Kim would be happy about that. We're going to go on digging round Shalamerg this year.'

At once the polite mask returned. 'Oh, many thanks for the offer, but my contract with you is over in a fortnight's time. I think it's better not to renew it. That wouldn't be suitable.'

He walked away towards Chowdhuri's tent, and she went up to the cage. The Esau rose to his feet and came to the steel mesh. He moved, she saw with concern, more slowly than usual, although that might be because he had been given a mild sedative to make it easier to get him from the cage next morning. Under the heavy brows his eyes glinted as he looked at her, though it was impossible to gauge his mood. She felt no sense of contact with him and, cautiously, she kept well clear of the fence.

'This is the only way.' She found to her astonishment that she was speaking the words aloud. The form on the other side of the mesh remained motionless, watching.

'We have different lives to live,' she said. 'Nothing else can be done.' She looked back after she reached the lamp-lit tent where others were gathered. In the darkness there was a yet darker outline where the Esau still stood beside the fence.

Inside Chowdhuri's tent a map was spread on the deal table, and Kimbell was tracing his finger along the purple and brown hatch which marked the range of the Pir Panjal, while Harry watched silently.

'Where do you imagine he'll head for, the minute he's out of that cage, Harry?'

The Englishman bent over the map. 'I still think north-east,' he said at last. 'Out of the Pir Panjal, as I've said before, because I don't think this is his territory. And then, maybe, out into Ladakh, or the Karakoram. That's wild country. You could hide a thousand Esaus there.'

Looking at the map's jumbled contours Liliane saw again how the shaded truce line ran diagonally across the mountain ranges, pointing steadily along the Esau's projected route.

'That's nearly a hundred miles?' she said questioningly to Harry.

His voice was impatient. 'We've had all this out before, Liliane. It's too late for second thoughts. Yes, it's around eighty miles—as the crow flies. But he's not a crow. He's going to have to move from valley to valley, peak to peak. And he won't trouble about the truce line, because he doesn't know it's there. But no one can stop him, wherever he goes. You could hire the best Pathan tracker between here and the Khyber Pass, and he couldn't keep up with the Esau over his own country. Wouldn't even see him move. The Esau will be fine as soon as he's free. All that lethargy will drop away. I've seen it with . . . well . . . other animals.'

'Yes,' Liliane said, with more certainty. Harry was right. Once in Esau country, no potential enemy or would-be observer could hope to follow him . . . as long as the prospect of freedom brought back his strength. And that was something they would find out at dawn.

Kimbell yawned. 'I'm going to bed for an hour or two. What time's Mohammad calling us?'

'Half an hour before first light,' Harry said. 'A good old Army time. You're all going to be out and about then, I take it?'

'Yes.'

'Good. If you want to watch him go, Mohammad and a cousin of his have brought up ponies—enough for everybody. You might find it interesting, though I don't imagine he'll be in sight for long.'

'Count me out,' said Kimbell, grimacing. 'My tall-in-the-saddle days are gone.'

It was still dark when Harry, lying fully dressed on his camp-bed, felt Meachem pull at his shoulder. Behind him was Liliane, buttoning up her drill shirt. Harry switched on his little battery lamp. Meachem looked worried. The wrist watch beside the lamp said that there was just an hour to first light.

'I want to show you something,' said Meachem. Harry followed them out, and they waited until his eyes became used to the darkness. Then they walked to the edge of the *merg*, and Meachem pointed up the dark hillside opposite.

'What do you think those are? I saw the first one ten minutes ago, but there seem to be more and more.'

On the black hump of the hill a dozen or so faint points of yellow light moved slowly upwards. Occasionally one would vanish, to reappear after a minute or two, always a little higher. Even with his binoculars he could not identify the moving dots.

'Lanterns,' said Chowdhuri beside them, so unexpectedly that they turned in surprise. He shivered in the cold morning air, struggling into his duffel-coat. 'Those are the lanterns they use for late harvesting in the Vale of Kashmir. We have the same in the Punjab.'

Harry stared upwards at the scattered points of light. 'They're climbing up to see the Esau off. At least, we can hope it's no more than that. Somehow, they know he's going soon, and they intend to be here. How the hell did they find out?'

'You can keep no secret in a bazaar,' Chowdhuri said. Harry strode down to the cage. Slumped, the Esau seemed to be still sleeping off his mild sedation, but now an extra soldier was patrolling beyond the cage. The Gurkha *naik*, the corporal in charge of the guard, was a little grizzled man with a straggling mandarin moustache. He emerged, blinking, as Harry opened the flap of the guard-tent.

'Yes, Colonel-*sahib*, I have already doubled the guard. I saw the lights half an hour ago. There are a few peasants out there—fifty, sixty, perhaps more. They will do nothing—we shall see to that. They are like stupid children, waving their lamps.'

'Good. Nevertheless, I think I'll stay around until—what in God's name is that?'

On the hillside opposite a tongue of flame leaped into the air, growing, swelling into a great patch of fire. A column of sparks swept upwards as the juniper bushes and azaleas, on the slopes, drying quickly after the rain, burst into flame. The fire was growing with incredible speed, stretching down towards Shalamerg. The *naik* grunted, and began to shout orders.

'Just watch those sparks,' shouted Harry, turning to run towards the tents to warn the others. 'The fire won't cross the stream, but the sparks might cause trouble. Those bushes dry

169

fast up here. Get your people beating at anything that lands.'

Standing in the darkness beside his own tent, Mohammad Pingnoo watched silently. In contrast with the dazzling blaze on the hillside, the Esau's cage seemed darker than ever. He pulled at the tent-flap. 'This is the time.'

The 'cousin' who emerged would have been recognised at once by Amrit Singh in Delhi, though not by any of Mohammad Pingnoo's family. He carried a plastic carrier bag and his spectacled face was anxious. Sixty yards away the bushes at the fringe of the *merg* went up in crackling flame exactly where, a minute ago, Mohammad had dropped some smouldering rags. Cursing, two patrolling Gurkhas ran over and began stamping and beating at the blaze, one of them turning to call out the guard for assistance. Mohammad and the man with the bag ran over to the unguarded fence. Quickly Mohammad unlocked the gate. The other paused, frightened. Mohammad hissed at him angrily.

'Be quick, you fool. They will be back here any second.'

'Is he . . . is there any danger?'

'No . . . of course not. I gave him extra drugs. He will sleep for another hour.'

Gingerly, the man with the bag went into the cage. With an effort he approached the Esau. There was a loud, rumbling snore and his confidence grew slightly. He took from the bag a steel collar lined with plastic, inside which was embedded a small transistor tube. From it sprouted, incongruously, a four-inch whip aerial. He forced himself to touch the hairy neck, and then snatched his hand away, watching. But the Esau's head still lolled, and the technician screwed up his courage. Stooping, he slid the collar through the thick hair above the great shoulders and snapped shut the lock. Then, triumphantly, he stole back to the gate.

Mohammad whispered from the other side, 'It is done?'

'Yes. Let me out.'

The keys scraped at the lock and the gate swung open. From behind, something hit him obliquely, but with tremendous force, sending him sprawling into the bars and breaking his spectacles. A great form filled the entrance for a second, and he heard a choked scream from Mohammad Pingnoo. Then came a strange bubbling cry, followed by a roar and a single rifle shot, the bullet whining away into the darkness. An English voice shouted: 'Stop firing. *Naik*, cease firing.'

One of the Gurkhas, stamping fiercely at a patch of flaming bush, glimpsed the Esau for a second against the light of the fire. Moving swiftly, silently, the bulky shadow vanished at once into the night. The Gurkha strained his watering eyes after him in the smoke, but the Esau was gone.

'Mohammad is dead—neck broken,' said Harry briefly. 'He had these keys in his hand—they aren't ours. I suppose he must have had them made secretly in town. And in the cage I found this . . . object.'

He thrust forward, into the lamp-lit hut, the shaking form of the technician. The Indian's face was bleeding slightly where the glass of his broken spectacles had cut his cheek. Liliane felt herself consumed with bitter anger. To have come so far, and to have succeeded so much—and now this. Where was the Esau, and was he safe? Suddenly, everything had changed. She turned on the Indian, almost spitting out the words.

'How did you get into the cage? Why were you there?'

The Indian drew the rags of his dignity around him.

'I have authorisation from Delhi. I have a right to be here. I do not answer questions from a foreign *memsahib*.'

'You have no right,' said Chowdhuri. 'You gave a false name.'

The Indian pointed to where Mohammad's body lay under a groundsheet. His assurance was returning.

'He knows why I am here.'

'And he can't tell us, can he?' Harry said.

'No—I will tell the police, when they come. I do not need to tell you. You are not Indians. I shall not speak.'

Harry turned and called into the darkness: '*Naik*, bring Rifleman Deobahadur Pun to us, please.' A moment later the little Gurkha was by their side, his face troubled.

'Colonel-*sahib*, I am struck with a deep shame. I left my post—it seemed right at the time, but I should not have gone.'

'You were still on duty?'

'Yes, Colonel-*sahib*.'

'All men make mistakes, Deobahadur Pun . . . even colonel-

171

sahibs. But not all men can redeem them. You see this man here?'

The Gurkha nodded. 'Bengali *pen-wallah*,' he said contemptuously.

'Just so. He is . . . having difficulty in explaining to us why he is here, and what he was doing. Perhaps he would talk to you, Deobahadur Pun.'

The Gurkha's teeth gleamed, and he pushed the Indian outside. As he left his right hand went down to his belt, and he unfastened the button on the toggle above his *kukri*.

The Indian gasped.

'I give him fifteen seconds,' said Harry. Chowdhuri looked away, his eyes wide.

Afterwards, Liliane realised that she had been steadily counting. She had reached thirteen when the Gurkha and the Indian returned. The Indian looked sick with terror. One side of his trousers flapped open to the chill night air.

'What were you doing in the cage?' Harry asked.

The reply was sullen but prompt. 'I fitted the creature with a radio-tracker.'

Liliane gasped. 'How . . . what kind?'

'A collar. It is locked—he cannot remove it.'

'Why did you do it?'

A shrug. 'I was ordered to—in Delhi, by the Government. Mohammad helped me.'

'He was your cousin?'

'No.'

She turned to Kimbell. 'It can't have been the Prime Minister who did this—it must have been Amrit Singh.' There was a confirmatory flicker in the Indian's eyes as he heard the name.

'What range do these things have?' asked Harry.

'Fifty or sixty miles at best,' Meachem said. 'In country like this, maybe quite a lot less. Valleys and rock-walls bounce the signals—it can be confusing. Otherwise, the sets are easy to operate. I know,' he added in answer to the unspoken question. 'I know because I once helped a biologist track a civet in Java. It was a holiday of sorts, after digging round the Solo River.'

He spoke again to the young Indian.

'Do you have a receiver?'

Silently the man indicated the plastic carrier bag. Kimbell drew from it a canvas-strapped plastic box, no bigger than a transistor radio.

'Why did you have this?' Meachem said quietly. 'You didn't need this. All you needed was the collar.'

The Indian's shoulders lifted in a sullen shrug. 'Mohammad told me to bring a set.'

'Why?'

Again a shrug. 'Mohammad always liked to have everything under his own hand. Perhaps he could have sold such a set. Perhaps—' his eyes lifted to Meachem's for a moment—'he might have sold it even to you . . .'

'Is is set to operate? What's the frequency?'

The Indian's lips tightened defiantly. Deobahadur Pun slid the *kukri* from his belt. 'Fifty megahertz,' said the Indian.

Tom whistled. 'On the low side, weren't you?'

'It is better in mountains,' said the Indian, almost proudly. 'There is less deflection than at higher frequency. We know that.'

Tom's fingers were busy on the setting band of the receiver. 'Fifty megahertz—well, he can't be far away yet. God, there he is—loud and clear.' The single set of head-phones still lay in the open carrier bag, but the steady bleep-bleep of the Esau's progress could be heard clearly all over the tent.

'He sounds so near,' Liliane said. She stared through the door of the hut as though expecting to see the familiar form back behind the mesh fence. Already the sky was streamed with the first hint of dawn.

'Where are the ponies?' she asked Harry abruptly.

'Down on the little bit of ground under the lip of the *merg*,' he said. 'But surely you're not thinking . . .?'

'I'm going to make sure he's all right,' she said, her voice calm though her mind raced. She felt a strange sense of exaltation, almost of renewal. Everything was not over yet . . .

'I've still got my bedroll packed—I didn't even unroll it, because I knew I wouldn't sleep. I can manage by myself. But does . . . does anybody want to come?'

Meachem was the first to speak. 'It's crazy. But I'm with you. I fancy a pony-trek in the Great Himalaya. Anyway, you'll need me to work the set.'

173

'I shall come also,' said Chowdhuri.

She patted his hand affectionately. 'Prakash, do you think you'll—'

'I shall come,' said the little man firmly. 'After all, he is *Homo kashmiriensis chowdhuri*.'

Kimbell shook his head sadly. 'I'm too old and too fat. Anyway, one of us will have to stay to tell the police how Mohammad died.'

'We'll start straight away,' Liliane said. 'Tom, you bring the receiving set. Prakash, Harry will lend you the rifle.'

Harry tried to control his mounting anger. 'You realise you might be out there for days? Of all the damn-fool ideas I ever heard . . . Liliane, don't be a fool. You'll be hopelessly lost in a few hours—this isn't a back-lot in California. And what good will it do? It's completely stupid.'

'There are people out there who wish him ill, Harry. They're not going to hurt him while I'm here. He's my responsibility and I'm going to see he gets well on the way to where he's going. You can do what you like.'

'Can I?' he said, his voice bitter. '*Naik*, saddle an extra pony for me.'

'You're coming?' she said, genuinely surprised.

'I have to, don't I? I still have a fortnight of my contract to run, and I always try to give good value.'

He stared at her and for a moment she dropped her eyes.

'Let's get one thing straight,' Harry said. 'We can't just ride straight out. We must organise a little. Pity . . . we can't take a couple of Gurkhas, because there's no time to clear it with the Army. And they don't ride well, anyway. We'll leave in half-an-hour, properly equipped—well, as far as we can be.'

From the headphones on the table the bleep-bleep of the moving Esau chirped steadily out into the dawn.

'Has there been anything since that gun-shot?' said Lieutenant-Colonel Azraf Khan. He lay on the dew-soaked ground, peering south over the crest towards the bulk of Shalamerg, his hawk-face faintly rosy in the pinkish glow from the distant fires. Below him two platoons of riflemen squatted on the stony slope.

'Nothing,' said the operator. 'But the creature is definitely free. Listen to this.'

He passed the headset with its steady bleep-bleep to Azraf Khan. The colonel held it to one ear, his head cocked to the side like a vigilant bird of prey.

'So,' he said at last. 'Nearly two hours early. Do you think they've found out that we, too, have a set? I never trust a damned thing that comes through Central Intelligence. For all we know, the Indians have sold us a decoy.'

'Brigadier Magib was very confident,' said the second-in-command tactfully. 'He said the set was supplied by a very high source.'

The colonel made a derisive sound, turning back to the operator. 'How far away is the accursed beast now?'

'A couple of miles, sir. Seems to be travelling north-west.'

Azraf Khan got to his feet. 'Time to move, then, Zulfikar. Let's show them whose mountains these are.'

18

He was moving steadily along the blind side of the crest above the lake, loping through a rough scrub of berberis bushes, just showing their first green shoots among patches of wild daphne blazing purple on the short turf. The sky was cloudless, blue as steel, and far below him the still surface of the water reflected the mountain. At intervals he stopped and put a hand to his left side, staring at the blood which quickly soaked his fingers. Once he swung up to the crest and lay for two minutes, watching. Three hundred feet lower, thirty or forty human creatures were climbing steadily, painfully upward, shouting and calling to each other. He observed them carefully, grunted with sudden pain as he stood again, and trotted slowly onward. He was travelling along the edge of the snowline, and muddy little snowfilled gullies seamed the mountainside all around him.

Above him lay winter, and hard, safe journeying, provided his body was still capable of meeting its challenge. He touched his side again. In seconds, his fingers were once more covered in blood. Below him lay spring, where rivers swollen with melted snow rushed down between broad, easy banks rioting with wild roses and yellow jessamine. It was an easier world down there, where he could move with less pain. But it was a world of men. He looked up into the vault of the sky where two crows flapped silently down into the valley. Again he felt the stab at his ribs, and he moved on just below the crest, neither climbing nor descending, but just out of sight of those behind him. Once or twice he pulled at the collar on his neck, but any attempt to break it caused such spurts of blood from his side that he stopped trying. Far, far ahead lay the white peaks of refuge, glittering in the sun.

'Well, it's pretty clear what's happened,' said Harry, cradling the old shotgun he had just picked out of the bushes. 'One of the Kashmiris was quite a bit higher than the others, met him, and got a shot in. Only one shot—there's still a live cartridge in the other barrel. But he got a hit. Look at the ground—there's blood everywhere.'

'It could be Kashmiri blood,' said Liliane slowly. She stood beside her pony, one hand resting on the bedroll strapped to its back as it grazed hastily in the fresh grass. She found herself hoping, slightly ashamed, that it *was* human blood.

Harry shook his head, and dipped a finger into the biggest blood patch. He held his hand out towards her, and she could see that among the glistening red was a strand of coarse russet hair.

'Then where's the Kashmiri?' said Tom Meachem, adjusting the dial of the little receiver.

Harry shrugged. 'He could have run back to his friends. Or he could be down there somewhere.' He pointed down the almost sheer drop, at least two hundred feet, at the side of the path. 'There's no way of knowing.'

'The others are still well below us,' Chowdhuri said, wheezing. Alone of the four, he had not dismounted from his pony when they found the shotgun. He was sweating heavily, and Liliane knew that the very act of mounting and dismounting was an ordeal for him. He should not have come, but—foolishly—she could not bring herself to stop him.

'They'll give up when the Esau climbs higher,' said Harry. 'They won't go out of country they know. But . . . now he's hurt, it may change things. We don't know how badly he's hit, but in any case he could be slowed down because . . . look . . . here and here . . . he's losing quite a lot of blood.' The receiver headphones bleeped suddenly and the intermittent note sang out into the crisp air.

'There he goes,' Tom Meachem said. 'Thank God he hasn't lost his collar.'

The bleep swelled loudly, faded, swelled again. Liliane picked up the headphones, though in the mountain silence the notice was clearly audible without them. 'How far away do you estimate he is?'

Meachem listened for a moment before he replied. 'These are pretty bad conditions for estimating range,' he said. 'The mountains form tunnels, so I'm getting a lot of distortion as the signals bounce to and fro. But, at a rough guess, I'd say no more than three miles.'

Liliane looked at Harry. For the moment the tension between them had gone. 'Then that argues that . . .'

He nodded. 'Yes. He's definitely been slowed down. He should be much more than three miles away by now, given the start he's had. He can move faster than the ponies—that's why I thought, originally, that your idea of going after him as a sort of escort was a non-starter. Now, of course, it's different. We can probably keep up. Maybe we shall even . . .'

'What?'

'Maybe we shall even find him,' Harry said steadily.

There was a cold feeling at her heart as she swung herself back into the stiff pommelled saddle, but her voice was determined. 'Then he needs us more than ever.'

Harry reined in his pony and looked back. The first added chill of the approaching evening touched the sweat on his forehead, and he shivered. He glanced at the little watch-sized altimeter he carried in his breast-pocket . . . 13,600 feet. At this altitude it was already cold, and with the spring night hurrying towards them, soon it would be colder still. The mountain wall reared to the side of the narrow, stony ledge along which they were slowly making their way. There was snow all around, though here and there, in a lee of the rocks, a primrose pushed defiantly through. A shaly slope was rising in front of them, and its top was crowned by a jumble of great rocks . . . probably, he thought, brought down by an avalanche long ago. One slab-sided piece of basalt lay athwart the jumble, making a cave about four feet high, its entrance fringed with stalks of dead juniper, laced with snow.

The other three riders were strung out along the ledge for about half-a-mile . . . Tom Meachem next, with the receiver, then Chowdhuri, then Liliane, who was riding last because they were worried about the elderly Indian.

'Can you get any kind of fix?' Harry said as Tom came up.

The American dismounted, and adjusted the frequency. He put the earphones on, and Harry could not hear the bleep, but after a few seconds Meachem nodded and passed the headset up to where Harry still sat on his pony.

'There he is, loud and clear.'

Harry listened while Chowdhuri and Liliane came slowly up to them. 'He seems pretty near.'

'Yes, I'd say within a mile.'

Liliane was startled. 'As near as that?'

'Seems like it. I think he's stopped. It's soon going to be dark and, of course, we don't know whether he likes moving at night. Or whether his wound is affecting him badly.'

Liliane considered. Harry watched her, his face neutral but attentive, and felt a strong impulse to put out his hand. Here she was, nearly 14,000 feet up in the wild Himalayas, tired, bedraggled, anxious, and inexperienced. She was trying to help a creature that, at best, none of them more than a quarter-understood. Prakash, too. The little man was exhausted, but all that long day he had not complained. Tom Meachem, of course, was younger and fitter, but none of them on this half-baked expedition had once suggested giving up.

'If he's so close,' said Liliane, 'do you think we should try to come right up to him?'

'To do what?' Harry said carefully. He did not wish to clash with her again.

'You have some anaesthetic darts, haven't you?'

'Yes. I brought the little dart rifle as well as the .300 carbine. But we'd have to get very close indeed with the dart-gun. It's not much more than a small air-rifle. It was fine in the compound, but I wouldn't fancy its chances at anything over ten or fifteen yards. And . . . do you think it's advisable? For him now, another bout of drugging might be the last straw.'

She felt helpless. 'I know. But we may have to. If he's really badly wounded, we could at least see what we can do for him.'

He nodded. 'Well, we've always got the dart-gun in reserve. We'll see if we have to use it tomorrow.'

'Why not now?'

He pointed to the fading sky. 'It'll be dark in an hour. We couldn't hope to come up with him before that, and we know how well he can camouflage himself. I think it's better to let him lie for the night. After all, he's stopped moving, so that's probably what he intends to do.'

'There could be another explanation,' Chowdhuri said gravely, blinking behind his spectacles. 'He could have stopped because he can no longer move.'

179

Liliane's pony shuffled suddenly, jostling against Harry's. Almost without meaning to, he put out his hand and took hers. 'If that's happened, then we probably can't help him anyway. But if he's just resting, then it's better we don't startle him into moving again. We couldn't follow him in the dark on these ponies—apart from anything else they also need rest. If that wound makes him lie up at night, then in one sense it's a godsend. Because if he decides to move, he could be twenty miles from us by dawn. It's best if we lie up ourselves now, and get some sleep.'

'One of us should be on listening watch, all night,' Liliane said. 'We can take it in turns, the three of us.'

'Agreed.'

'There are four of us,' Chowdhuri said.

Liliane smiled at him. 'No, Prakash, I insist. You must rest as much as you can. You're the oldest of us, and it will be no good at all if you're exhausted tomorrow.'

He began to argue, until he saw it was useless. Harry dismounted and walked up to the cave. The entrance was deep in old, drifted snow, and long icicles hung down from the basalt roof. He scraped away enough ridged and crusted snow to squat inside the entrance. The cave ran back about eight yards into a jumble of loose rock. A first gust of the usual night breeze stirred the disturbed snow, scattering the frozen particles into his face. He turned to the others.

'I think this will be better than the tent. There could be a bit of wind tonight, and I'd hate to lose the tent. We could be quite snug in here, as long as we all lie close together.'

They tethered the ponies in a little flat amphitheatre of rocks above the cave. No grass was visible beneath the smooth snow, but the animals pushed their noses under the white surface and began to graze, tearing out long wet tufts of yellow vegetation. Inside the cave, behind the snow-filled entrance, Meachem was lighting the little paraffin stove. It was dry back there, though the sandy floor was marked with greyish slime, which gave off a sharp, ammoniac smell.

'Bat-droppings,' Meachem said, wrinkling his nose. 'Not exactly the Himalaya Hilton. And you'll have to wait for tea. That stove doesn't burn well as high as this.'

They ate without much conversation, while the twilight

advanced. There was no variety in the food. All that they had been able to pack, in the scramble to get away from Shalamerg, had been a basketful of flour-and-water Indian *chapatti* pancakes, tins of corned beef, and some canned fruit. Tom had opened a tin of apricots for the evening meal. Harry finished quickly, drank the hot milkless tea, took the carbine and went outside. This diet, he knew, was inadequate, even temporarily, for days of riding, and served to emphasise the hopelessly improvised and improvident character of the whole affair. They needed more protein—especially Chowdhuri. There wasn't likely to be much about, but even a squirrel, well roasted, would be acceptable. Squirrels lived hundreds of feet lower, amongst the cedars of the down-slopes, but sometimes, long ago, he had seen them above the snowline in spring, taking azalea buds. He lay above the cave for twenty minutes, watching, but there were no squirrels. It was now almost dark, and very cold. He was about to go back to the cave, when he sensed, rather than saw, a movement in the rock corrie above him. Straining his eyes, he gradually picked out an unmistakable goat silhouette . . . long legs braced against the slope of the ground, horns curving back in a graceful parabola. Ibex . . . there were five . . . six of them. They were at least 300 yards away, but upwind, and he was certain they had not seen him. Nevertheless, they were shifting about uneasily, and the leader—the one with the great horns—whistled at intervals in the creaking ibex way to keep his females alert. Even as Harry began to work out the route he could crawl to get within range, they were gone, melting like shadows into the darkness. Something had disturbed them. It could be anything, of course. A leopard, perhaps. But was it, so very close, the Esau?

At the mouth of the cave Tom Meachem took the first bleeper-watch. Lying close together, Harry and Liliane pulled their quilted sleeping bags close around them. Liliane lay in the middle, between Harry and Chowdhuri, since Harry's was the next watch, and Liliane's the last. Chowdhuri had taken a tablet, and was lying on his back, breathing stertorously. In spite of herself, Liliane shivered inside her bag.

'Cold?' said Harry beside her.

'Yes, a little.'

'I'm not surprised. My thermometer read 26 Fahrenheit

about an hour ago. There's one good tip, though. Pull the flap of your bag up over your face. That way you warm yourself with your own breath. See what I mean . . . is that better?'

Her voice was muffled. 'Yes, Harry, that's a lot better.'

'Good.' He settled himself back into his own sleeping bag, only half-awake now, but still conscious of her form beside him. Suddenly she moved sharply, and he felt, very briefly, the touch of her lips on his.

'Goodnight, Harry. Sleep well.'

'Cold rations tonight,' said Azraf Khan. 'I don't want that pony party warned by a lot of cooking fires. They're only a mile away.'

'But,' said his second-in-command, 'on the other side of the truce line.'

The colonel laughed, putting his binoculars back into their stout leather case.

'They haven't spotted us yet, but I got a good look at them this afternoon, when they came through that defile below us. One of them is Kernow. I remember him—he was lecturing at Camberley when I was on the overseas staff course. He was—probably still is—very efficient. Retired now, of course. I don't understand what he's doing out here, now that they've released that damned animal. There's something funny going on.'

'And the other three, sir?'

'Didn't recognise the young one . . . doesn't look much, though. The woman, of course . . . not easy to forget her. And then there's the Indian—rides like a sack of maize. A real liability, that one.'

The telemeter operator came up, saluted, spoke briefly to the second-in-command, and went back to where the riflemen were rolling themselves into their blankets in the lee of the rocks.

'It seems the beast is still stopped,' the second-in-command said. 'Do you think we could . . .'

Decisively, Azraf Khan shook his head. 'No, Zulfikar. Not a night operation. As long as he stays stopped, we can get him tomorrow. He's moving more slowly than I'd imagined. Maybe he's weaker for some reason. We'll keep listening watch on that set, of course. And double the guard . . . two hours on, four hours off.'

'You don't think the beast would . . .?'

The colonel laughed again. It was, his companion thought, a peculiarly mirthless sound. 'You never know, Zulfikar. He might double back on us. He's killed Rifleman Gundar Ali already—that's why we're here. I don't want him killing somebody else. At present, it balances. A life for a life.'

The second-in-command was startled into a question. 'But I thought we were here on specific orders from the General to bring the creature back alive?'

'If possible,' the colonel said smoothly. 'If possible. But a lot of unpredictable factors may intervene . . .'

He squatted in the corrie. The wound in his side had stopped bleeding for most of the time now, and had stiffened into a throbbing area of pain. A little stream, mostly melted snow, ran down the side of the rocks. Searching along it, he had found frogspawn and new buds on the sparse bushes. He ate both, all the time steadily watching the mountainside below and ahead of him. Only one human was now in the mouth of the cave: the others were inside. On the distant slope the bigger party—each of whom looked like the human he had killed above Shalamerg before he was taken—were settled for the night. His hand explored the wound in his side. It seemed to be wet again. He lifted his fingers to his mouth in the darkness and tasted the salt of blood. Breaking some branches from the bushes he wedged them round his body as he shrank into the rough shelter of the rocks. He must not sleep, but he could rest. Eyes half-closed, body aching with pain, uneasy, he watched the camp-sites of the humans who were following him better than any animal had ever followed him before.

19

At noon on the following day Tom Meachem's receiver lost the Esau. Since shortly after dawn they had been moving steadily north-east into the towering range of the Great Himalaya, traversing a jagged, jumbled litter of razor-edged slopes. It was a country with no natural grain: its defiles and crests ran at odds with each other, criss-crossing in a tangle of lines on the map. Yet the ponies picked a way easily enough. Even in this wilderness there were trails used by nomad *gujars* on their way to summer herding. But the going was very hard, and frequently they had to dismount to lead the animals across great areas of fallen rock. Each of them felt the effects of altitude . . . shortness of breath, sweating, chill, headache. Yet, Harry knew, they were still only a little higher than 14,000 feet, and the Esau might choose to go higher. He looked back at Chowdhuri, who was on the pony behind him. The Indian's face was grey. Soon they would either have to leave him or all turn back together. And, of course, they couldn't leave him . . .

Then, at the rear of the little spread-out column, he saw Meachem waving. He reined in while the others came up —Chowdhuri slumped in weary silence; Liliane strong, keeping that eager quality that still made him catch his breath; Meachem baffled and angry.

'He's gone,' he said, slithering from his pony and again unshipping the set. 'He's damned well gone. Not a whisper of a bleep.' He adjusted the dial, handing the headphones to Liliane. There was a steady roar of static but nothing else. Worried, she passed the headphones to Harry.

'Do you think he's managed to break the collar?'

'Could be,' Meachem said. 'He wouldn't know what it was, of course, but it may have irritated him. Or these rock walls could have bounced the signal right out of our listening area. Either way, we don't have the faintest idea of which way he's moving now.'

'He could be dead,' Harry said.

'Meachem shook his head. 'Even if he was dead, the collar

would go on transmitting. Only two things could stop us hearing—bad physical conditions, or a break in the collar itself.'

Harry cleared his throat. 'I hate to say this, because I suppose I now feel as involved as any of you, but in fact we should turn back in any case. We haven't got adequate food, and I've had no luck at all with the rifle. My compass tells me roughly where we are, but rough estimates aren't really adequate up here. I don't have any clear idea of which side of the truce line we are now. And one of us can't go much further, anyway.' He dropped his voice as he said the last words, and Chowdhuri did not hear.

Liliane's heart sank. Harry was right. Although she had nothing like his experience in these mountains, even the little she knew told her that their chances of following the Esau, without the help of the transmitter in the collar, were negligible. It was possible, of course, that if they pushed on in a direction which seemed a likley one for him, they might eventually re-establish contact. But the chance was very, very small . . . and it might be bought at the price of Chowdhuri's life, or at least of his future health. They would have to go back, and now she might never know . . . The broad hairy face with the great jutting brow and the deep-set eyes came back into her mind. For a moment she seemed to feel his presence and she shivered. But it was imagination only, and nothing like the contact he had sometimes been able to establish with her in the past. The Esau had gone.

They rested for an hour before turning back, the delay giving Chowdhuri a chance to rest and the ponies the opportunity of a brief grazing on the thin mountain grass. Tom continued to fiddle with the receiver, trying to pick up the signal—if indeed it was still available to be picked up. Watching Chowdhuri's exhausted face, Liliane found herself almost hoping that Tom would be unsuccessful. The loss of the signal had made turning back the only practical option. But if Tom re-established contact, what then? But Tom didn't, and by mid-afternoon they were picking their way west, along a trail they had already travelled.

Once more Harry rode first, with Chowdhuri next, then Meachem, and last of all, Liliane. Liliane was strong—much stronger than Chowdhuri and probably fitter than Tom. The last place in the line was the hardest one to ride, more tiring even than Harry's position, leading. But he had to lead because he knew more about the country, and because he was by far the best shot of the four. They needed meat if they were not to be very hungry indeed by the time they got back to Shalamerg.

Harry was approaching the lip of a crest. Beyond it stretched a short, almost rectangular mountain meadow, at the far side of which was the fall into the valley. It was a likely place for goat . . . either feral goat, escaped generations ago from valley domesticity, or even the wild, spiral-horned markhor, much rarer, hunted by sportsmen with implacable assiduity in the days of the Raj. He slipped from the pony and crawled on his hands and knees up to the crest. But the little natural meadow was empty. There were few trees at this height, and across the valley he could see only a scanty stand of pine and a couple of scrawny stunted birch. The ground on which he lay was covered with a pink carpet of some small flower whose name he did not know. Through it brown and yellow fritillaries thrust on long thin stalks. A little patch of white saxifrage grew within reach of his right hand. Absently, watching the mountainside, he broke a piece off and sniffed at its aromatic scent. In the same instant he glimpsed a movement on the opposite slopes. Carefully he raised his binoculars to his eyes. There was a little shelf-like plateau there, and a patch of ferns which meant that probably there was also a pool. Again there was a flicker of movement . . . was it the Esau? He looked again, and he felt a tug of apprehension. Clear in the lens he saw two soldiers. They were dressed in Pakistani green combat fatigues, and both were lying full-length among the ferns, filling their water bottles. They were probably more than a quarter of a mile away, and there was no sign that they had seen him. He wriggled back from the crest and went down to where his pony grazed below. The others, strung out on the trail, were just coming up into the meadow, and Harry signalled them to dismount.

'There are a couple of Pakistani infantrymen over on the other side of the valley. And where there are two, there'll be more. I don't have any idea of what they're doing—it may be

186

quite innocent. Perhaps it's just a company exercise. But I think we ought to keep out of sight.'

He turned to Liliane. 'Want to take a look?' She crawled beside him to the crest and looked through the glasses. There was no movement now by the patch of ferns, but a little further up the mountainside she caught a moment's glimpse of a small green figure as it dropped out of sight.

'But what are they doing here, in India?'

He shrugged. 'I'd lay a good bet that we aren't in India any more. The truce line's pretty hazy in these parts, but I wouldn't be at all surprised if we're on their side of it. And if they pick us up, we'll be spending a long time in Gilgit—that's their regional headquarters, a few miles down from here. And there'll have to be a lot of very embarrassing explanations.'

She handed him the binoculars, and as she did so her shoulder touched his. Deliberately, she kept it there, and he did not move away. At once there flashed between them a strong confident sexuality. Harry half-turned to face her. Almost savagely, he reached towards her, and the back of his hand lay snug against her breast, warm under the thin silk shirt. Slowly he turned his wrist to cup his hand.

'Not . . . not here . . . the others. We can't . . .'

He took his hand from her breast and raised it to her hair, running a shining curl between his fingers. 'We're going to have to talk about this . . .'

'Not talk, Harry. There's too much talk. We know what we both want. All we have to . . . what is it?'

His eyes narrowed, looking over towards the mountainside once more. He raised the binoculars. 'Well, I'll be damned. Look at that.'

On the opposite slope six or seven soldiers had come into view and were squatting in a circle at the centre of which was a man with a small rectangular box. In the twin circles of the lens the nature of the box was clear. It was a receiving set, exactly like the one Tom Meachem carried. Liliane stared, her eyes wide.

'Then they're after the Esau, too?'

'Yes. Somebody in Delhi must have given them a set.'

'But why?'

He gave a little mirthless laugh. 'Somebody wants Pakistan

to get hold of the Esau. Indian politics is a riddle within a riddle.'

She thought of the Indian Prime Minister, and of the cold vain Sikh who served as her minister. If the Pakistanis captured the Esau, the Prime Minister would look very, very silly, not only at home but also abroad. Silly enough, perhaps, to affect her whole political position. She opened her mouth to speak to Harry, but stopped short. He had the binoculars to his eyes again. After a few moments he passed them to her.

'You see the man in the middle of them . . . the one with the badges on his shoulders?'

She re-focussed the central screw. 'Yes.'

'I know him—he's Azraf Khan. Commands one of the Pathan battalions . . . 8th or 10th, I forget which. I met him at Camberley, a long time ago.'

'Yes?'

'Well, he's not out here for his health. He can't possibly have more than a half-company over there—probably not even that many. And yet he's taken command himself. It must be pretty important.'

Something in his tone worried her. 'I suppose the Pakistan Government do regard capturing the Esau as important,' she said.

'Yes,' Harry said. 'It could be that. Or . . . it could be that Azraf Khan regards it as important. Important to him.'

'But why?'

He turned to face her, leaning on his elbow. There was an absurd smudge of dust on her cheek, and again he felt desire.

'You remember the soldier the Esau was supposed to have killed, above Shalamerg?'

'Yes.'

'He was said to have been a Pathan. God, I was stupid. I should have realised, but it simply didn't occur to me.'

'What do you mean?'

'Pathans are hill people––they have a simple morality about the death of another Pathan from their own grouping. They want a life for a life.'

Her voice was incredulous. 'You mean they want to kill the Esau?'

'I wouldn't be surprised. That's why Azraf Khan's here in

person. He takes himself pretty seriously, that one.'

'But if they kill the Esau, there'll be an international scandal. Surely the Pakistan Government wouldn't be so mad . . .?'

'I don't imagine the Pakistan Government knows anything about what Azraf Khan intends to do. He's no doubt been told to bring the Esau back alive. And so he's out here with twenty or thirty hand-picked men, probably every one of them a Pathan, whom he can trust to keep their mouths shut. They'll find the Esau, kill him, and then go back and report that they couldn't find him at all. Nobody will be able to prove differently, and Pathan honour will be satisfied.'

She looked at him unbelievingly. 'You don't seriously mean that to do that would be regarded as "honour"? We aren't living in the Middle Ages.'

'They are in some of the hill villages up in Waziristan and Baluchistan, or east of the Kyber,' Harry said soberly. 'And Azraf Khan has to think about his battalion, in a way no pen-pusher in Islamabad could understand. If he balances the books, his men will continue to respect him. If he doesn't . . . well, who knows?'

'You sound as though you agree with him.'

Harry smiled, and put a hand on hers. 'I can see how it looks from his point of view. But no, I don't want him to kill the Esau. Not a bit.'

'Good.'

He looked at her inquisitively. 'There's . . . something . . . isn't there? . . . between you and him. I knew it back at the compound.'

Her voice was uncomfortable. 'It isn't sex, if that's what you think, Harry.'

'No? I didn't think you'd been in his arms, so to speak. Of course not. But there's rather more to sex than half-an-hour's bashing about under the sheets. As I hope you're beginning to discover.'

Briefly the old chill returned between them. Liliane cut through it, putting her hand on his arm.

'We don't need to quarrel, Harry. Perhaps . . . perhaps each of us has something to learn. And you're right about the Esau. There is something, but I don't know what it is. When it comes, it frightens me. It's as though we had one mind. I

189

suppose it *is* sex, in a way. A sort of unity . . . for those moments I can't think about anything but him.'

'It's not easy, being a woman, is it?'

She smiled. 'What do you know about it?'

'I've watched you. And I've—'

She interrupted him before he could continue. 'This isn't the time or the place, Harry. There are decisions to be made. Let's get on with them.'

Again he stared through the binoculars at the opposite slopes. There were several flickers of movement now, and once a group of green-clad figures crossed a small gully, out in the open for a second or two, moving east. Harry put down the binoculars.

'I think they've still got contact with him, over there. They're following the same line of country. So either our set's not working properly, or we're in a bad reception area, and they're in a good one. But they're definitely going on. It gives us a chance, but a risky one.'

'You mean we can follow them . . . let them lead us to the Esau?'

'Exactly. But remember . . . they're trained soldiers. They'll have a rearguard, and there are far more of them than of us. And, of course, even if they lead us to the Esau, it's difficult to see how we could help him against so many.'

'We'll decide that when the time comes. We must follow them, Harry. We must.'

'Right . . . but not all of us. It will have to be just you and me. Chowdhuri can't go on, and he can't go back alone. So Tom will have to take him. I'll take the set—it's easy to operate —I've watched Tom often enough. But I doubt it will be much more use to us. We must be getting pretty near the Esau's destination.'

The Prime Minister regarded Richard Kimbell thoughtfully, where he sat in the opposite armchair in the cool, shadowed room in York Road. A glistening sunbird, purple in its male breeding plumage, flashing golden tufts of feathers beneath its wings, flew in and out of the tree on the lawn, busily nesting. What did we call it when I was a child? she thought, her mind skidding away at a tangent for a moment. *Shakarkhora*, that was it. The sunbird seized a spider and disappeared into the foliage. The Prime Minister turned back to Kimbell. He looked older, greyer, slightly more defeated than when she had last spoken to him, several months ago. He was not a young man, of course—and by Indian standards he was old. Yet somehow one expected a little more energy, a little more cutting edge, from western men . . .

'So you have no idea where they are now?' she asked again. He spread his hands.

'Well, they must be somewhere within a certain radius in the Great Himalaya. There's a limit to the distance they could have gone on those ponies in the time available. But, as you know better than I, the Himalaya is chaotic country. Even a force of helicopters would be lucky to spot them.'

Her hands moved impatiently, but her voice remained even and unexcited. 'There will be no force of helicopters, Dr Kimbell. The area in which they are . . . well, wandering . . . is the truce line, the demilitarised zone, and beyond it Pakistan-controlled territory. I do not want a major incident with Pakistan over this relatively trivial matter.'

Kimbell was surprised. 'Trivial? I should not have thought so. There's much prestige involved. And the issues, scientifically speaking, are also important.'

'Have you ever walked in the streets of Calcutta at dawn, Dr Kimbell?'

'No.'

'That is the time when they clear away those who have died there during the night . . . of hunger, disease, deprivation. That is what we call an important issue, here in India. I should take such a walk, if you get the opportunity. It will help to clear your mind.'

He did not answer, feeling helpless. After a small silence, she spoke again. 'It was an impulsive decision by Dr Erckmann, wasn't it? Did it take you by surprise?'

'Given the circumstances, Prime Minister, any decision taken could only be impulsive. She had only minutes—literally minutes—in which to make up her mind.'

She nodded, waiting, but he did not go on. There was something, she thought, that he did not want to talk about. She tried again.

'As you know, they were a party of four when they started, of course.'

'Were?' he said quickly.

'Yes. I have information this morning that an army patrol met Dr Chowdhuri and Dr Meachem riding back down into the Vale of Kashmir. Apparently Dr Chowdhuri was badly affected by altitude. The Army took him to hospital in Srinagar.'

'I'm sorry to hear that Prakash is ill,' said Kimbell. The courtesy sounded a trifle mechanical, she thought.

'We shall know more once Dr Meachem has been asked some questions,' said the Prime Minister. 'Though he's already said one or two interesting things.'

'Did . . . did Liliane go on, then?'

'Not alone. She had Colonel Kernow with her.'

'Ah, yes . . . of course. They would go on together. Obviously, they would do that. Obviously.'

So that was it. Poor, unhappy man. But surely, he didn't imagine that a woman like Erckmann would . . . Desire deceives us all, she thought. There is no arithmetic for what happens in our loins. And perhaps there was something between Erckmann and Kimbell . . . once. Erckmann had always seemed cold, or at least unaroused. And some cold women would give themselves easily, to someone they liked and respected.

'Colonel Kernow knows the country,' she said.

'None better.'

'So we must hope that they stay out of trouble. And that they stay on this side of the border. Because I cannot help them if they stray too far north. It was not a good decision, by Dr Erckmann, though I am beginning to see how it was made. The intention was good, but I fear that the result may be bad. However, we shall see. Meanwhile, I have a small political crisis on my hands here in Delhi.'

He was astonished that she should take him so far into her confidence. She saw his surprise and laughed, sounding genuinely amused.

'I would not normally trouble you with our political trivia, Dr Kimbell, but I think you should know that Amrit Singh handed in his portfolio this morning.'

'Resigned?' he said stupidly.

Her shoulders lifted. 'That's one word for it, I suppose. He's under house arrest at the moment. While we make certain inquiries.'

Kimbell still remembered the swift cold purpose on her face long after he had left the room. When he had gone, the Prime Minister drew aside a small curtain covering a recess in the wall. The small carved stone figure of a god stood there . . . Siva the four-handed, the Destroyer, the Terrible. In one hand he held a noose to bind his enemies, and at this the Prime Minister gazed for a long time.

20

Harry and Liliane were lost once more. It was now more than six hours since Meachem and Chowdhuri had left them. The American had grumbled briefly when asked to turn back, but one look at Chowdhuri's grey, pinched face was enough to convince him. They had taken the receiver-set with them, after Tom discovered that the reason they heard no more bleeps from the Esau was because the tuning dial had become detached from its whorled column. There was no way of repairing it without a workshop, and the receiver was now simply dead-weight.

For as long as they could, Liliane and Harry followed the Pakistani soldiers. This had proved, in the end, to be impossibly difficult. The soldiers, trained and agile hillmen, moved more quickly on their feet than Harry and Liliane could manage even with the ponies. The need to stay far behind them, out of sight, meant that frequently they lost the soldiers altogether. This had happened for the last time more than two hours ago, and as Harry came back from the top of a ridge where he had been looking out for them, he shook his head.

'Not a sign. Or a sound. The trouble is, once we lose them in this kind of country, they could be anywhere. They're following an unpredictable creature, and we can't even guess at what route they might have taken.'

Liliane sat down beside her pony. Her limbs ached—another of the effects of altitude, she thought dully. There was a dull pain inside her skull that seemed to have been there all day. The warmth was going out of the late afternoon quite rapidly, and in a couple of hours it would be dark.

Harry looked at her, worried. 'It's no use, is it? We're not going to help . . . him . . . or ourselves by thrashing around here. We must go back—it's two days' ride to Shalamerg, maybe more. We've got one tin of beef between us—enough, but only just. I can lay a course with my compass that will certainly take us back into Indian Kashmir. I think we're probably in the demilitarised zone at the moment.'

She nodded. 'Do you think the soldiers will catch up with him?'

'Maybe. I don't think they'd stand a chance in hell if he wasn't hurt, but he's moving much more slowly than I'd imagined, and I think his wound is slowing him down.'

Her voice was flat. 'And when they catch him, they'll kill him.'

'I think they may. It will depend on Azraf Khan.'

'A damned savage.'

He shook his head. 'Not a savage, Liliane. Just a different kind of man. Perhaps he's a man the Esau would understand better than he was able to understand us.'

When night came, it was very cold. They had put up the little tent in the shelter of a jagged corrie, halfway down towards the thin line of the stream in the valley below. Half the tin of beef made their supper: the rest Harry wrapped carefully in a polythene bag. When they got lower he might well find a goat or a hare. But there was no certainty about that, and they would have to be careful. They huddled together, sleeping bags touching, taking comfort in each other's warmth. Liliane slept fitfully, never entirely unconscious. There were sounds all night long. Once some animal called, far down the valley . . . a high keening note which ceased abruptly as though cut off. Once she thought she heard a distant roar, not unlike the sound the Esau made. But she was half-asleep when the sound pierced into her consciousness, and it was not repeated. Perhaps an hour later there was a single distant crack. Harry sat upright instantly. Liliane pushed the hair from her eyes.

'What was it?'

He sank back into his bag after a few seconds. 'Could have been a rifle shot—it's hard to tell. Sound plays funny tricks up here. And it could have been a bit of the old glacier cracking. The surface begins to change in spring.'

They pushed on again, at dawn, working along the high rim of a saucer-shaped valley of which Harry had never previously heard. There was no sign of the soldiers or of the Esau. Nothing moved below them but fifty feet above their heads two big, dark-brown, crested birds soared in wide, sweeping circles.

'Serpent eagles,' Harry said, pointing upwards. 'That's a sign we're getting lower. I've never seen them much above nine thousand feet. They usually fly like that, in pairs.'

One of the eagles called, a thin whistling 'kek-kek-kek' sound, ominous, disturbing. They did not move either down or up the valley, but remained circling.

'Something's bothering them,' Harry said, shading his eyes.

Liliane turned to him sharply. 'Could it be the Esau?'

He shook his head. 'I don't think so. And I don't think it's Azraf Khan's little lot, either. Could be anything—a snow leopard, perhaps. But if it is a leopard, we shan't see it. They keep out of the way of human beings.'

At noon they rested the ponies. Both Liliane and Harry were hungry, but they contented themselves with hot tea. They would eat the remaining tinned meat that night, after which there would be nothing unless Harry's rifle could be made to earn the weight of its carriage on the trip. Tomorrow, then, might be a day without anything to eat, but by its end, they would be in striking distance of Shalamerg or one of the tiny villages along the Lidar River to the east.

Harry took the rifle and moved off among the scattered stands of trees. At this height they were still not thick on the ground but straggled in groups of three or four . . . birch, pine, weedy-looking oaks, and even a single half-grown cedar, seeded by some natural accident from the valley floor. Liliane lay back on the thin, tufty grass and let the midday warmth soak into her. She felt tired, but not unduly so. Hunger was her chief concern, but the hot tea had helped to comfort her stomach. And perhaps Harry could find a squirrel. Or even one of those circling eagles. What would breast of eagle taste like, she wondered sleepily. God knows, I'm not as fussy as I was . . .

Dimly, in her sleep, she heard the ponies neigh. The animals had not been tethered, for they never strayed, but as she struggled awake she heard the thump of their hooves as they galloped down the trail. She sat up instantly. A new sound was coming from the thickets of azaleas and juniper below their halting place . . . a grunting snuffle, followed every few seconds by a sobbing whimper. Cautiously, she crept to a large boulder beside the trail and looked down to the tangled scrub of bushes a few feet below. With its back to her, reaching into the low trees and pulling off handfuls of buds, was the largest creature she had ever seen standing on two feet. It was a black bear, fully eight hundred pounds in weight, massively tall. It did not see her, continuing to eat and to whimper. Down its left shoulder and arm blood appeared at intervals, falling in sticky red patches round the great claws of the feet. As slowly as possible, she turned her head. There was no sign of Harry. He had the .300 hunting rifle, but the little anaesthetic air-gun they had used on the Esau lay beside his pack, about thirty feet away. And it was loaded. Harry always kept it loaded. Would it work on the bear? She did not know, and she had not the faintest intention of trying to find out, unless she had to. But she would feel safer with it in her hand. Quietly, she slid down behind the boulder. There was only the faintest whisper of a sound, but the bear looked up, turning the great pointed head with its cruel teeth towards her.

She gasped. The face was like a map of hell. A dreadful wound had destroyed the left side of the head. One eye was hanging low on the cheek, and from the red socket and the torn flesh beside it, blood was dripping, though part of the injury was already congealed. The bear saw her and gave a shrieking, high-pitched roar. In the same second it charged.

Despairingly, she flung herself towards the little rifle, but the great bear moved faster. As it came up behind her it dealt her a blow on the right shoulder which sent her staggering to her knees. She was halfway to her feet again when the bear seized her at the waist. Her face was squeezed into the matted blood on the chest: the heavy fur and the rank smell stifled her. Her consciousness was going fast.

Then there was light again and air as the bear dropped her, and roared and screamed where it stood, facing the trees. Her eyes were still masked in the injured animal's blood, but as she scraped the mess from her face she saw the Esau. He stood a few feet from the bear, circling like a wrestler. The bear roared again, and cuffed towards him. The Esau swayed backwards, a fraction of a second too late, and the very tip of the bear's claw ripped a line of flesh from his shoulder. And the whole of the Esau's right side already seemed to be a matted scab of dried blood. Now he moved in quickly, and his hand shot out to the bear's injured eye. With a terrible scream the great animal turned away, dropped to all fours, and lumbered down the slope, half-running, half-sliding in a shower of dust and stones.

The feeling was coming back into Liliane's numbed shoulder. It hurt badly. Again she cleared the bear's blood from her eyes. The Esau stood ten yards away, watching her. He was slightly stooped, breathing heavily, and new blood was oozing through the dark-red, gluey tangle round his ribs. Again, as at the compound, she felt the sense of oneness with him. Stiffly, she hobbled towards him.

'Liliane, Liliane . . . where are you?'

Harry ran down into the little clearing, the rifle cradled in his arms. The Esau turned, dropped down the slope, and vanished.

'God, your face. Here . . . let me . . .'

She pushed him away. 'It's nothing. There was a bear, a wounded bear. It charged at me. It's not my blood—it's the bear's. But it hit me. It hit me.'

'Let me see.' His fingers explored her arm. Gently he flexed the muscles, bent the elbow.

'It's not broken, thank God. But it will be damned stiff in a couple of hours. Do you think you can ride?'

She laughed a little shrilly. 'If you can find the ponies. They bolted when the bear came.'

Harry went to the boulder above the trail, looking out carefully. At last he came back, his face troubled. 'Not a sign of either of them. You say the bear was wounded? That's why it charged, of course.'

'It was terribly wounded.' She shuddered. 'Its eye was nearly torn out. And the Esau—he was hurt, too. But he saved me, Harry. I thought I was dead.'

'He must have doubled back, to shake off Azraf Khan. Thank God he did. But . . . you say he rescued you. Did he mean to? Or was he just fighting a bear?'

'I think he meant to.' But did he? she thought. Yes, of course. I felt it again . . . that feeling with him. Until Harry came. Oh, God, why did Harry come just then?

Harry spoke again, looking at her curiously. 'Well, you may be right. I wonder what wounded the bear, though? Perhaps the Esau fought it earlier, and was simply following up for the kill.'

She did not answer. Harry went over to where the Esau had been standing.

'Two kinds of blood here. Look . . . this . . . quite fresh. New blood. And this, much more gooey, darker. That's the blood from the old wound, the one he got outside Shalamerg. The other's something else.'

'The bear clawed him, just once,' she said dully. 'I saw the skin come away.'

Harry dropped to his hands and knees. After a few seconds he looked up at her. 'It doesn't look good for him, Liliane. He's losing an awful lot of blood. Just look at this. Any man—any ordinary man, that is,' he said hastily, looking at her stony expression, 'would be on the way out by now, without a massive transfusion. He's immensely strong, but even his strength must have its limits.'

'He'd have killed the bear,' she said, 'if he'd been himself. He'd have killed it.'

Though her voice was flat, there was a strange note of suppressed pride behind it. She stood there, holding her shoulder, her face still smeared with the blood of the bear. There was blood in her hair, and on her hands. The thought flashed into his mind that she looked like a Stone Age woman.

'Probably you're right,' he said. 'But that's something we'll never know. Well . . . now we have to find the ponies.'

Two hours later even this hope disappeared. The ponies could not be seen from any vantage point along the rim of the high ground, and reluctantly Harry concluded that they had gone so far down into the saucer-valley that it was unlikely that they were any longer within walking range. The tent and camp equipment were still on the ponies' backs, but luckily both Liliane and Harry had unloaded their own packs to give the ponies easier grazing. The two packs, each wrapped in a sleeping bag, were now all they had, and Harry knew that it was not practicable to return to Shalamerg on foot, unless they could get food, and enough rest to allow Liliane's shoulder to become less stiff. They had to find a human dwelling, and for that they must go down into the valley. The valley was not marked on the map, but, Harry thought, that was not very surprising. There were hundreds of square miles in this region that had never been surveyed, mainly because they were broken, useless, surpemely wild country which was not worth the labour. There might well be a shepherd's hut down there, or at least tents of wandering *gujar* herdsmen. And, in any case, the lower they descended, the more chance there was of finding food.

Huddled in a sheltering outcrop of boulders they spent the night lying together for warmth, their sleeping bags tied one to another so that they could not roll apart. Even so it was cold, very cold. They had eaten the last of the tinned meat—a few ounces each—with some biscuit, and only a piece of biscuit each remained for next day. Harry was not unduly worried —at a pinch he could hope to shoot an eagle, and as they got lower there were certain to be birds. The single-shot .300 rifle was unsuitable for the purpose, but he had no shotgun, and he was sure that he was a good enough shot to pick off a big bird, even if it was flying. The birds here were unwary of man . . . quite often they circled slowly only a score or so feet above the ground. The problem, he thought ruefully, wouldn't be killing the bird, but retrieving it, if its body dropped deep into the valley. He drifted into an uneasy doze, while beside him Liliane breathed evenly, deeply asleep, except for a moment or two when she rolled on to her bruised shoulder and, half-waking, grumbled for a second or two at the pain. It was still dark, and the short grass was dusted with a ghostly film of frost, when Harry opened his eyes and heard the voice above him.

'A very touching sight, Colonel Kernow. Like one of your English stories . . . the babes in the wood, eh? The babes in the wood, ha-ha.'

Harry squinted upwards. Above him, outlined against the faintly paling sky, stood Azraf Khan.

21

'He seems a perfectly civilised man,' Liliane said, looking over to where Azraf Khan was standing, a short, erect figure in camouflage jacket and brown beret. He was talking to a young junior officer, and his hands were sketching quick, explanatory gestures, emphasising his words. His body was thrust slightly forward, as though he was impatient to move.

'Well, he serves a good breakfast, anyway,' Harry said, noncommittally. Their stomachs were comfortably full of hot curried lamb from the infantry stewpot, now being packed up ready to move. This was a tight, efficient little force—thirty riflemen and two junior officers, apart from Azraf Khan himself and the major who was his second-in-command. Four officers for such a small body of men . . . it was obvious that Azraf Khan was taking his mission very, very seriously. One of the unit's three mules was being brought up the track, and the stewpot was now loaded on to it, quietly, efficiently. The other mules waited below . . . one was loaded with tents and groundsheets, the other with a tarpaulin-covered burden that might well be bridging equipment. Azraf Khan walked over to them and spoke to Liliane.

'Your Tarzan is moving again, Mademoiselle Erckmann.'

She shaded her eyes, looking up at him against the brightness of the sky.

'Why do you call him that?'

'Oh, I remember the films when I was a boy. Even in my village, we knew of Tarzan. He leaps, he bounds, he swoops, he saves the heroine from the tiger. Or the bear.'

His smile showed a gleam of white teeth below the black moustache. A funny little man, she thought, but really quite attractive. He had a curious style of spoken English—like a British Army officer straight from the old Raj.

'I don't think he's anything like Tarzan, Colonel. Quite different . . . not a man in the sense that Tarzan was a man.'

He shrugged. 'We agree on that. I think he's like your bear . . . a dangerous beast. You say the bear was wounded? I think one of my chaps may have done that. One of the picket-sentries got a shot off at a bear when it came grubbing round an outpost last night. Probably the same bear—my chaps don't often miss. They're both dangerous beasts—the bear and the ape-man. And dangerous beasts must be checked. Made powerless.'

Her voice was sharp. 'But how?'

'Oh, we shall see. We have to wait to find how the cookie crumbles, as the Americans say. I don't believe in rigid planning. A soldier must learn to seize the moment, eh, Kernow?'

'That's what they teach us,' said Harry drily. 'The problem is identifying the moment.'

'You will come with us, of course,' said Azraf Khan. His tone was perfectly polite, but there was no mistaking the steel behind it. Nevertheless, Harry decided to try.

'If you could give us a little food, we can go back down to Shalamerg. We shall manage well.'

The colonel laughed. 'No doubt, no doubt. But you are no longer in India, Kernow. You are in our territory. A natural mistake, of course. This is confusing country, even for those who are born in it. There will be no real difficulty, I will see to that—but there are formalities. So I shall be glad to keep you with us while we complete this operation. It will be a pleasure . . . and, forgive me, Kernow . . . it will be an especial pleasure to have the company of Mademoiselle Erckmann. If the beast is indeed Tarzan, then it—or he?—could hardly have discovered a more attractive Jane.'

He walked jauntily away. In spite of herself she felt a little stab of pleasure at the compliment. There really was something about Azraf Khan . . .

'He's taking no chances,' Harry said.

'What do you mean?'

Harry rose to his feet, brushing biscuit-crumbs from his bush-shirt. 'He doesn't really want us with him. No soldier wants to tote a couple of civilians along on an operation—from his point of view, we're a damned nuisance. In ordinary circumstances, he'd probably just show us exactly where we'd gone wrong, on the map, point us in the right direction, and wave goodbye. But, as I say, he's not risking it. He thinks we'd head the Esau away from him if we got the chance while we were alone—and, of course, he's right. So he'll keep us where he can see what we're doing. And he may even have another idea at the back of his mind.'

'What idea?'

Harry's voice became quite expressionless.

'Well, he keeps joking about Tarzan and Jane. But, after all, we told him about how the Esau tackled the bear. Suppose Azraf Khan thinks it might happen again?'

She was derisive. 'What . . . another bear? Oh, really, Harry . . .'

'Of course I don't mean another bear. But has it occurred to you that if the Esau *is* keeping a watching Tarzan eye on you, he might feel he had to do something about your situation now?'

Liliane said nothing.

'So it seems to me,' Harry said, 'that Azraf Khan may think that if he's got the bait, he might as well set the trap . . .'

The Pakistani unit was made up of Pathan hillmen—small wiry soldiers who moved easily and naturally. Two dozen of them were in the forward party, sending scouts out ahead, following the information given out by the operator with the set, round whom Azraf Khan formed his moving headquarters. The remaining six men remained with the mules, also advancing, fully a half-mile to the rear. It was as neat a little operation of its kind as Harry had ever seen. Azraf Khan must have worked Hunza Rifles up to a very high peak.

Harry and Liliane were kept with the headquarters section, and at their two-hourly rests for water—and sometimes food —the colonel would sometimes come over to chat briefly with Harry about mutual acquaintances at Camberley or in the British Army. He was always affable and pleasant. To Liliane he said little, apart from polite small-talk, but he allowed her to see that his eyes rested on her with admiration. Occasionally the bespectacled second-in-command would join their little group. He was the only one of the soldiers who was not a hillman, and this set him slightly apart. He seemed watchful, saying little. When he did speak, he would look first towards Azraf Khan as though gauging any remark against the colonel's possible reaction. Harry noticed, too, that there was a marginal but perceptible difference in the way the second-in-command was treated by the rest of the unit. Azraf Khan was unquestioned, total authority . . . so easy a dominance that his men almost anticipated his orders. For the subordinate major, it was different. He seemed to have to explain more, and his instructions, sometimes, were obeyed with the slightest of hesitations. Occasionally a soldier or even one of the two junior officers would glance towards Azraf Khan as though seeking a confirmatory nod. If I were the second-in-command, Harry thought, I'd be thinking of arranging myself a transfer.

And yet the general atmosphere in the unit seemed relaxed, almost easy. At the regular halts men squatted on the ground, playing complicated games of pebble-tossing on the palms and backs of their hands. There was much quiet laughter, genuine enjoyment. If a man achieved some unusual feat in these contests, it would be followed by flashing grins in the dark, cruel faces, and then by a round of polite clapping. Clapping, not cheering, was their tribute—the deliberate underplay of men completely confident in their own masculine ethos.

Walking beside Harry, Liliane felt better than for the past three days. The warm food had revived her, and though her shoulder was still stiff from the bear's blow, Azraf Khan had given orders that both her pack and Harry's must be carried on the mules. The old injury to Harry's leg had troubled him a little since the ponies had bolted, but he limped along at a brisk enough pace, and she herself had no trouble in keeping up with the rest of the party. She worried about the Esau, but she knew she must accept that for the moment, at least, the matter was out of her hands. And she would be present at the final outcome, and could give advice and help when they captured him—which they certainly seemed likely to do. The operator with the set was now reporting that Esau was travelling more and more slowly, possibly no more than three-quarters of a mile ahead. Yet there was no touch of him on her mind, no awareness that he was near. Perhaps he was dying . . . perhaps he no longer thought of her. Perhaps, now, his thought must be only for himself.

During the course of the long day they climbed over a giant inverted geological bowl of mountain, measured at 12,000 feet by Harry's pocket altimeter. It was country with which even the Pathan soldiers were unfamiliar, and they chattered among themselves as they wound in slow single file along makeshift paths. Ahead lay a triangle of peaks towering in the afternoon sky. The ground sloped down towards them, a jumbled, jagged detritus of the birth of mountains aeons ago, with a deep, dark ravine on one side and a rising slope of old, crusted snow on the other. The day had been warm, but the chill of the coming evening was already upon them, cooling the sweat on their cheeks.

One of the Pathans came running back down the path and spoke rapidly to Azraf Khan. He grunted a reply, and began to follow the man back up the path. Then he turned towards them, speaking to Harry, but looking at Liliane.

'Perhaps you would like to see? They have sighted him, about six hundred yards ahead. But you will have to hurry.'

Harry grimaced. 'I'm sorry—I think I'll follow you up as best as I can. This damned leg stiffens up a bit at the end of the day. You go on ahead.'

Azraf Khan trotted up the path, with Liliane beside him. They passed a line of infantrymen, each in position among the scattered boulders, waiting to move on. As they came up to a small crest Liliane saw the second-in-command with two of the Pathan scouts. He came forward and said something unintelligible to Azraf Khan. The colonel unbuttoned his binocular-case and put the glasses to his eyes. After a little, he nodded, and beckoned to Liliane.

'You see . . . there? To the right of that outcrop of yellow rocks, perhaps eight hundred yards away.'

It took her several seconds to focus the binoculars on to the Esau, but then she saw him clearly. He was several hundred feet below them, moving slowly across a small bare plateau towards the yellow rocks. To his left rose the dark wall of the ravine. Once he stopped and stared straight back towards her, almost as though he could see her as clearly as she saw him. His face leapt into the powerful glasses, but he turned away and began to move again just as she picked him up. Azraf Khan rubbed his hands with satisfaction.

'We have him, I think. But we must get him before it is dark.'

He talked quickly to the two junior officers, who nodded

and ran back down the path. A few moments later a file of a dozen soldiers began to snake down towards the near-edge of the ravine.

'A simple outflanking movement . . . basic battle drill,' Harry's voice said behind Liliane. She turned, surprised. She had not heard him come up, but Azraf Khan nodded and spoke without taking the binoculars from his eyes.

'Yes. Simple tactics are always best. I don't imagine an ape-man is going to defeat the infantry manual—especially one that has only a little time to live.'

At once Liliane was chill with fear. 'What do you mean? You aren't going to kill him?'

Azraf Khan turned his face up to her as she stood above him. He scrambled, smiling, to his feet. 'If I do, mademoiselle, it will rob him of no more than an hour or so. Look at him.'

Again he passed her the binoculars. The Esau was in sight again, still travelling away from them, but slowly. Sometimes he staggered, sometimes stopped completely. There was a shining red patch at his side. One of the Pathan scouts worked the bolt of his rifle and moved into the aiming position, steadying the butt where he lay between two rocks. Gently his fingers slid the range-band to 700. Then he glanced up at Azraf Khan, but the colonel shook his head, speaking sharply in a dialect Harry did not know. The scout relaxed, laying his rifle on the rocks. When Azraf Khan spoke again, his voice had changed. His face was pinched, remote.

'You have a saying in the West,' he said. ' "Justice must always be seen to be done." That is what I am going to do now. That . . . that creature . . . killed one of my men. In the hills a death must be paid for. But with a rifle, at such a range, even the best shot might miss. We will make certain. Your friend's Tarzan days are over.'

In impotent, sick despair, she swung towards him, but he was already walking away, and Harry put his hand on her shoulder.

'It's no use,' he said. 'He won't listen now. He can't change his mind, in front of his men.'

'He's a barbarian. He'll pay for this.' There was a sob in her voice.

'He won't,' Harry said. 'He's acting within what he believes

206

to be his rights. Not everybody on this planet thinks as you do. Or as I do, for that matter.'

Harry had picked up Azraf Khan's binoculars, and now he passed them to her.

'He's gone down among those rocks. Look . . .'

Down below them the little file of infantry were distant dots, unmoving. They seemed to be lying down, about three hundred yards out to the flank of the yellow boulders where the Esau had disappeared. Behind them four men brought the mules up, and began to unload the tarpaulin-covered packages from their backs. As soon as he saw the dull green metal, the stout tripod legs, the squat stubby tube, Harry understood.

'What are they going to do?' Liliane whispered. Her whole being seemed filled with a dull ache. Everything had moved now into an unfamiliar world, where she was a stranger, an unwilling spectator, uncomprehending and not consulted.

'That's a three-inch mortar,' said Harry. 'Old-fashioned, but it works. And over much longer ranges than this.'

'Yes?'

He cleared his throat. 'Well, they'll lob a couple of mortar bombs into those boulders, I imagine. I don't think that . . . he . . . will have much chance of surviving that. And even if he does, and he runs out of the rocks . . . well, look. The riflemen are waiting.'

The Pathans took their time setting up the mortar, laughing and joking amongst themselves. Four pairs of binoculars were trained on the yellow boulders, making certain that the holed-up Esau did not move, though Harry thought privately that, judging from the Esau's condition as last seen, he might already be dead. How could any living creature lose so much blood and continue to make such enormous effort?

At last the mortar was ready, standing on the pebbly ground like a squat metal insect. A Pathan knelt beside it, adjusting the trigger, angling the barrel into his estimate of the range. One of the junior officers nodded. The mortar crew stepped back, the man beside the barrel slid the finned bomb into its muzzle, and there was a sharp thudding crack. For a fraction of a second Harry saw the black speck of the bomb as it hurtled away from them on its long slow parabola into the sky. Seconds ticked by and then, a hundred yards to the right of the boulders, a great brown cloud of dust and stones erupted noiselessly. After a moment or two came the crumping roar of the distant explosion, followed by a slight vibration in the ground beneath them.

'They missed,' Liliane said. Harry shook his head.

'Just a ranging shot. They fired it on the far side to make sure they didn't put it short, among their own infantry. The second one will . . . there it goes . . .'

A thud, and once more, infinitesimally, the black dot in the air. The very centre of the yellow boulders towered in smoke and flame. Again, and then a fourth time the mortar fired. By now the cloud around the boulders was impenetrable to the eye, and fully a minute passed before they could distinguish details again. There was no movement from inside the rocky area where they had last seen the Esau. Azraf Khan grinned at his second-in-command, and spoke into his radio headset. The Pathans again laughed amongst themselves, happy and relaxed. Below them the waiting riflemen were already moving into the rocks, moving like small green bugs amongst the pulverised basalt, searching. In the binoculars Harry saw one of them talking quickly into the radio. Beside them Azraf Khan listened, his face puzzled. Liliane watched him, hope rising. At last he spoke to them.

'Well, there's something very peculiar about your Tarzan, Dr Erckmann. He isn't there. Unless we've blown him to bits, eh, Kernow?'

'There'd be something there,' Harry said. Azraf Khan nodded, and spoke sharply to the second-in-command, who shouted to where the headquarters party waited below. There was an answering yell.

'And he's still transmitting,' Azraf Khan said slowly. 'Of course, that collar would transmit even if he's dead. But, no, I agree, Kernow. It doesn't seem that we've blown him to bits.'

He walked to the edge of the little escarpment where they stood. 'Now I wonder just how—'

From below them came a terrible scream. There was a chorus of shouts, a shot, then a ragged rattle of rifle fire. Azraf Khan spun on his heels. 'What . . .?'

For as long as she lived, Liliane was never able to erase the next few seconds from her mind. Something came up over the lip of the ridge behind them, something dark, bulky, moving fast . . . the Esau. His mouth was open, his eyes wild. In one hand he held the head of a soldier, swinging by the long dark hair. Desperately, Azraf Khan fumbled to unbutton his pistol holster, but he stood no chance. The Esau struck him in the same second, towering above him. Azraf Khan was grasped by the waist, whirled above the Esau's head, and then cast out, out, out from the escarpment, turning silently over and over until he hit the rocks eighty feet below, bounced once, slithered in a cloud of dust, and lay still. The Esau was clambering with amazing speed down under the overhang of the escarpment. The Pathans nearest to Harry and Liliane shrank back from the edge, crying shrilly to each other in high-pitched voices. Only the second-in-command took any action, leaning over the escarpment and firing his pistol, vainly but determinedly, trying to get a sight of the vanished Esau. The bullets whined away, ricocheting off rocks far below them. At last the firing stopped and, almost fearfully, the infantrymen went down to get Azraf Khan's body.

Ten yards ahead of Liliane the corpse of Azraf Khan, shrouded now in a broad tarpaulin, swayed on the back of its plodding mule. Her eyes smarted with the greyish dust of the small area of flattish ground, perhaps half a mile wide, which lay between them and the yellow rocks which the mortar had bombarded . . . oh, it seemed a lifetime ago, though no more than an hour had passed. Everything had changed. The whole mood of the little Pathan infantry unit was transformed. There was no more of the easy laughter, the relaxed discipline, the high tuneless singing that had marked the earlier pursuit. The Pathans around them seemed half-fearful, half-vengeful. The scouts ahead reported constantly, and the second-in-command—now in sole charge—moved with uneasy energy up and down the moving line, questioning, demanding, handing out orders. Looking at them, Harry felt a quiver of doubt. The Pathans were in a curious mood, and their attitude to Liliane and to himself was different. They were now made to move in the dust at the rear of the column, and a couple of Pathans had been ordered to guard them.

'But how in Heaven did he do it?' Liliane asked again. 'We

saw him down there, among those rocks. And a few minutes later he's up amongst us . . . killing.'

'He came round the long way, on the blind side of the crests we could see. We used to have a saying in the Army: "Sweat saves blood. And brain saves sweat." I reckon it must be the Esau's motto. And it means either that he was deliberately deceiving us about the extent of his wound—or that from somewhere he got immense reserves of strength. Because he must have run very fast. But even accepting that . . . there's another very odd thing.'

'What?' said Liliane dully.

'When he got to us, he killed an outpost sentry on his way up. He'd have to do that to get past him, of course. But then he came right through us and killed the man who really mattered . . . the commanding officer. How did he know Azraf Khan was in command? He was wearing combat fatigues like the rest of them—and I can't believe the Esau can recognise a colonel's rank badges.'

Liliane coughed, and spat out rough grains of dust before she spoke.

'I think he's always . . . grasped . . . more than we realised, more than he wanted us to know. Somehow he can get inside your mind, just for a little. He didn't know Azraf Khan was a colonel, of course . . . in any case, he doesn't know what a colonel is. But he did know that Azraf Khan was the one who was organising things against him—that he was the one to kill.'

The yellow rocks were scarred and chipped by mortar fire, and flakes of stone lay all around. There was no blood: no physical evidence that the Esau had been there. Across the ravine to their front more yellow rocks were piled in haphazard heaps . . . witnesses to the slow passing of a glacier thousands of years before. Somewhere down in that ravine was the Esau, hiding. Harry and Liliane knew it, and the bespectacled second-in-command and all his men knew it also. They unpacked the mortar from its mule and set it up among the rocks. Intently, the second-in-command began to quarter the ravine through his binoculars. No binoculars were offered to Harry or Liliane. Harry wandered aimlessly around the area, watched keenly by the two soldiers set to guard him.

Liliane sat at the edge of the rocks, staring out towards the ravine, silent.

It was by the sheerest chance that Harry saw the skulls. He was examining, with a mild professional interest, the point of impact and the beaten zone of one of the mortar shells when he saw the first piece of bone lying in the dust. Wondering, he picked it up. It was about four inches of a jawbone, with some of the teeth still in place. Around it were dozens of pieces of bone—far too many to have belonged to a single skull. Quietly, he went over to Liliane.

'Come and look at this—but don't show too much interest. It might get our friend there excited.'

Together they walked over to the bones. Liliane picked up the largest—the vault of a cranium. It looked old, very old . . . not unlike one of the craniums from Shalamerg. She turned it over in her hands, and then dropped to her knees, looking at the other fragments. Her mind registered almost automatically that at least four skulls had been grouped together before the mortar bomb reduced them to fragments. Something tugged at her brain, but she felt astonishingly uninterested in the discovery. The Pathan soldier had walked over, holding out a hand in demand. She passed the piece of jawbone to him. He looked it over uncomprehendingly, and then threw it back on the ground contemptuously. Harry picked it up and put it in his pocket.

'What do you think?'

'Another group of skulls,' she said wearily. 'Rather like Shalamerg, but more of them. Badly smashed now, of course —it would be hard to reassemble them. And the age . . . anybody's guess. They obviously mean something to the Esau, perhaps that's why he came here today. But we knew already that skulls have some significance. I don't think this —what's happening?'

There was a chorus of excited shouts from the Pathans at the edge of the rocks. They were peering intently across the ravine.

'They must have sighted him,' Harry said. 'No—they haven't. God, look at that.'

On a ledge about a quarter of the way down the far wall of the ravine several dots, just distinguishable as human figures, had appeared. It was impossible to see from where they had emerged, but the rockface opposite was seamed by gullies and honeycombed with caves. The infantry sergeant beside Harry was staring through binoculars. Sharply, Harry tapped him on the shoulder and held out his hand. Almost without thinking the sergeant gave them to him. He looked through them for a long quarter-minute and then, his face expressionless, passed them to Liliane. The group of dots leapt into the lens, but now she could see what they were. They were a group of Esaus —nine, no . . . ten . . . eleven . . . Several were males, who looked so exactly like the Esau they knew that they might have been clones of the same individual. At least three were young, perhaps no more than ten years old. And two were clearly females, one carrying a baby. They stood in a group looking downward, and then two of the young males began to clamber lower into the ravine. And below them the Esau —their own Shalamerg Esau—came into sight, climbing painfully upwards. He was no more than fifty feet below the larger group, and now the two males had reached him, helping.

The Pathans beside Harry and Liliane exploded into a series of shrill cries and commands. Three ran to the mortar, while a fourth took three of the finned bombs from the green ammunition boxes stacked twenty yards behind it. The second-in-command had given no order yet, but the mortar was ready. Liliane pushed aside the sergeant's restraining hand and ran to the officer's side.

'No, no. You can't. Please, you can't. Don't do it—it will be a crime.'

For a few moments he turned his face towards her. Doubt struggled in his features, indecision, even a sort of compassion. But Harry's heart sank. The Pathans were watching the officer like hounds on a leash. Azraf Khan might be dead, but his tarpaulin-shrouded corpse still commanded all. It would need a bigger man than the second-in-command to decline to give the order to fire. Azraf Khan alone might have done it, but Azraf Khan would never give an order again. The major tore his eyes from Liliane's and nodded to the mortar crew. Liliane screamed.

The first bomb burst to the left of the main group of Esaus. Watching through the glasses, Harry saw one or two of them go down, lying motionless. The others, including the two females, began to scurry about. A great cloud of brown dust hid the three climbing Esaus. The mortar cracked again. The second bomb burst directly above the Esau group, and the whole face of the mountainside changed in a continuous titanic movement. The rock wall above the Esaus began to collapse, ponderously, as though in slow motion. From where they watched the first moments were silent, but then the delayed sound reached them in a dull unceasing roar. The whole Esau area plunged into the gulf, passing straight through the climbing trio, thundering down to the valley floor, thousands of feet below. Harry thought he saw an Esau whirling over and over at the edge of the dust cloud, but he could not be sure. The Pathan sergeant turned to them, grinning.

'It is finished,' he said. 'No more ape-man.'

Liliane sank to her knees as though she would never stand again. Across the ravine the dust was slowly clearing, but the whole mountainside was completely changed. Nothing remained of the rockface where the Esaus had stood, where they had, presumably, lived. From far below the sound of its fall still grumbled and muttered. Harry put his hand on Liliane's shoulder, and painfully she struggled to her feet. Her face was a mask of despair. She spoke to the sergeant, and not to Harry.

'You're right, it's over. Everything is over. A million years are over.'

Unheeding, the sergeant turned away. A burst of excited chatter swept through the surrounding Pathans . . . laughter, back-slapping. They formed around the mortar-crew, and quietly at first, but more and more vigorously, began to clap their hands.

MEMORANDUM

From Dr Liliane Erckmann and Dr Richard Kimbell, Srinagar, State of Jammu and Kashmir (Indian Zone).

To Director-General, United Nations Educational, Scientific and Cultural Organisation, Paris, France.

Subject Provisional Conclusions on the Destruction of *Homo kashmiriensis (chowdhuri)*.

ONE: We regret to inform you that following unofficial military action on the truce line (reference JG 584 OD 522 on the attached map) the specimen of *Homo kashmiriensis* (popularly known as the Esau) released in the Great Himalaya by agreement with the Government of India is now dead.

TWO: In addition, what appears to be the sole remaining community in the Himalaya of this *Homo* species was also totally destroyed. Unofficial reports from Pakistan suggest that the physical evidence reveals that the community consisted of approximately thirty individuals. Nineteen positive reconstructions of individuals have been made. Scientists from Islamabad are now reported to be examinining this physical evidence, but no report has yet been issued.

THREE: This is an irreparable loss, since even so small a community was viable, and had apparently been so for many thousands of years. The mechanism by which this population survived would have been of surpassing interest and importance.

FOUR: On the basis of the examinations carried out in preceding months by specialists in various fields (and of which you have received a number of reports) we believe that the significance of *Homo kashmiriensis* can hardly be over-emphasised.

FIVE: In imaginative terms, this might be compared to the first pictures of the Earth from the moon, which dramatically revealed to mankind the fragility of our position in space.

SIX: The discovery of *Homo kashmiriensis* is already—though slowly—changing not only our view of human evolution but also our estimate of the place of ourselves in the universe. It could be compared with the gradual realisation, in the nineteenth and twentieth centuries, of the exact significance of the evolutionary doctrines propounded by Charles Darwin.

SEVEN: It was shocking for nineteenth-century human beings to be told that they were kin to the apes. Throughout the subsequent history of palaeo-anthropolgy, the whole weight of our research has been to seek ever-older 'human' ancestors, as though by finding older fossils we could in some way distance ourselves from the apes.

EIGHT: Such an attitude has carried with it the scientifically unspoken feeling that man is the pinnacle of creation . . . the 'reason' for the evolution of life on earth.

NINE: We now know that this is not so. Very recent studies with *Homo kashmiriensis* and before that with chimpanzees and gorillas combine to show us that our own line separated from the common ancestors of us all only about four million years ago.

TEN: We are brothers to apes, and twin-brothers to *Homo kashmiriensis*. We have already, in *kashmiriensis*, seen an alternative to us waiting in the wings. Typically, we have destroyed it.

ELEVEN: It is as though the dinosaurs of sixty-five million years ago— the most formidable creatures of their own time—had in some way realised what evolution could bring, and had therefore deliberately exterminated the rat-like primates which would one day develop into man. Yet such an extermination would not have saved the dinosaurs from vanishing for ever as a dominant life-form on this planet.

TWELVE: We are ourselves now in the position of such intelligent dinosaurs. We know that we are not evolution's last word. And we have two possible paths before us:

(a) Faced again with such a situation—and similar situations involving creatures can be found all over our planet—we can behave in the same destructive way. This will demonstrate that the evolutionary 'experiment' of human intelligence has failed and that like the dinosaurs we are doomed.

(b) Or we can try, slowly and with difficulty, to appreciate our responsibilities to a future which we cannot foresee—least of all our own part in it. Yet it is a future which even now we can do something to protect. In other words, we have a responsibility to life itself, as well as to what we imagine to be the short-term interests of our own species.

THIRTEEN: If there is to be such a hope as we have outlined in (b), it is first with organisations such as yours that the beginnings of effective action can lie . . .

22

'There's been no official comment at all from Islamabad,' said the Indian Foreign Minister, smoothing his chin. In the other armchair in the garden-room at York Road, the Prime Minister stirred impatiently.

'One would hardly expect the General to apologise for what is done within the territory under his control,' she said.

The Foreign Minister shrugged. 'Well, the map is none too clear at that point, but . . . yes, I concede that probably he was within his rights. If you can call it a matter of right to kill people.'

She smiled faintly. 'People, Krishna? That's what all the argument is about. I—we—think they were people. The General thinks they were some kind of ape. I doubt he intended to kill them, in any case. I think the matter was taken out of his hands.'

'International scientific opinion . . .' the Foreign Minister began, but the Prime Minister interrupted him.

'The General doesn't care a fig for international scientific opinion, Krishna. And nor would I, in his place. International science is in a poor position to lay blame for extinguishing lives, whether of men or animals. There was a furore, of course, but it will die down . . . is already dying down. Tomorrow there will be new problems, new scandals. You will see.'

'I agree. But perhaps we should make the General sweat a little. The truce line where all this happened—it could be redrawn somewhat to our advantage.'

'The extra battalion we sent is in position?'

'Yes.'

The Foreign Minister got out of his chair and walked to the big map spread across the desk. The Prime Minister joined him, looking down at the jumbled contours of the Great Himalaya.

'What a country to try to rule,' breathed the Foreign Minister. 'If any opposition really organised itself in Kashmir, how difficult we might find it.'

He glanced warily at the Prime Minister. Her mouth was set in familiar rat-trap lines.

'Exactly. You are right, Krishna. Let us make the General sweat. If we advance the truce line even half a mile here—' her finger stabbed at the map—'then, according to the Defence Ministry, we control the valley path. And that means we can oversee the movement of the Gilgit *gujars*. They'll be able to bring in fewer agents when we can do that . . .'

After the Foreign Minister had left, the Prime Minister stood looking unseeingly out at the green lawns where the glossy mynah birds hopped. What was Erckmann doing now? She hadn't seen Erckmann since the Esau debacle, but she had received a letter . . . anguished, perhaps, behind its scientific detachment. With the death of the Esau community, something had gone for ever, Erckmann said . . . something that could never come again. Well, I didn't do it, the Prime Minister thought, turning back to her desk. Though, if I'd been the General—or that dead Pathan colonel—who knows? I might have. Erckmann was upset, of course. That was understandable. She'd been very closely identified with the whole project. Yet was there something more? Sometimes, talking to Erckmann about the Esau, the Prime Minister had sensed a secret behind the woman scientist's eyes. Desire? Surely not. Identification? Perhaps. Again the first word thrust itself insistently into her mind. Desire? Well, it could take curious forms, work in strange ways. But . . . we shan't ever know. Perhaps Erckmann herself doesn't know. And as for me . . . mechanically she put on her reading spectacles, and opened the topmost Government-green folder on her desk . . . as for me, what do I know about desire?

'So, in the end, we failed,' Chowdhuri said, plucking fretfully at the white sheet which covered him where he lay in his bunk in the big stern stateroom of the houseboat on the Nagim Lake. A kingfisher, blue and green, perched for a moment on the deck-rail beyond the open door. Liliane watched it for several seconds before she answered Chowdhuri. God, how grey he still looked. Tom must have done wonders to get him back to Srinagar alive. Absently, she fingered her copy of the memorandum that had gone earlier in the day to the Director-General in Paris. There they were . . . thirteen paragraphs, for what they were worth. Thirteen . . . some people thought it an unlucky number. She shivered.

'Yes, we failed,' she said.

Harry was sitting in a canvas chair in the doorway, holding a small black book. That little involuntary shudder had not escaped him, and he spoke more to give Liliane a chance to recover than for any other reason.

'There were really very few of them,' he said slowly. 'Could they have survived, even if . . .?' His voice trailed away. The kingfisher came back to the rail, carrying a small green fish.

'I don't know, Harry. I think they might. Species have survived for centuries on a handful of individuals—there's a famous herd of primitive cattle in England, and the Arabian oryx, though both species have needed human help. Of course, the Esaus were intelligent beings—as intelligent as we are, in their way. They knew about themselves, just as we do. You remember the pieces of skull you found . . . in those rocks where . . .' She could not go on. He nodded.

'Well,' she said, 'the dating shows them to be roughly like the Shalamerg skulls. Some ancient, some modern. Somehow the Esaus knew where a few, at least, of the ancient skulls

218

could be found—an almost unbelievable feat of race memory. And then, for a reason we can only guess, they placed the modern skulls side by side with the old ones, as though they drew strength from it. Maybe it symbolised their access to their own past—a facility we've always assumed was open to man alone. Exactly how it worked for them we can't know. But it made him—our own Esau, the only one we ever had contact with—very formidable.'

'More formidable than we are, on his own ground,' Harry said. 'And that's not true of any other land animal.'

'He wasn't an animal,' she flashed angrily. 'He was like us.'

'I thought that was the whole point.' Harry's voice was deceptively mild. 'I thought we were all animals.'

Unexpectedly, from the bunk, Chowdhuri laughed. 'He has you there, Liliane.'

After a few seconds she smiled, but without real conviction. Lately she had looked a little beaten, more vulnerable than before. That wasn't hard to understand, Harry thought, but somehow it had made her even more sexually attractive. And she had needed something . . . physical satisfaction . . . comfort . . . reassurance . . . perhaps even friendship. Because for the past few days on the houseboat she had come to him night after night. Sometimes her lovemaking had been wild, painful: sometimes gentle and tender. Yet even when she was loving, it had been, he remembered suddenly, a loving courtesy, a sexual politeness, almost abstracted, as though her body was his but her mind was elsewhere. She still used him, though not as crudely as on the night they had first coupled—for that was the only word for it—on the houseboat. He was a man and she needed him. But she didn't need him as Harry Kernow, as a man she found unique. Not in the way he needed her.

There was a soft snore from the bunk. Chowdhuri was asleep. With a finger to her lips Liliane motioned to Harry to leave. They walked along the side of the boat and up the small companionway to the top deck. The lake glittered silver, and the kingfisher swallowed his fish, and dived again. The wind tugged at Liliane's shining hair, and instant desire made Harry's voice thick. He touched her bare arm.

'Tonight?'

She looked at him with a half-smile. 'Perhaps.'

'Tonight,' he said again.

'I expect so. But . . . Harry . . .'

'Yes?'

'It doesn't mean anything permanent, you know. I like you, Harry. I'm even very fond of you. But I can't tie myself to you, or you to me.'

'We could make a go of it, you and I.'

She turned away sharply. 'No. We couldn't. I don't think I will with any man.'

He felt a choking in his throat. 'Do you still think about him?'

'What do you mean? I don't want to talk about him.'

'You still do,' he said wearily. 'I don't blame you. He was a killer, I suppose, and he couldn't speak, and we thought he couldn't understand. But he understood you, didn't he?'

From across the lake came the thin high hoot of the midday bus. The kingfisher came back with another fish. She looked at Harry, at his tanned, battered face, his square shoulders, his look of dependability. Swiftly she put her hands on his shoulders and kissed him.

'Thank you, Harry. Thank you for that. I'll never forget you said it. Because until you did . . . well, I hadn't thought it even to myself. But it's true.'

He smiled, but there was pain in his face. 'So I *have* lost you, haven't I?'

She did not reply, and after a little he took from his pocket the black book he had brought from the stateroom. It was a Bible.

'I was reading the Esau story last night. Strange stuff . . . it seems to echo from a long way back. I marked the place. I thought it might comfort you.'

He turned and went down the companionway. He'd marked the section with an old sepia postcard of Srinagar. She took it out and looked at the page heading . . . Genesis, the story of how Jacob tricked his hairy twin Esau out of his birthright. She began to read.

'And Esau said unto his father, Hast thou but one blessing, my father? Bless me, even me also, O my father. And Esau lifted up his voice, and wept.

'And Isaac his father answered and said unto him,

Behold, thy dwelling shall be the fatness of the earth, and of the dew of heaven from above;

'And by thy sword shalt thou live, and shalt serve thy brother; and it shall come to pass when thou shalt have the dominion, that thou shalt break his yoke from off thy neck . . .'

She went over to the rail and looked out to the blue bulk of the mountain beyond the green fringe of the far lake shore. Soon she would be leaving Kashmir. Richard Kimbell and Tom Meachem were already in California. They were going to see Judy Agar. People said she was beginning to recover, though she was still under psychiatric care. And now there was Harry . . . what was she going to do about Harry? The Bible he had given her was still in her hand, her forefinger marking the Book of Genesis. 'Thou shalt break his yoke from off thy neck.' That was the promise made to Esau. Well, it hadn't been kept. All it had taken to destroy Esau was a few vengeful Pathans and a simple invention of *Homo sapiens*—the three-inch mortar.

The surface of the lake was still, but a white streak of cloud, blown by some distant wind thousands of feet higher, crept steadily along the far mountain peak. Somewhere beyond that mountain barrier lay the valley where the Esau had lived—and to which, unwittingly, he had led the destroyers of himself and his kind. Was he there now, crushed beneath a hundred thousand tons of rock? Or was his dead body, what remained of it, under the post-mortem knives of inquisitive scientists in Islamabad?

Sharply, something tugged at her mind. She gasped, the blood rising to her face as though she were a young girl. But then, almost at once, it ceased, and although she reached out for it desperately, it did not come again. So even memory could trigger it, she thought. Perhaps that was a kind of comfort.

EPILOGUE

In the dying sunshine the steep mountainside seemed asleep. A scattering of markhor goats, among them three small kids, grazed on a small grassy expanse that was little more than a ledge, tearing at the fresh shoots of juniper and azalea on the scattering of bushes which the thin soil supported. Below them stood the sentinel of the herd—a big bearded animal, old in mountain ways, with a set of twisted horns that sprouted fully four feet from his head. As always, the herd had lain in cover all day, high above where they now grazed, in a corrie so inaccessible that even the agile ibex, with which they competed for the sparse vegetation, had ignored it. Above the markhor herd the looming overhang of the mountain made approach impossible: below them stood the sentinel, watching the downward slope.

The old markhor stirred where he stood, reaching out his leathery mouth to a green sprig on a bush almost within reach. He tore it away and champed at it, never taking his eyes from the slope. There was a tiny splinter of sound, and for a few seconds the markhor's ears went back. But the flycatchers on the nearest bushes, busy taking the evening midges, did not cease their activities or fly away. The markhor relaxed, and stretched out for another branch. Instantly, his head was seized by the horns and forced back. The neck vertebrae stretched and cracked. Twitching, the markhor died. A tall shadow fell across the little ledge where he had kept guard. The flycatchers watched from the bushes for a few moments, and then resumed their feeding and quarrelling. A first chill wind of evening stirred the scrubby grass, but there was no further sound. Once more, the mountainside seemed to slumber.

WHALE

JEREMY LUCAS

A classic story of the sea, WHALE tells of the love, loyalty and life of Sabre, a killer whale.

'We believe in Sabre, the killer whale whose fortunes we follow. Jeremy Lucas' respect for the species is infectious. There are some awe-inspiring descriptions of the way these intelligent animals care for each other, how they comfort the wounded and dying, protect the cows and calves . . . this is a fascinating piece of work.'
Daily Telegraph

'Mr Lucas' whales are capable of grief, clemency, conscientious leadership; they can harbour old grudges, adopt orphans and extend a helping fin in trouble. He knows his whales, and brings a lyrical determination to the *life-and-death dance of creation.*'
Observer

'This excellent first novel is moving, original and *enlightening. It ought to become a classic of its kind.*'
New Statesman

GENERAL FICTION   0 7221 5640 5   £1.75

A selection of bestsellers from SPHERE

FICTION

ONCE IN A LIFETIME	Danielle Steel	£1.95 ☐
WHALE	Jeremy Lucas	£1.75 ☐
THE NEXT	Bob Randall	£1.75 ☐
REALITIES	Marian Schwartz	£2.25 ☐
PACIFIC VORTEX!	Clive Cussler	£1.95 ☐

FILM & TV TIE-INS

WIDOWS	Lynda La Plante	£1.50 ☐
THE YEAR OF LIVING DANGEROUSLY	C. J. Koch	£1.50 ☐
E.T. THE EXTRA-TERRESTRIAL	William Kotzwinkle	£1.50 ☐
HONKYTONK MAN	Clancy Carlile	£1.95 ☐
INCUBUS	Ray Russell	£1.50 ☐

NON-FICTION

THE SINGLE FILE	Deanna Maclaren	£1.95 ☐
NELLA LAST'S WAR	Nella Last	£1.95 ☐
THE NUCLEAR BARONS	P. Pringle & J. Spigelman	£3.50 ☐
THE CONTAINED GARDEN	K. Beckett, D. Carr & D. Stevens	£6.95 ☐

All Sphere books are available at your local bookshop or newsagent, or can be ordered direct from the publisher. Just tick the titles you want and fill in the form below.

Name _____

Address _____
_____

Write to Sphere Books, Cash Sales Department, P.O. Box 11, Falmouth, Cornwall TR10 9EN

Please enclose cheque or postal order to the value of the cover price plus:

UK: 45p for the first book, 20p for the second and 14p per copy for each additional book ordered to a maximum charge of £1.63.

OVERSEAS: 75p for the first book and 21p for each additional book.

BFPO & EIRE: 45p for the first book, 20p for the second book plus 14p per copy for the next 7 books, thereafter 8p per book.

Sphere Books reserve the right to show new retail prices on covers which may differ from those previously advertised in the text or elsewhere, and to increase postal rates in accordance with the PO.